THE LAST THING THE ANGEL SAID

Nick Sweeney

Auctus Publishers

Auctuspublishers.com

Published by Auctus Publishers

606 Merion Avenue, First Floor

Havertown, PA 19083, USA

ISBN (Print): 979-8-9894812-9-3

ISBN (Electronic): 979-8-9915910-8-9

Library of Congress Control Number: 2025931133

Dedykuję tę książkę dwóm Joannom

Also by Nick Sweeney

Contents

ONE

Masked Dance Saturday Night, Midnight Bells And Angels

———◈———

As the bells stamped midnight onto the town of Balz, Milo Galitzki was having the best night a boy could have. On a creaking bed high up in the old Zacharov mansion, an angel pinned him with her legs and squeezed him with muscles inside her whose names he didn't know. Milo gasped on contact with her pubic bone. The angel's eyes rested an inch from his own and he felt her breath through her mask.

She didn't make the noises Milo had imagined girls did when engaged in that midnight thing. It was his own sound she made, of the heart-busting effort a bike rider made when ascending.

"It hurts," she whispered.

"Hurts?" Milo knew only later that she didn't mean the kind of hurt that could be mended, like the rips in his knees and elbows collected from contact with the road during his foolish racing of bikes.

Milo traced a vein on the angel's breast and walked fingers down her ribs. "Now," came from the painted bow of her lips. "Hold your tongue and let me love."

That was a quote, Milo knew, though from which of the thousands of books in his head, he couldn't say.

He and the angel thrust and finally juddered to a halt in a tumult of blankets and feathers. "Oh," they said. "Hey."

1

Milo remembered that angels were boys, and that no girl angel would invent herself just to love him that way. He was certain too that angels weren't equipped with the... wherewithal. And they never smiled. Why? Answers to these conundrums escaped him. He released his breath as the words, "Angel, what's your name?"

That got her saying, *"Never* ask that of an angel." She stood. Her wingtips scraped the sloping wall and her robe cascaded and made a secret of her. She snatched a towel and wiped herself with it before opening the door. "You'll know." He sensed a smile in her voice. "Someday."

"Hey." Milo would think of his call echoing for a long time after that best night of his life.

It was only later that it turned into the worst. Milo told me all this after we married. He told me all the things that happened to him, except the last thing the angel said. I had to find that out for myself.

Years before, when Milo found his legs, and his sister Mila made a prayer to angels

One day Milo walked into the kitchen and startled his mom into dropping a knife. He saw it fall and walked away. He was six months old. Later he fancied he was born with the urge to work those legs and escape: out of the womb and keep going.

In his genes were imprinted a bike racers' slipstream, he decided, defying headwinds on cobbled European roads to Hell. He had the fear of them in his legs, he said, and in his head the names of mountain passes the mention of which made grown men cry. Or so he said. Out of these thoughts rose a trail of scree up a mountain from whose top he would treat a crowd to disbelieving blinks as he held up a race winner's bouquet.

He led his sister Mila up the steps of Balz's fort, a place of laments moldering over the town. He was six. He looked over the salt flats and wondered what Balz might have become had the water stayed, link to the ocean and infinity. He parroted the names of maritime cities learned from books. In the marshes lay galleons and clippers, he was sure, full of soapstone and amber, gold and silver, crucifixes and talismans clutched in the fleshless fingers of mariners.

Milo wondered how many other kids sat over dry seas, a little sister by their sides. "Not so many," he declared. To Mila's puzzlement, he said, "I got to tell *some*body."

Fearless, she let him draw her to the edge.

"See that?" His finger followed the eye in his mind. "Schooner out of Hong Kong, bringing tea. You know all that tea people drink?"

"Yeah." To Mila it looked like pee. It disturbed her that people drank it out of china cups.

Milo showed her steppes horsemen, heads of enemies bouncing off saddlebags, and camel trains laden with silks and spices. He pointed out a pack of bike riders breaking up and unraveling like a jersey caught on a nail. Mila saw wagons with elephants and Arabian horses, bearded ladies and geeks and midgets and clowns, acrobats cartwheeling, come to capture the town's wavering souls. Out there she saw soldiers tramp their cart horse feet, going no place at all.

They watched a plane crash and burn in a smoky swoop. Milo said, "People are on fire out there." He hadn't needed to tell her that. Their eyes became a canvas for the oranges and yellows of flames.

Mila didn't speak for a week. Mrs Galitzka knew her daughter was turning all the goodness in her to prayers for the dead airmen, Ganser and Weiss. "They're in Heaven, Mila," Mrs Galitzka whispered.

Mr Galitzki let out a laugh in a cough and said, "They're going to name a street after them in town."

As well as the dust of aviators, Balz's beaches were strewn with bones bleached white by the sun and the salt and the centuries. Milo was disappointed to find out it was the wind whipped up bones, clay pipes and combs, underwear and old magazines, and banknotes from faraway robberies, and sent the whole mess through the air, showers of fishes and frogs, even a sheep once, carried by a tornado. Or so people claimed. They also claimed that pigeon feathers, infected with crop and cattle death, found their way into the air from military testing labs.

Milo walked out through the sagebrush that hid the homes of scavenging creatures, not for a second taking his eyes off what turned out to be a cogwheel with eleven teeth on it. He remembered the skeleton of a machine in his dad's yard and put flesh on it, saw it in movement. He saw that the cog belonged to a bicycle and that, on a bicycle, he could challenge and subdue the wind.

He hurried back to the beach to tell his dad, by then discussing the question that sometimes claimed him on the beach, namely: did God live in the sun or the moon? He only entered into it to humor the blue-haired green-nosed pink-eyed women who congregated there. Milo tried to show Mila his cog but she had eyes shut and hands clasped for the souls of those who dared to take to the air. He heard the bells in the cathedral of the Holy Apostles strike noon and knew she was saying the *Angelus*. "Pa," he called. "She's doing it again. She's praying."

The jeremiad goes on despite the wishes of boys and the prayers of girls

Milo looked over Balz as if seeing it for the first time. The peat fires smelled stronger than ever. The washing had colors in it that never existed till then. The glazed tiles over the doors of houses were gleaming. Milo thought if he listened hard over the keening of the town's creaky windows he would hear everything said in the streets. He saw men with dusty faces tilting broken hats at lemon-faced women whose headscarves concealed hair crimped with twists of newspaper. He made out the air forming pockets around their bad teeth, saw them give pain a face as they muttered, "Goddam it if we're not the most unlucky people in the world." At the

4

windows of second-last chance saloons and fat-chance cafés he saw the faces of dead flyers, ghost motorbikers, future presidents, bike-pushing Belgians, Jesus, drowned children, Lucifer and men who got taken into forests by soldiers and never seen again. He spied traders cursing the saboteurs who spoiled their wares, glued their locks tight shut and sugared their gas tanks. Milo learned later that he was having what is called *the sight of things already seen.*

Mrs Galitzka said people's bad luck started when some clan left its village in some corner of Europe without paying dues to some saint in its midst. For this they carried a saint's curse in the form of a jeremiad, a long sad story to be told till time ran out.

"Is that true?" Milo asked his dad.

Mr Galitzki said only, "Beware of people who talk about saints."

Milo's mom did, and his sister did, and his friends, and their parents, and so did his teachers and the priests and nuns – the whole town, the voices on the radio; everybody talked about saints.

Mr Galitzki said, "Beware of people who tell you about angels, cherubim, seraphim, divine messengers, devils and demons and all that kind of whatever." A laugh guided his voice. "They are fools and liars of the deepest shade."

"They *are* not." A small voice, ignored. Mila's.

"Beware them all, Milo. They're crooks, cheats and corrupters of the mind."

"They are *not*." Mila stamped a foot.

"People should forget the bad things." Milo sounded as if he mistrusted his own sense. "And then they won't be cursed with the long sad story."

"It's the things that *happen* that are the curse." Mr Galitzki pitied his boy's lack of intellect. "The story's going to get told whether people like it or not."

They were on the ramparts of the fort on a winter afternoon after school. Below on Glass Beach, soldiers marked time to the barking of a drill sergeant with a head like a dog. They watched the men fade in the fog. Milo spied a child figure pirouetting on one leg on top of a twenty-foot flagpole. It was a sight so fantastic that the sense of the already seen deserted him. He grabbed at his dad's sleeve and pointed and said, "Lucy." Mila repeated the name as a question, and clapped hands urgently.

"The little saint herself." Mr Galitzki was compelled to watch the alarming dance. He was reminded that he owed the enignmatic acrobat, and always would. He put a hand onto his son's head and remembered that Milo might not have been there were it not for Lucy Ephraim. He tried to blot out the vision of Lucy, but then all godless Witold Galitzki could see was an angel, dancing on the head of a pin.

Milo at age five, meeting two saints on the same day

Milo and Mila knew already that bad things happened. One day on Reformatory Beach a woman in white put a hand on Milo's shoulder and said, "Hey, you seen a little boy out here?"

Milo blinked up at a cat face framed in a veil. It occurred to him to say, 'I *am* a little boy out here.' He said only, "Uh-uh."

The woman said to Mila, "How about you, sweety?" She knew girls noticed things boys didn't for all the foolish things in their heads. Not this one, who shook her head and said, "Nah."

"You stay right here," she said over her shoulder. She walked out to where the sea used to be. When Milo told me that I saw the shape she shimmered, bright ghost against the dung color of the salt flats.

That was Sister Adelheid from Balz's Charity Mission. She was looking for a kid called Michael Sheltz. "His aunt was his mother," Milo would hear his dad say of Michael, an uneasy loading in the riddle. "His mother was his aunt," Milo would hear. "And that tells that poor kid's tale entire."

Milo didn't warn Sister Adelheid that the clouds were coming down, just watched her move in and out of them. He lifted the cogwheel he'd found not an hour before, and framed her in the perfect hole at its center. "There she is," he observed for Mila.

"Where?" Mila said.

"And there she isn't."

"*Where* isn't she?" Mila looked hard, saw nothing. When she turned back, Milo too was gone. The cliff behind, gone. The whole world – gone. She cried till she saw a yellow square of window in the home for destitute girls. Balancing herself carefully in case she upset the gyros in the void and lost that window, she made her way toward it.

She ran into women on the promenade and made herself and them scream. They were busy lamenting the missing Michael, but encircled Mila when she told them that Milo too was gone.

The lighted window was Lucy Ephraim's. She soon joined that gaggle of mothers haunted by lost children. She drew the hand-wringing to a close by asking, if children were missing, how come the women didn't go out there and *find* them? But no, the men would take charge once they had been drawn out of their daytime business of beer and cabbage, chess and cribbage, their barbershop Babel.

Lucy said, "I make it a point never to wait for a man to do *any*thing."

The women's faces said, 'Oh *yeah*,' down at her. 'Like any man would ever want to do anything for a stunted little creature like you.'

7

If those looks hurt Lucy, who at age sixteen was three feet six, she didn't show it. She showed those women her back. Next thing she was out on the flats, a Stroh violin under her chin, its horn resonating an urgent call.

That day Michael Sheltz walked out of the fog singing for his supper, but Sister Adelheid never saw suppertime again. She stepped through the salt crust to rest among sailors' bones and pipes and pistols, and parts from watches.

The people of Balz didn't want to be told that the crucifix Sister Adelheid wore on a diaper pin on her shoulder had not protected her. They filed in and out of the masses said for her and, no grasp of canonical law, droned righteously how she was truly a saint. The people of Balz mumble complaints to this day, fleeced out of their Saint Adel.

Half an hour after Lucy had gone out on the flats she ran into a group of searchers that included Milo's mom and dad. She handed over their silent, dust-covered child. Nobody suggested that day that what Lucy had done was a miracle. That's the people of Balz for you. They wanted Sister Adelheid, who had simply sunk into the salt, for their saint while denying that Lucy had done anything at all. It was not so many years later that the suggestion would arise that because of her act of rescue, Lucy could be Balz's saint instead. The main drawback, and never mind that Lucy had pulled off nothing miraculous, was that saints, to be declared saints, had first to be declared dead.

Graduation summer, funeral of a lost saint

Lucy Ephraim obliged. She died the summer we graduated from the Balz Lyceum high school. I stood on the wall of Balz's fort and looked through the scum of smoke and flies and stories to a child's daub of houses with crooked windows and spidery afterthoughts of smokestacks, cables and stair rails. Balz was no place of saints. On the contrary, people followed luckless lives behind those facades and on the streets of steps

8

between the domes of the churches. Balz's apartment buildings were full of people who wept and drank green vodka in secret, laughed only sometimes, loved each other only one time then dwelled on that instance forever.

I wore my blue serge cape over my nursing whites, my starched cap and my clogs. I carried my Spanish guitar, off shift and on my way to a lesson. I knew nursing would never save people from their luck, and that music would only soundtrack their misery. I thought of taking my uniform off and flinging it into the air to treat the town to the illusion of an angel. It was late afternoon though, and Saint Anna's Day when, church-haunting crones claimed, the summer winds turn cold. I thought too of freeing my guitar and letting it plink and clatter down the wall, but knew the music would stay in my fingers.

I watched Lucy Ephraim's funeral. She had tumbled through a chain of events starting with her faith in the power of growth and ending in God's empty space. The middle part had gotten filled by Milo Galitzki's big mouth. As the casket was borne in procession from Lucy's house to the graveyard behind the Holy Apostles I prayed for Lucy.

And I cursed Milo for the things he hadn't been able to learn.

"There's hope," I heard him say one time across a school corridor to his friend Eurydice Armentiere. "People have got to have hope." The words made the troubles pour out of Eurydice's tan southern face for a second. They thrilled me, too. I hovered, but couldn't intrigue Milo to look my way. Didn't Milo Galitzki know hope was never enough? Even so, I wanted to tap him on the shoulder and tell him, "*I* am your hope, you sap."

Hope deserted our town the day Lucy was buried. It was the day Balz lost its second saint, and just how many chances did some podunk town get at having a saint of its own?

The cortege was more carnival than funeral, led by the people of the Udino Brothers Circus, where Lucy had worked. Fanfared by the ringmaster and a brass band looping a slow waltz, there walked the bearded lady, the man-woman, the strongman, the lion-tamer, with two lions, and some long-faced clowns. Stoic acrobats bore the child-sized casket. Balz's Father Ignatz Vishnevski officiated.

At the gateway to the graveyard, Balz's Bishop Tauber raised a hand. He commanded Father Vishnevski to step away from the procession. The brimstone bishop declaimed that the funeral was not the work of God, only of gravediggers. It wasn't Father Vish who brought speechlessness to Bishop Tauber. It was four people under three feet seven, sitting two each on a lion. The priest was borne forward by the other members of the cortege, grinning. They left the silenced bishop in the gateway.

Lucy Ephraim had been everything the people of Balz hated and feared. She called to mind folk tales about vengeful sprites. Lucy's job had prompted old yarns about the circus stealing souls and children. She was a Gypsy too, it was said, and were they not from Egypt, land of the Saracens, so wasn't Lucy only pretending to worship the true God of the Romans? I think what the people of Balz really couldn't get over was that Lucy was smart. Brought up in the home for destitute girls, Lucy should have been pregnant at fourteen, on welfare at sixteen and in jail at eighteen. She was none those things.

All it took for them to love her was a little blood. Lucy had revealed her stigmata, the marks of Christ's wounds, when she reached eighteen. She then took the saint-in-waiting place of that silly Sister Adelheid who, they dimly recalled, did nothing but kill herself, foolish thing. At Lucy's funeral, while the townspeople did their sheepish best to honor somebody they despised, the circus people carried Lucy's body toward its final dignity.

The citizens of Balz didn't know canonical law, which decreed that to be a saint you have to be declared one by the Pope in Rome and a bunch of cardinals incanting Latin. For them to do that, you have to have worked a no-shadow-of-a-doubt miracle. Lucy had not done that, though the people of Balz argued that some things she did had been miraculous. The holy had walked among them, and they ached for that claim to have been the truth; it could have been their redemption, but that wasn't to be. As our generation grew up in that town we watched people imprisoned by their bad luck, helpless as it ate them up and churned their guts each time they passed the Holy Apostles' bone orchard and its plot laid out, grudgingly, for suicides.

When Milo was ten, and still believed in angels, and why Ulysses did all that stuff

From the ramparts of Balz's fort, Mr Galitzki and his kids were mesmerized as the fog enclosed Lucy Ephraim. The Glass Beach flagpole was gone, and there she was in space, turning.

Witold Galitzki had a pitted white pancake for a face and the unsettling eyes of an Ottoman cat, one almost green, one verging on blue. His hair was what you saw sprouting out of the cables worming their way out of the walls of the fort. He was long and spare and his dark clothes hung off him like he'd just lost forty pounds. He was bearded and bespectacled and, under the brim of his hat, rabbinical. He was the wisest man in Balz. Everybody said so. Even Galitzki himself.

Milo said, "She'll fall."

"Not her," Milo's dad said with an air of the wise guy, as if he knew different but wasn't saying.

Milo knew he ought to pray that Lucy didn't fall, but something stopped him. Mila would pray, anyhow. He asked his dad, "But if she did?"

"Then… nobody could help her."

"Not even her friends?"

"Your friends are the last people who'll help you."

Milo's dad joined his son in thinking of his own little friends. Wire-headed long-nosed kid that reminded Witold of an animal that chewed through people's things. Straw-haired kid with broad cheeks, sized the world up all the time with urgent, insolent eyes, and his kid brother, his eyes friendly but empty. The weasel-faced twins belonging to that insufferable Peterlejtner guy who had the grocery store. Child with long hair of the richest brown and an unearthly smile that didn't hide some deep feminine misery. Bible-quoting neighbor kid born the same time as Milo, head of sprouting gold flames, with her matricidal kid brother. That pitiful Michael kid. There was the fat kid, too, the hirsute fat kid, the hirsute fat fatherless kid, eyes deeper and darker than those of a Kolinsky mink.

Milo changed tack without his dad able to anticipate it, asked, "How about angels?"

Mila clapped her hands. It hurt to know it, but she had been aware since the day Sister Adelheid died that angels couldn't even help themselves. She had on a brown wool coat buttoned up to the neck, and sported a white angora beret. Milo thought she looked like a rum baba. He put his tongue out at her.

They were standing near one of the wells in the west gate tower of the fort, where soldiers used to stand on platforms and bang drums that echoed around town. It was like one of the holes in the walls of Chinese towns that Milo saw in a book, down which unwanted girl babies were thrown. He thought how easy it would be shove Mila down to crack her skull open on the bottom. Right at that moment Mr Galitzki caught Milo in cross-hairs he made with his eyes, and Milo vowed never to harm his sister. Unfortunate timing, because he'd spotted the bulge of Mila's Bible in her pocket, and could have told his dad and gotten him mad at her.

"Angels?" Mr Galitzki let fade those pictures of his kids' friends. Friends didn't mean a thing. In the Galician village in which he'd been raised, soldiers in the Tsar's livery had marched men into forests and shot them in the backs of their heads. They'd been pointed out as Bolsheviks

12

by people they'd sat in school with, with whom they'd shared jokes and first cigarettes and slugs of vodka, peeks at girls undressing at the swimming hole and all the startling watery mischief of Easter Monday. A few years later the finger-pointers were denounced as Tsarists to the Bolsheviks, by other friends. Witold Galitzki had decided he wouldn't make any more friends in his life, would support neither Tsars nor commissars, nor make peace with God, and wouldn't believe in God's angels. "There *are* no angels."

For an agonizing second the sight and smell and sound of Sister Adelheid came back to Milo. "But Pa," he began.

"*No* angels." Milo had the oddest feeling that his dad was mostly in a daydream, his head full of workmen raising towers and gantries and whistling at women passing below. "And if there were, they wouldn't come and help you out."

"There are *so* angels." Mila tugged her dad's hand.

Milo knew his dad was forming cities in his head; he was walking under the awnings of hotels and casinos, dodging streetcars on boulevards and ducking down alleys to stand reflected in the rainbow scum the oil left on the river.

Witold snapped out of it and became aware of Mila. He barely knew her, the child who came to light once the first enervating spark of love had passed. He gathered her into his arms. "Our children," he declared into her ear, "though conceived in a bitter age, may build better than their fathers. Hey." He found his engineer's voice again for Milo. "Why did Ulysses do all that stuff?"

"What?" Mila's smile said the world was a confusing place described, what was more, by words that only some people were allowed to use.

Milo said, "Because he wanted to go home."

13

"*What?*" Mila turned her head from one to the other of the men in her life.

"Home." There was a pause, as if their dad was trying to work out what the word meant. Then he put Mila down and herded the pair together with his long arms. He set them walking. "Here we go."

My childhood tainted by wisdom

It's me borrowing the eyes of God and framing this tale, so you need to know that I started out as a compact child with hair plaited painfully, and who was dressed younger than my years my whole life. I had stick-out teeth. It was an overbite, Mrs Chomska the school dentist told me, which didn't sound so bad, except when I said that to kids they said, "Yeah, like an alligator." I guarded those teeth under a pout that made me look like an argument that had happened. Later I wore correction braces on them, a feat of engineering that gave me the smile of a tin can automaton. I kept my pout to cover them up and was stuck with it. I damned the slanty eyes I got from my great granny until a fire inside them made them glow. I had skin that wanted to be brown but was in fact just tinted yellow. I didn't look like I had a right to hair so blond it was almost white but that's what I had.

I had no sisters. I had a brother name of Calloway who lay in his crib and turned the deepest blue and died six days after he was born. His remains lay in the graveyard behind the little black church of the Holy Virgin under a stone that puns *Little Calloway Called Away*. Like most babies in Balz, Calloway wore a red thread around his wrist, supposed to protect him from the evil eye till he got baptized. I swore he'd be the last baby came out of our family to wear that thread.

When my dad's noisy friends stopped by in their shiny suits and twinsets, Dad jumped me through hoops to show what a clever girl he had. My teachers at Christ the Almighty elementary school didn't see me that way, sent me smiles as they told dad I was a little slow, maybe. The gaze he rested on them said something like if they wanted him to arrange for the

14

new heating system to be put in at cost then I'd still pass all my tests, wouldn't I?

I had friends who didn't think I was slow, mainly because they were slower. I hung out with the rich set from where we lived over Mozhay Beach. They were my own kind, or so I was led to believe.

Dad's money came from his being a hotshot building inspector. He was a regular building inspector till he blundered into a contract with a client by the name of Theodore House. Dad traveled all over for Mr House and attested that perfectly safe buildings were about to fall down. Sometimes he attested to the perfect safety of buildings that really were about to fall down. And sometimes, safe or not, those buildings collapsed, mysteriously, often left blackened holes behind. Somehow, Theodore House made money on the deals, and so did Dad. He got behind the worsted shoulders of financiers and put his money into savings and medical and pension plans wrapped up in this clause and that for this eventuality or that.

"Where does the money come from?" I got to wondering.

Dad said, "My princess doesn't want to know *that*."

I had to ask Mom, who said, "I just spend it, honey." I ha-hahed at this invitation into her women's conspiracy but had an instinct that there was more to money than that. I don't know how I knew. Maybe I wasn't so slow. The silver we had, the china, the cut glass, the chatchkas on shelves, the garish oils on the walls, I knew it was no earthly use to a soul.

I said we could easily give some money away to people who needed it, I didn't know who or where. Mom said Dad's money would get passed on to my husband when Dad got old. I thought, 'Husband – what?' I caught a flickered scene of some leering fat boy who slapped my ass every time he came home demanding dinner. I blinked it to a close and said, "Then I can start giving it away?"

"My money is like an agreement, honey." Dad winked. "Between gentlemen."

I stated, "I'm no gentleman."

Gentlemen or not, what would they be able to do once I'd given the money away to feed starving people?

"Hey, us gentlemen would be mad as hell if my princess turned into a pinko."

"What's that?"

Dad didn't let me raise the subject of money with him again. He didn't get old, either. The summer I graduated, he shot into a canyon when the brakes gave out in the new Packard he was driving. He flew, then clattered down the scree and rolled to a dead halt. It dawned on me that Mr House and his friends did it to fit into the logic they had, all their own.

I also thought I knew what happened to people caught in the orbit of that kind of gentleman. I kept my face from Mom, didn't want her to see the knowledge there. In her widow's weeds she attested that she held ownership of a roll of phony companies, and got a deal that left her cautious but comfortable.

Once that was done one of the shiny-suited swells came by around ten one night. He assured Mom that he wasn't going to let no family of no friend of his go to no wall. And could she just sign these papers, please? He came up the stairs and in my room to tell me, "Anything I can do for you." He wet my ear with his breath. "You tell me." I said there was one little thing. "That's what, sweetheart?" He thumped his chest. "You tell, I do." I said he could certainly take his hand off my knee. He looked at me a long time, then got up promising, "You and me are going to be *friends*."

I fretted about this and about the papers Mom signed till six weeks later when a circus troupe of guys in more somber suits swarmed over the house. They carried Internal Revenue and Customs Department ID cards

16

and carried out shedloads of documents from dad's study to put an end to the whole thing.

It was the end too for me and Mom of Mozhay Beach life, the parties and the friends and the noises they made that echoed through my childhood that, no matter what people said as they witnessed me dressed up as a child, got tainted by wisdom.

Prize day at the Balz Lyceum, and the embarrassment that helped me fall in love

Milo Galitzki didn't go to Christ the Almighty elementary. He went instead to the ruin of a school inside the walls of the old Civil War fort. That was where he made his friends and where they made him.

If Milo was content to be just strange, those friends were persistent oddballs. Richard Szczur, called Richard Rat, and Maciej Krzeski, known as Moby, looked to me like prototypes thrown together by God on a bad day. Moby's younger brother Stanislav, known for some reason as Selby, was hardly impressive either. Axel and Illona, the Peterlejtner twins, shared a room their whole lives despite living in a vast place over their dad's store. Their sass had a scary intensity, as did the red tantrums they threw to get their way. Eurydice Armentiere had to have been born with the look of noble Latin contempt she wore. Nobody saw her any other way, though her black eyes maybe just served to hide the troubled thoughts that roamed her head. She certainly wasn't born with her beauty mole, which she got from absentmindedly scratching a zit with an ink-blacked pen. There was crazy moppet Loretta Churchyard too, who shared Milo's belief that angels would come to Balz, and her seemingly catatonic brother Dominic. There was poor Michael Sheltz. There was Orville Charleroi, with the sweetest face under the sleekest blue-black hair in the world, but he was the kind of kid who blew his nose and checked his hanky to see if what lay in it was as big or as green or as sticky as the time before, and would kindly show you. Milo brought them all, except Michael, to the Balz

17

Lyceum with him, where the things they did got fixed in people's minds as their collective work.

I never got to know Milo in our years at the Lyceum. Outside school he rarely came near Mozhay Beach. He lived at the other end of town in a house painted German mustard yellow. It had windows shaped like dogs' teeth and half-moon tiles on the roof, had projecting corbels that cried out for gargoyles, had a tower on it, for Chrissake. It had a part-covered yard that looked like it'd been blown intact from some fledgling industrial nation, with forges and lathes and generators and chimneys plus piles of metal and wood, tools that looked like torture instruments and the carcasses of dead machines.

Milo was gawky, with big hands and feet and long limbs. He had no stomach and no ass, just legs that were by his mid-teens knotted into clusters of muscles and veins. He had stupid hair of no discernible color, that always seemed wrong, like he'd gotten somebody else's haircut by mistake. He had earnest blue eyes whose irises didn't match exactly, a nose that flattened at the end and a chin that projected his voice loud and clear.

Maybe because his mom ran the town library and he was often seen there, not to mention heard, he'd gotten a name as a bookworm by the time he was at the Lyceum. He made it plain he could take or leave the disdain that brought. What saved him from being seen as a schmo in the boys' eyes was sport, as it didn't take him but the blink of an eye to be known as a jock. He didn't charge into football, but he did pole vault, long jump and high jump, ran long and short distance and went without reverence through the rituals of baseball while dismissing it as a child's game. He didn't box, like the grade-A marsupials, but, as he sometimes had to show, he could throw a concrete punch if he had to.

What Milo was a nut about was riding a bike around the town and up and down its hills, the fastest thing there that didn't have an engine attached. "A crazy thing to do," people agreed as they stepped out of his way. He didn't see the fists they shook at him, had left them behind in the history that bike riders perceive to lie in seconds and their divisions. He was dreaming already of legendary French mountains and the mud-spattered glory of northern European races, of being a heroic race leader, object of awe and envy. He was fixed already on how he would live in France and do the whole French thing, all for the chance to show the world that maybe he could do nothing else, but he sure could ride that bike.

Milo seemed to do more or less what he wanted. When he was fourteen he hung out evenings with the war veterans at the roadhouse and persuaded them into letting him open up their motorbikes and spread them on the ground to check how they were put together. His hook lay in a promise that with a little fooling here and messing there he would make those bikes go fast enough to beat the Horsemen of the Apocalypse, never mind traffic cops. Those suspicious biker eyes lit up when he managed to bring them a click nearer the chance to be ghosts on the highway. He also took days off school to mess with the planes at the airstrip outside town and, later, to do bike races in other towns.

I always felt it was a measure of how he saw those friends of his that he didn't do all this stuff with them, but never found friends anyplace else. There was no question that he was going to join up with the roadhouse bikers, so he would be with them sometimes, but never *of* them. I thought he felt that way about school too, and about most of the kids there.

So I didn't get to know Milo, and yet I had always loved him. And then I didn't; I dismissed him as a child's fancy. I realized I was stuck with a thing about him though when I backtracked through years of thoughts about him. I knew then that what stood out from them was the question mark he made with his body when he hunched over that bike. I never dreamed it would follow the two of us together to Europe one day, nor did I think it would fall to me to erase it.

At the end of our first year at the Lyceum I got a prize for flower arranging, a pretty lame thing to do. The winners sat in the front rows. There I was among the kids with glasses who'd scooped the academic kudos, the gorillas who'd sweated for the sports prizes and the usual Mozhay Beach girls' club types who'd done the cheerleading and painted eggs and charity Christmas cards, not to mention flower arranging, again. When called, I traipsed up to get my prize, some stupid book for little girls. Mr Leeward the principal shook my hand and I did the curtsy I'd been told to make.

As I walked off, my foot got caught in the microphone cable, and down I went. I guess I got the comedy prize too, because after a pregnant second during which everybody was able to inspect my dark blue drawers, the assembly erupted into laughter. Mr Leeward, after breathing out the name of Jesus, waved to somebody to help me up. I thought how it wouldn't have killed him to do it.

As I rose I tried to make a dignified face to cover the tearful one I had on. I lit on the front rows, saw all those teeth on show, all those eyes wide with cutting merriment, all the meatballs, all the nerds, all my so-called friends, all laughing, everybody except Milo Galitzki. He had his head down. I could tell it was for shame and embarrassment, and that he was sharing mine. I never forgot that. Maybe that was why I went on many years later to share in his own embarrassment and shame, and in the pain that burned inside him and came out to burn me in my turn.

TWO

Masked Dance Saturday Night, Eleven Forty Five To Twelve Fifteen, And Milo's Moments Of Mesmer

◆————◈————◆

S trings of colored bulbs blinked, and illuminated mirrors reflected the animated faces in the Zacharov mansion. Swaths of material were tacked onto walls or draped over chandeliers, moth-eaten satins catching the light, moldy velvet drinking it in. The walls were graffitied with suggestive figures and faces, the doors with aphorisms that occasionally transfixed dancers in the middle of a step or gesture, warning that the dance could turn into something to haunt them.

In the ballroom a boy in lederhosen had saluted Milo Galitzki and a black cat had leered at him. He'd loomed at himself in a reflector when a dentist shoved past calling him by a name he didn't own. He brushed them aside as he felt his hair stand on end, knowing he was captured in somebody's gaze.

The sensation was obscured by Balz's bikers arriving in the grounds, the roars of their mounts bringing thunder. As the machines settled to purrs, Milo stepped back from the surge to the windows. He could do without the stink of gasoline and warm denim and the gleam of leather and chrome and in biker eyes at whatever the night might bring. 'Like heraldic beasts,' he started to think. What was the word? 'Oh… yeah – *rampant.*'

The angel stood still as the voyeurs tripped past her toward the windows. She filled the space with wings and white and looked Milo's way, a hand up in a wave. "Angel," he called, the value of one word that said it all.

21

Drapes were drawn back to reveal a scene in Milo's head, and he saw Balz's lost Saint Adel in the gloom of Reformatory Beach, her eyes appalled. He made those drapes close. This time he would catch the angel. He kept her wingtips in sight.

The music had become maudlin. People sashayed through a sad dance, though a drunken sailor ignored the tempo and did a hornpipe shuffle on top of a stone urn. Near Milo a bear removed his head and, out a window, greeted the night with convulsions. The year before, Milo's friend Eurydice had tumbled out of that same window and snapped one of her legs. She never again did her famous fencing.

Milo's moment of mesmer was halted by moonstruck Michael Sheltz. On Michael's marrow-shaped face his bottom lip was spread pinkly and his pupils were dilated. He looked at Milo but seemed not to know him. Milo took Michael's hand and said, "Go *home*."

It had always been Mila Galitzka who brought Michael home when he was adrift in town. It was Mila who pushed through chittering circles to stop Michael doing whatever people had persuaded him into for their amusement. Always Mila, who told them they were the most pitiable of God's belly-crawling creatures for their lack of decency. That was before, though. Michael was the same but Mila wasn't. She had slammed her door on that despicable world and, it was rumored in town, talked to nobody but God. Mr Galitzki had told Milo, "She talks to your ma, too." He arched an eyebrow. "The Holy Trinity."

"Michael, scram." Milo was trying to spook Michael with a stern tone, but was also anxious not to lose sight of the angel.

Michael's half-closed lids striped his eyes with veins. He said only, "Buh."

"*Beat* it." Milo felt an old anger grab him. He wanted to drop the business in hand and go drag Michael's old man Bible Jack Sheltz out of bed and show him the frontier justice of a leather boot. And he'd tell

Michael's stepmom Hornrim Jane Sheltz a thing or two, letting Michael roam the town the night of the dance. "Go *home*."

"Buh."

"For Chrissake, go *home*."

Milo got the barest impression of Michael's hand held out. Was that a cogwheel embedded in Michael's palm? Panic came and went when he lost sight of the angel then sensed her next to him. He forgot Michael and Hornrim Jane and Bible Jack and Mila and Eurydice and the bear and the sailor and the whole damn town and swapped Michael's hand for that of the angel.

"Angel." The word told the story trapped inside him.

She bobbed her head and said, "Hey, soldier boy."

"You're dancing?" he asked.

"I'm… romancing." Milo *had* heard right. There was a frightening beauty in the words. "Milo?"

"How do you know I'm Milo?" He'd reached up and felt for his mask. "I could be anybody."

"No." Something funny in her voice when she said, "You're… *definitely* Milo." The words shone a light through him. He wanted to communicate to her that he too knew what it was to soar to the Heavens and see what a no-account kind of place the world was.

"So, Milo?" His hand was clutched tightly.

"What?"

"Come upstairs."

Set into his mask, Milo's eyes shone out a hunger. Then the angel led him up to that best and worst night of his life, marking the occasion in his wrist with her nails.

He felt for the marks as he cleaned himself up twenty minutes later. All those pockets in soldiers' tunics were for the erasing of traces: Kleenex and gum, toothbrush and paste, aspirin, pen, paper, rubbers.

It seemed as if he was only just realizing he hadn't used a rubber, but in truth it had nagged at him. Something in the... *etiquette* of the proceedings though had prevented him from interrupting their motion.

What if a clot of blood inside her grew into their own little soldier angel? He tried not to think about the crushing cruelty of childbirth. He resumed his cleaning.

In the scrap of moonlight in the room, Milo saw feathers on the bed and picked one up. He stuck it in his buttonhole. He touched the metal knob of the bedstead and got a charge of static. It startled him into the anguish of seeing something that didn't quite make it to a memory, like the murmurs after a dream, then into thinking, 'Hey, Milo, go find that angel, and then you can do that again, mark each other, love each other. *Go.*'

It was as a knocking sounded at the door that he fell to the knowledge that he was in love. He smoothed the front of his tunic and stuck his chest out. "*For God's sake,*" he quoted carefully, "*hold your tongue and let me love.*" He knew words were wonderful things, especially when punctuated sweetly by what he'd lain under the angel and done in that room whose borders expanded to keep up with the raging landscapes in his head. He marched to the door.

When Milo was sixteen and had wings to fly fools who looked for angels.

Michael Sheltz saw the angels of Balz the All Souls' Day Milo took him flying. Milo learned to fly firstly out of wanting to know how a plane worked its magic, but his urge incorporated his unhappiness with the confines of gravity. He was twelve when he accompanied old farmer Shilnikov in his shuddering crop duster and fourteen the day he debuted alone in one of the airstrip's Pipers. On his way out Mila had held his arm and urged him to stay on *terra firma* but he'd unfastened her fingers, with some difficulty, and headed for the skies.

He wasn't to know she was thinking of the plane they saw belly-flop local hero pilots Ganser and Weiss to their flaming doom that day so long before that neither would have trusted their memories of it had the people of our town not spoken of it so often. A flying sheep, men still stated in barfly awe, elevated by a freak tornado, hit the propeller, and that was that. No, the duo got shot down, barbershop talkers declared, by a National Guard unit out on the flats on maneuvers, driven nuts from thirst and flies.

The widow Ganser said what happened was the men took three days to drink their month's pay, went up to clear their heads and got exactly that wish: euphoria, then oblivion. Mrs Weiss came clean on that one too but the men of Balz could not credit a story as far-fetched as that.

All the same, a check for sheep in the air and guardsmen on the ground had worked its way into Milo's routine. Sometimes as he followed the aces' vodka vapor-trails he imagined a clunk, the propeller slicing mutton chops before standing still, and sometimes he imagined a shell slamming into his throat to reveal its meat. There were other demons for him up there though, and he soon forgot those bar-room fancies.

I saw Milo the day he first went up alone. I knelt on my fake sick bed when I should have been in a classroom at the Lyceum. My radio was cowed by the growl of engines. I didn't know it was him, just saw that flimsy contraption on a sky washed with yellow, pitting itself against what height and ground combined had waiting for anybody crazy enough to rise above them. I saw the wives of the Mozhay Beach big cigars stop their backyard prattle when they caught on that the sky wasn't there only to allow the sun at their hides.

The day he took Michael up, Milo knew everybody he could think of would get mad if they saw Michael within even whistling distance of a plane, but there was something in him that wanted to make Michael a gift

25

of the sky, the horizon and the Heavens. He drove his dad's old pick-up to the hangar and got them airborne without incident.

Once they were up, Michael made faces Milo could sense rather than see. Michael brought them to life by saying, "Jesus Mary," over and over. Then he began squawking, "Down. *Down.*"

Milo quieted him in the usual way, which was simply to point until Michael got so absorbed in what he was supposed to be looking for that he found something to focus on. "We're in the sky, Michael," Milo hollered. "Nothing bad's going to happen up here. It's down there you've got to worry about."

Two days before, Mila had come home in tears saying only Michael's name; it was quicker than saying the names of all the people who were mean to Michael. Milo pressed her as to why and what and who and she demanded of him, "Just how many heads are you going to punch for Michael?" She'd hidden her face with her hair. "Not even you can punch out the whole town."

No, not even Milo had enough fool's enthusiasm for that. He'd put a hand out to Mila and she took it, ran her fingers over its bones and let it fall.

"Look out the window," Milo mouthed to Michael up in that big sky. "Watch for angels."

Michael took to that. As Milo traced figures-of-eight over Balz, Michael started to yell, "Milo, they're there."

"Sure they are." Milo was fixed on a dial whose needle was, he hoped, having a machine's joke on him. He banged it, got that needle jumping. "I told you, already." He put his ear protectors on, blocked out the drone that signaled the chemicals coming to completion inside Michael's head to bring him light, color, choirs of angels singing, maybe – who knew? Nobody ever would.

Milo sighted a disfigured column of black bricks topped by a pyramid roof, all that remained of a structure raised by his grandpa, Waldemar Petrov. It was the clock tower of a department store to be called Modz. It never got filled with rows of goods nor browsed by shoppers or thieves, had no thousandth lucky customer nor even one, got burned down two nights before its grand opening. Milo's mom said, "That's why you're not heir to a store fortune right now." Milo never knew whether his mom was kidding when she said that. "Living over Mozhay Beach." Nor was he sure why, but he was glad about that. That non-existent store had always been bad news as far as Milo was concerned. His grandpa had been driven to distraction by all the what-ifs, and there was his mom, still airing them.

Balz was no monumental town, except for its churches. Milo liked seeing the cross shapes they showed when you saw them from the air, like their architects knew all along how people would fly one day to see them how they looked on plans.

Michael swiped him on the head. "I see the angels," Milo read on his lips.

"Sure."

"They're *there*." Michael swiped him again.

"I *know*, goddammit."

They were, too. All Souls' Day got the graveyards speckled with candles. In the square by the Holy Wisdom cathedral, Balz's white holy sisters were in procession to serenade the dead. What for, he had come to understand, didn't matter.

From the skies that threw their atomic light onto the day, Milo saw his pal Moby Krzeski schmoozing Csilla Kodaly, the schoolteacher's sister, in the kitchen gardens behind where the Kodalys lived. He saw Eurydice Armentiere. She was all the more beautiful on account of being escorted by her dog-ugly brother Benny. Milo wished he could swoop low and yell out the window, 'Hey, Eurydice, where did you get the chimpanzee?'

I thought about that a long time after Milo told me about it. With all he had to think about up in the sky, that was his wish: to make Eurydice froth out her rare laughter. Why did he want to do that for her, I wondered, when he wouldn't do it for me? In return, I would have given him a view of infinity much greater than any he could spy from some plane.

If he'd looked for me on that All Souls' Day I would have been on that same trail to the Holy Wisdom, candle in hand, prodded up the hill by the ghost of my cot-dead brother. How would he have seen me, though, taken up as he was with that frosty uptight bitch Eurydice?

I wish I could say he just forgot Eurydice, but he had other things on his mind. He banked away from the town and scanned the highway for the man who nearly ruined Mila. He saw him time and again, then didn't, a lone figure with the power to tramp in and out of time on roads that let the bad out but let it in, too. *It was* you, *goddammit, who nearly ruined Mila.* He liked to think that was his own voice saying that into the man's road-weary eyes, but it wasn't: it was his mom's, and she wasn't saying it to the man. Those same eyes lay in Moby's painting in the entry hall of the Holy Apostles, of Christ riding a bike on which the pedals were without toe-clips, so no advantage on the upstroke. "Christ didn't ride a *bike*," he'd told Moby. "For... uh... Chrissake. He *walked* the roads." Like the man who nearly ruined Mila.

When you were flying a plane, it wasn't a good idea to watch the roads. Milo looped the loop over Old Balz, a cluster of ruins filled with specters, then got air under the wings. He had to imagine the grace of the movement. Up there he could feel only the reluctant grind of its compliance.

Michael signaled an end to his terror with a susurration of exhilaration. 'Born to fly,' Milo thought he could hear him say. It sounded as though Michael was feeling a tuneless song coming on, so Milo pointed. "Angels," he said. "Don't miss a single one."

The day a man nearly ruined Mila Galitzka

The day the man nearly ruined Mila, Milo was diverted by police officer Edel in the Galitzkis' kitchen holding a bundle. Edel called Officer Protzner over and pushed the bundle at her, saying, "We've got to, uh, examine these."

"Eh?" Protzner held up Mila's gray and blue check dress. "For what?"

"Uh." Edel found himself stuck with Mila's sky blue panties intertwined with a white sock. "Huh-hmm." He summoned up a look that said he didn't get a job in the police department to look at kids' clothes. "I don't rightly know."

"Hey." Mr Galitzki tapped on the table to regain Milo's attention. "I'm *talking* to you. You look at my face, you see what?"

"I don't know," Milo said. Why was his dad talking about his own face? It was the other face that Milo had to remember, the man with the country's underbelly in his eyes. Milo looked at the officers passing Mila's clothes between them in hot-potato slapstick, hissing at each other like snakes.

"Smartass Milo Galitzki doesn't *know*." Witold Galitzki bellowed the words into a crescendo that stopped the officers and made them pantomime a tiptoed exit. Mr Galitzki said, "You don't *know*? You don't see my... *frustration*, actually, Milo? You don't see a man who has been... let down further than he thought there was... *depth*?"

"Pa?"

"You listen to me. And remember this forever. You meet a man who's hungry in the face, whose hands itch to do harm, you stop whatever it is you're doing, you watch that man, and even if your life hangs on it you don't give that man an *inch* of space. Be careful with your sister." He squeezed Milo's shoulder. Milo could tell that his dad wanted to slap him, but that something wouldn't let him. "She *hurts* right now. Careful what you say in front of her. Careful with the language of your body, Milo. Look at you now, your tongue on your lip like a fool. Careful."

That afternoon Milo had been on his way out when the man appeared at the porch, asking, "Your daddy's here?" A bum looking for work, Milo guessed, drawn by the engineering yard by the house. He yelped for his dad to come out of his room, then rolled his bike onto the path and freewheeled down it, thinking of the time he had to make up Universe Hill.

Mila came down calling to Milo that their dad was out walking, and their mom out too. "Stocktaking." She was saying that to a silhouette framed by the fly screen door. "Whatever that is," she finished as the man shut the door behind him.

Mr Galitzki told Milo that the man carried his sister upstairs and made her undress, then kissed her mouth and her chest then ran his tongue down her body to the place where her body vanished inside her. He stopped this distressing business there.

Officer Edel had said, "She was lucky." In answer, Milo's mom slapped the bright side of the officer's face for him. Milo heard the report echo around the flags of the kitchen.

The man locked Mila in her room, ate leftover meatloaf and pickles in the kitchen and glugged a bottle of chokeberry wine. He took the few bucks he found and an old Russian greatcoat, later found dumped near the railroad.

Mila was in her room two weeks, drapes drawn, door closed, the only sign of congress her and her mom talking into the nights. Why couldn't Milo's mom talk to him that way?

30

Mrs Galitzka spoke to Milo only one time in those two weeks. Eyes shimmering, she asked why Milo had told people about what had happened to Mila. Milo's heart went to jelly and leaked to his toes and he said, "I didn't mean any harm." He watched his mom pick through the words and, even more so than with his dad, got a sense of violence reined in. "I didn't want it to happen to anybody else," he blurted out. He hated the way his face must have looked as his mom made and unmade her fists.

She said, "And but? You got it to happen to your sister, didn't you?"

He wasn't to know the kids in the streets would stick their tongues out and wiggle them at Mila every opportunity they got, wasn't to know every smartass storekeeper would look at her like she'd brought it on herself just by being a girl who was alone and defenseless. Why didn't he know? His mom said, "God forgive you your big mouth, Milo."

When she said that, Milo wanted to wander the world and die at a roadside in a ruined and spooky place like Old Balz and be buried with the legend *Unknown* on a stick in the dirt above his sorry head. What he wanted more though was for his mom to put her arms around him and tell him he was a one hundred and one percent A-one klutz, but that she forgave him.

She caught sight of his cycling cap and reached over and picked it up. She jammed it on his head and said, "Now scram. Leave us to get on with the business you've brought on us. Go ride that bike of yours, little boy, and pray God that's not all you're ever going to be good for."

When Milo was five and got lost and saved and struck dumb both times

The original settlement of Balz was no more than broken houses converging on a square with the remains of a well and a carpet-beating frame. It lay off Route Thirteen in fields of scrub. People said the roadhouse bikers hung out there and got up to black masses and Roman orgies. I suspected the bikers had never even gotten to grips with regular

31

Catholic mass, and had only vaguely heard of the Romans, and just got drunk and shot at empty liquor bottles. Milo said the bikers were rebel angels after their fall. "They saw Hell in Europe and Japan in the war," he told anybody who'd listen, especially when at times the whole town blamed them for anything from sheep stealing to store sabotage to first-degree murder. That hangout of theirs was named Old Balz on the map, but people called it Miss Agnes'. This was because on one of the walls somebody had scrawled *Czy tutaj mieszka, Panna Agnieszka*, meaning, *Does Miss Agnes live here*? Nobody knew who had written that nor why, nor who Miss Agnes was. In any case, the answer was no.

Mrs Galitzka told Milo the jeremiad exploded into life in Old Balz the All Souls' Night a guy named George Vrona killed every man, woman and child in them with a shotgun and an ax then hanged himself from a tree next to the little church they were raising, called Our Lady Patiently Waiting. Almost hidden in the grass were the postcard-size grave markers. Every All Souls' Day women made schmatters by tearing strips from old clothes then hung them from the tree, set candles by the graves and bowed heads for an *alfresco* mass.

Nineteen people died that night. Only one person was missing when George Vrona did his crazy business. A kid was lost on the salt flats, scared to move and thinking he was going to freeze and die. In fact he was the only one going to live. That was Milo's grandpa Waldemar Petrov, who would go on to be architect, builder, dreamer of and loser of store fortunes. He hanged himself from Milo's dad's derrick truck when Milo was three and left neither a cent nor a word. People guessed he was just sick of living.

Milo remembered his own time on the flats off Reformatory Beach when he was little, when he followed the blue-eyed sister through the sagebrush. The silence had filled gradually with the squeaking of sand squirrels, the buzzing of flies and the coughing of crows.

He might have called out to her to watch her step, but he found himself with a mouthful of glue, his teeth coated with the alkali in the air.

When it set his tongue went as hard as the those on the sandstone lions guarding the war memorial.

In time he heard a melody played on a violin. He hadn't turned, knew it was foolish to look for something you could only hear, but just the same his quaryy dissolved into the lapse in his concentration. When he went to transform his anguish into words it was like an arrow had punctured his throat, and no sound came.

The lady in white had appeared again in a break in the fog. Her arms were making movements that signaled the distress of any creature caught in a trap. Milo watched her struggle and sink.

He had to have his mouth washed out with lemon juice and warm water by Mrs Panufnik the district nurse. "Angel," he kept trying to say, which didn't please his dad at all. When Milo got his tongue to move he said the word again.

Mila clapped and said, "Angel? Hoo!" and let out her little girl's laugh that didn't care about a thing.

Mrs Panufnik said, "*Now* now, I think you got a vivid imagination, child," but they were all thinking the same thing: about the sister who was missing and the nuns and soldiers and townspeople looking for her on the flats.

"No I don't." Milo brought them back to him with his muddled defense, but Mrs Panufnik was right. Milo's head was full of other people's words and pictures that he had changed into his own. His dad had told him that books were the only reality and held the world entire in their pages. At school Milo had already made his teachers Miss Kodaly and Miss Ostrovska mad by knowing everything before they taught it because he'd read it already in some book. What was more, if he hadn't read it he was willing to improvise. "I heard music," he ventured.

They were thankful to be able to say, "Sure you did." They moved aside to reveal a girl who perched on the edge of the chesterfield clutching a little glass of something the color of piss, Mr Galitzki's white port. She had a strange instrument by her feet, a violin with a metal horn on it. She sported plaits that shone with oil. She had the biggest most liquid eyes Milo had ever seen, and a little red bow of lips. She was short of four feet tall and pretty in the way a tiny Japanese tree was. Her smile tickled Milo's guts. That was Lucy Ephraim.

Mr Galitzki said, "How are you going to thank this little lady for bringing you back, Milo?" Milo didn't know how to thank her but there he was, willing to improvise. He walked over to Lucy and picked up the edge of her long dark flowery skirt and smelled it. The salt and fog dust couldn't hide the scent of sandalwood. He heard a voice say his name sharply but went on holding the hem of Lucy's skirt to his nose. "Now, Milo," his dad said into his ear. He let the hem fall.

His dad looked at his mom. Milo followed his dad's gaze. He caught a current passing between his parents. Lucy never saw it, Milo was convinced later, because she didn't want to see it.

Milo knew his dad was kind of mystic, though that wasn't a word either of them used. Sometimes he was able to tell Milo about things that would happen the next week or the next year, and they would. Milo's mom too knew all kinds of stuff nobody should know, but things had happened to her when she was young that taught her that it was foolhardy to say so.

That day, Mrs Galitzka looked at Lucy then bent her head and shut her eyes. She didn't see Lucy's smile at all, just saw her in a dark hallway, crying in the kind of distress that was never going to be eased in this world. After Lucy went, Mr Galitzki took his wife to one side and hissed, "You saw what? *Tell* me," but she kept her head down and took to her bed with a migraine.

Was I looking in the window as all this happened, you may wonder. I wish. No. Milo told me, after we married. Mrs Galitzka told me some of it too, after I took charge of her boy. Mila told me some of it, eventually. Through their eyes, I see it all.

Mrs Galitzka's eyes were a mahogany polished black, and her long dark hair was neatly tied up. Her cheekbones made her look determined. She walked tall and straight when women of her time bore kids and waddled out of elegance.

And I may as well trace a line here and tell you that Mila got her mom's eyes and her poise and those cheekbones. She had a year of being curvy when she was about twelve. That was the year the traveling man nearly ruined her. Maybe it was to do with that day and that man, but those curves became angles and she grew big and lean like an athlete, despite never doing a stroke of exercise. She too wore her hair long, a rope of it trailing down her back. She had good teeth on account, according to Milo, of brushing them almost before she'd finished eating, had eyebrows that looked as if they had been magically calligraphed and an unremarkable, proportionate nose.

"Fine kids," Lucy said as she took her leave that day. "A handsome boy and a pretty girl. Well, Milo Galitzki, I'll remember you, so don't you forget about me, eh?"

"I won't," Milo promised.

"And keep imagining, now." That impressed Milo. He didn't know why, just had a flash that told him that life wasn't meant to be about imagination in a town like Balz. "Milo Galitzki." Milo saw that Lucy just liked saying his name, and made no answer. "*Well* now."

Galitzki is my name now – I didn't take the Polish prerogative of a feminine -a on the end – and it's a good name to say. It looks kind of crazy written down, though an improvement on what it was back in Europe, when it was written Galycki. An early memory of Milo's was of being in Peterlejtner's store with his dad, who sounded the -ej in Mr Peterlejtner's name like in *light* and not in *late*. Mr Peterlejtner muttered a correction.

Milo's dad shot back, "You think you got problems? My name is Ga-Frigging-Litzki."

Everybody knew that, because there were metal plates scribed with his name on all the things he built in Balz. He put up the big roof of the train station, beauty out of nothing but space and abstract math. He built the tanks and their connecting walkways and bridges at the refinery. He rebuilt the cooling towers and gas burners that projected a tiny city of light that fanciful old Balzers claimed aped the skyline of night-time Warszawa from the Wisła river before it suffered Nazi bombardment and dynamite, whether they had seen that venerable stretch of real estate or not. Milo's dad also strengthened the arches in the Rink, Balz's town square. Witold Galitzki's name was everywhere in Balz, and Milo liked that. Maybe that was why he felt he had to forget angels and junk the imagination, take a turn to the practical and become an engineer too.

Before Milo was born, and his mom and dad's preoccupations with Roman miracles

Witold Galitzki never set foot near a church ceremony. The idea of Balz's miraculous churches, raised, it was said, from nothing, turned the skin on his face the color of rare roast beef. Mr Galitzki reminded anybody who'd listen that bishops and priests were grifters and crooks. He told Milo you couldn't be an atheist until after you'd been a Catholic, because how could you not believe in something if you didn't know what it was?

Milo knew his dad as an engineer, and also as a man who lived somewhat discontentedly off investments and the income from patents, board membership stipends and payments for consultation on theoretical projects. Milo had only the faintest picture of Engineer Galitzki in the square-cut suits with the swish office on the Rink in town and the big yard by the railroad, wasn't aware of the building boom passing over and his dad growing richer but grouchier. He noticed one day years later the way his dad had devolved, in those same suits gone threadbare.

Everybody who got an education in Balz knew Romualda, Milo's mom, from her job in the town library, because every schoolkid got a trip there about every two weeks. They saw her kind face and knew she'd find them any book they wanted.

The year Romualda was twelve, not long after her mom, Eulalia Petrova, had died from eating amanita toadstools, Romualda had visions of the Blessed Virgin Mary in Balz's cathedral of the Holy Wisdom. They drew in half the girls in Balz. My mom was among them but said later she wasn't sure if she ever saw anything at all.

I agreed with commentators who worked out that the visions were signs of a population susceptible to mass hysteria while being stung by bad luck. But then I would.

Whatever they were, once they stopped, Romualda was left with catatonic trances, then diabetes, that nobody wanted to claim. She also got a nervous disease that broke her out in zits; this grounded her for the rest of her teens and for much of her twenties. People assumed she'd never marry, and were surprised to see her walking out with Galitzki, who lodged in the Petrov tower house when he came to Balz. It beat everybody as to why Romualda married an outsider, at least till eight months on and the birth of Milo. She bloomed again then. Even when she got to middle age there was something about her that stayed young, and if you caught her face the right way you got a picture of the girl she was once.

At the same time you saw the woman Mila would be. Mila's face was handsome and kind, but in it you caught the knowledge that there were troubles to be faced, forgiveness to summon up and, an awful thing, the options that remained when forgiveness ran out.

Mila at fourteen, the call to sisterhood drowned out by believers and unbelievers

All Souls' Day didn't matter to Balz's white sisters. They chanted their vows of poverty, chastity, obedience and joy any time of year. Milo always heard the vows replaced by the neighing of mares and snorting of stallions. Those came through the noses of my Mozhay Beach friends, who led the school in snickering at Mila when word got around that she wanted to join the sisters.

The first Milo heard of it was when he got home one evening and was on the porch covering his bike with a tarpaulin. He heard Mila cutting through his mom's and dad's voices to say, "I got *what* to look forward to in this town? Waste my days away in some factory, maybe. And for *what*?" Milo felt himself nod. "And then I'll *what*? Get my tush pinched at dances all my Saturday nights till I meet some... *schmo* I marry and make babies with? That's me, is it, Ma? I wheel a buggy through the park and talk about diapers with other mothers? Don't you know, the only people who do any good around here are the sisters? The rest of the people in this town plug away at their dumb lives, kidding themselves into a dream made of automobiles and washing machines."

Milo heard his dad then, drawling, "Mila, you want to wash bums' socks your whole life? You want to watch them slobber their soup down them like animals? You want to wipe their asses for them? Kiss their sores better, like... the man from Assisi? And in return you have them praise the Lord with their whiskey croaking? Poverty?" He spattered the vows out in a laugh. "Chastity? Obedience?" He made them sound like the worst sins in the world. "Hear me, Mila. I promise you, you're better than that."

Mila said, "I despise your pride," so low that Milo had to press his ear against the fly screen to hear it. "Nobody's better than that, Pa. Trouble is, everybody thinks they are. And anyhow, Pa?"

"What, child?" Through the screen, Milo made out the ectoplasmic figure his dad cut as he headed for the stairs and the refuge of his room. That was his way of closing the debate when he wasn't likely to claim the last word.

"The vows are poverty, chastity, obedience and joy," Mila called. "You forgot joy. You know why that *is*, Pa? It's because you haven't got any."

That was a family conversation. How did word of Mila's consideration of the vows get around town?

"That was a thing I had to think about without people's opinions, Milo." Mila's words chased Milo each time he saw one of the white sisters. That got him believing that what people said about it being bad luck for a nun to cross your path had to be true. "Do you know how hard it made it, with every kid in that freaking school chanting the vows at me, and every know-nothing asshole in this town giving me their advice?"

"I didn't mean to tell anybody." Milo wasn't lying.

"And but?"

"Well, uh… I did." Nor was that a lie.

"That hurt, Milo."

"I only told Richard." Milo had been trying to concentrate on his plan, which had Richard Rat standing outside under Mila's window at that moment, trying his damnedest to look nonchalant. "He's our friend."

"He's *your* friend."

"Oh." Milo ached then to learn that Mila no longer counted Richard as a friend. "Well..." Sorry wasn't enough, not then, talking to her through her bedroom door, behind which their parents locked her till she quit the idea of joining the sisters. "I'm *sorry*," he offered anyhow. It was all he had. Almost. "Uh, Mila?"

"*What*?" It was the worn-down voice of a girl with things on her mind of which he had no part.

"Richard's outside." Milo's picture of himself and Richard rescuing Mila paled now beside that of Mila sitting with dignity in front of her dark icon of Saints Barbara and Katarzyna and looking in onto her life and its

39

direction. Milo told his sister, "He's got a ladder." He felt the words burn through seconds of silence till he heard Mila at her window, singing out to Richard to stick his ladder up where the sun didn't shine and then climb up it, a series of impossible demands that would challenge even optimistic do-anything Richard Rat.

Balz girls' different hearts' desires, the time Mila and I were sisters for a minute.

I understood Mila's complaint that night Milo eavesdropped on her: Balz girls' hearts' desires led them to getting hitched to some chump, driving convertibles timidly around town, having their hair and fingernails done often and buying stuff for their kids they thought their friends' kids wouldn't have. That was what I'd been raised to think about when the future was mentioned. I *did* too, for a time. It doesn't come to mind now exactly when I stopped thinking that way. I only know that one day I looked at my mom and dad and knew I didn't want to live the way they lived. First thing I did was tell them I wouldn't go to the secretary college to do the program that would book my place on the lap of some sweaty-shirted executive.

I told them I wanted to be a nurse. I'm pretty sure I never thought about it till that second. I got the same kind of grief Mila's mom and dad gave her. Did I want to wipe people's asses for them all my days? Was that really the worst thing in the world people could think of? Was I going to break their hearts that way?

I said, "Your hearts get broken that easy, better get new models, just like you do with every other goddam thing." After the usual reminder to watch my young lady's language there was a suggestion that I'd grow out of it. "No doubt," I gave in and said. "It's just an idea." That brightened them a little but under my breath I gave the Balz Lyceum counter-curse of the one word, "Doubt," and knew it deserved a shot.

Mila's dad being disdainful of God, you could see why he was against Mila joining the sisters. Mila's mom's problem was what, I never found out for a long time. Some of it was to do with Mila being Mrs Galitzka's child and hers alone, the old man not wanting more than his little engineer. Mrs Galitzka wasn't ready to lose Mila to anybody, not even Jesus. At the time I guessed she had a vague idea of something better for Mila, but my mom hinted at those crazy religious things that happened to Romualda Petrova when she was a girl, inseparable in mom's mind from insulin and zits. I didn't know what the sisters got out of their vocation but knew it had to be something more than the accomplishment of clean asses. Whatever it was, Milo knew there were worse things Mila could want to do, so he told people about it.

Mila was confined to her room for a week. Everybody at school was assuming she'd taken the veil already, was at those low tasks that burdened their bad dreams.

Once Mr Galitzki got out of Mila a cross-fingered pledge to give up on the sisters and she was back in school, kids made a gauntlet of the sisters' vows for her to run. In her defense, Milo tugged on a few lapels and punched a few snouts but even if he'd been able to punch out the whole school it wouldn't have helped Mila.

At morning recess of Mila's second day back, I was sitting in a classroom over an Aunt Flo pain piercing through to my back. In came Mila, sick of people going to her, "Hey, Sister Mila." On an impulse, I asked how she was. She claimed to be fine, though the face she treated me to said something more like, *what do* you *care*? She went and stood at the window.

I said, "Tough, huh?"

She admitted to the window, "It is." All thoughts of Sister Mila vanished when she said softly, "Some days you just want to fuck off and *die*. You know?"

41

"Um, I know." I joined her. "Hey. Listen."

"Yeah – what?" Without any sign of humor Mila put her head on one side and cocked an ear. "I'm listening." That got me on the cusp of a laugh and of the urge to touch her.

I said, "I'm sorry about my friends. They're assholes."

Her eyes said, *and but? So you're not?*

I said again, "It's tough," then heard myself telling her about my wanting to nurse, and how my mom and dad had been. I wasn't sure how that was going to sit with her, especially as I was making a comparison between Jesus and the Balz General Hospital. I hadn't been locked up in my room over it either, nor had a brother with the loudest voice in town broadcasting it.

Mila pushed her hair back from her temples. I thought how handsome she was, and how I'd not noticed that before.

"You've got to do what you think you need to do." Her voice steamed the window. She spotted the vapor with a finger. "No matter what obstacles you got." She waved them away.

"Yeah, I guess."

"Wise." She avoided my eyes and yet still I felt her stare the word at me.

"Sure."

"Or stupid. If you really want to do it," she said, "you'll do it." She looked at me then. "Jesus will help you."

I kind of hah-hmmed nervously at that, but said a quiet *yeah*.

"Sometimes whether you want His help or not."

In her voice, it sounded as true as anything you heard in the classrooms at the Lyceum. I hadn't thought about Jesus helping me, but maybe it was at that moment that I knew that after school I would go to the

Balz General Hospital and ask a starched, supercilious matron just what it was I had to do to get into nursing. She'd give me a withering look and a fan of forms. That evening I would dust off my science books and hardly be without them till I graduated with distinction in the sciences a few years later.

On the campus, groups of girls stood in their gossiping gaggles, while gangs of boys did the same but tried to dignify it with the name of *talk*. Richard Rat was remonstrating with two of my neighbors. I had an idea what about. I guessed Milo was nearby doing the same till he turned a corner, Loretta Churchyard burying his head in her huge head of bright hair as she spoke urgently into his ear.

Mila said, "That unfortunate kid," which was just like her, with all she had to think about at that moment.

"*Howl, shepherds.*" I didn't know what that meant, had just picked it out of the loopy things Loretta was heard to say.

"*Cry aloud,*" Mila finished for me with an acid little smile.

Rumor had it that Loretta was about to get bumped from school for setting a heap of gym mats on fire in the shed out back of the sports fields, while declaring, "In Egypt shall they all meet their end." We had to guess that this was her way of talking about the sinners who'd done their own gymnastics on those mats, though as far as anybody knew they were never going to head for anyplace as outlandish as Egypt. Loretta was being shown the door because she was crazy and poor and not good at anything except declaiming parts from the *Bible*. A lot of kids at the Lyceum were crazy, but if their parents had money, or if they could chase a football around a field with pointless expertise, it didn't matter.

I looked at Mila and thought then how she had to have the patience of those saints that surrounded us in Balz with the memory of their suffering. I sensed even then that there was a lot of hurt between Mila and her brother, but it was nothing to what was going to pile up in graduation summer, when Lucy Ephraim died.

THREE

Masked Dance Saturday Night, Twelve Twenty And All The Artifice Of The Orient

◄─────◈─────►

The attic door opened onto Milo Galitzki lit by moonlight, and a Chinese mandarin entered the room. Milo took in the looping mustaches, the blue silk jacket with its high collar and the yellow pants tapering to neat black shoes. Even with all the artifice of the Orient the apparition looked like Richard Rat. Some girl followed him. She was supposed to be Cleopatra. She was straight out of the children's encyclopedia, but all the same no less grandiose in the shabby room. The blond pigtail hanging out of her head-dress did little to diminish the effect.

"You all done in here?" Only unintentionally threatening, that was Richard.

Milo nodded but couldn't resist saying, "It *looks* like I'm busy, Richard?"

"Hey." A light little laugh died in the mandarin's throat. "I'm not Richard."

Cleopatra snapped fingers and said, "Richard?" in a shocked but comic tone of voice. "Jesus *Mary*. The *rat*?" Then, as if she were surrounded by grave robbers, she about-turned in a shimmer of lamé and a rattle of beads and made for the corridor.

The Oriental face remained inscrutable as the mandarin cursed. He pulled that face off and threw it at Milo's head.

"Richard, sorry." Milo bent and picked up the mask. He handed it back with the action of the guy at the zoo feeding the alligators.

"*Milo?*" There was something about Richard Rat's face that prodded people into bad-mood memories of damp locker rooms and lines to see the school dentist. Right then though Milo saw the face of a dog who got shown a bone but given a stone. Richard got distracted by a zap of static from the handle as he reached behind him to shut the door, and bared his teeth. He said, "Why ask, even? *Had* to be you."

"Sorry."

"You didn't come by." Richard's tone was sore.

"No. Sorry." Milo hated that forlorn tone, and hated having brought it to his friend. "I haven't been home too long."

"Well." Richard spread hands. "Now you're here, thanks a bunch. You know who that was?"

"Yeah." Milo didn't know anybody in town, he remembered: a guy went away to college for four years, came back and everybody was a stranger, behind masks or not. "In fact, no. Cleopatra?" he ventured.

"That was Bronia Chambers." Richard let out a groan.

Milo was about to say, that *pint-size Minnehaha,* but didn't think it so wise.

"Bronia Fucking Chambers." Richard's hand-movements would have looked expressive in the glare of footlights.

"That was *not* Bronia Chambers." Milo thought he ought to at least try to make his friend feel better, although his memory of Cleo certainly fitted the shape of Bronia, who had moved in and out of the background of their school years. "Too tall," he lied. Richard ignored that, repeated Bronia Chambers' modified name like some profane prayer. Milo improvised, "Too small, maybe."

On one of his trips home Milo remembered Richard enthusing about how Bronia Chambers, a habitual feature in the top five, at least, of boys' votes for most hideous girl at junior high, had turned from an ugly duckling into a swan. "Not one of the real *humdinger* swans," Richard had admitted. "But a swan nevertheless anyhow, just the same."

"Too fat." Milo searched the ceiling for adjectives. "Too *Egyptian*," he risked. That got half a smile out of Richard's good heart, which just couldn't resist the little comic ghost that hovered around all our heads in that miserable town.

Richard kept that half a smile frozen onto his face. 'There's Milo,' he was thinking. 'College boy all done with college, Milo G stood tall on his big strong legs that don't do him any good now, anchored in this town, his eyes dull with the dead wood of this town, my oldest pal Milo Galitzki.' He made a swift fist and punched Milo very hard on the chin.

"*Fuck.*" Milo reached up, felt the numb chin of his mask. He tasted cabbage iron in the blood on the tip of his tongue. He pulled the mask off and threw it down. "What did you do that for?" His stance changed: fists up and legs apart.

The sight made Richard's smile break out and blaze in an old competitive excitement. He saw the lights in Milo's eyes, a fire consuming that dead wood. Richard called, "You earned it." He put hands up as Milo advanced, and said, "Now come on, Milo, let's not get into this. We're quits, right?"

"You are growing into a violent man," Milo observed. "That's not a good thing. You ought to learn to control your aggression."

"Control your mouth." Richard's reply was like the slapping back of a medicine ball through the close-packed air in the room. "And I'll worry about my aggression."

They weren't thinking anymore of Richard's ruined chance of being a Chinaman on Bronia Chambers' Silk Route. Both were thinking of how

Milo's mouth had always revealed the lives of others and foretold their destinies. They were picturing Lucy Ephraim. They saw her in her yard, going around on her unicycle. She was using a stick not to balance with but to show her sense of balance. The stick was the same height as her. Richard remembered Milo telling him about Lucy's stick, remembered his exact words, recalled them echoed back at him from every corner of town. Both saw her climb up the stick and disappear like a boy in a sideshow in India, fear of growth in his eyes because he knew that when he grew he'd go from sideshow star to sidestreet panhandler. It was soundtracked by Milo, talking. Richard hadn't meant to bring such a vision between them, and it was his turn to be sorry.

"Well, so, now." Richard thought it the decent thing to change the subject. "You're not busy in here? I mean, I am *understanding* the situation?"

Milo rubbed his chin and put on a lantern show of expressions to display his discomfort. He recalled that Richard had seen it all his life and was waiting for it to end. Then he remembered the angel. "Listen," he said. "You didn't see an angel, huh? On the stairs?"

"What?" Richard flickered his interest. "That big tall angel?"

"*Yeah. Who* is she? Do you know?"

Milo could see Richard think up some lie, and Richard managed, "It was Kasia Krantz."

"No." The Lyceum's basketball star would never have even sniffed at Milo, let alone say the things the angel had said. It was rumored that she'd put out for anybody who asked nicely, as long as they were hulking football player types. "It wasn't her." Milo was caught on a sliver of memory, that of the alluring operation of the angel's sex, its doors that opened to reveal doors, its ridges and floodgates: miracle of biomechanics. "Might have been Bronia Chambers." Mischief made the casual suggestion. "Except," he improvised quickly as he saw Richard's hands crunch into fists, "she was maybe twice as tall."

"Jesus." Milo registered one more time the injury he'd done his friend. Richard slammed a palm with a fist. Milo was glad it wasn't aimed at his chin again. "Bronia Fucking Chambers."

There really was no telling whether the queen of the Nile had turned on a heel because Milo had said it was Richard in particular or just because his name had been uttered. The routine at the masked dance was that you didn't exchange names, though people often did, especially if paternity suits might later be involved. You could also make an exception if you fell in love, Milo thought with some excitement. Was that what was hanging over his head, love? Lovers could break any rules.

"Well," Milo reasoned, "this is the *Ladies' Excuse Me*." That was just something to print on the dance tickets; it didn't matter what the theme was, as everybody went got up in the same old things anyhow. Milo didn't recall angels ever coming to the dance, though. "And that's exactly what Cleo just did, Richard."

"Thought it meant you should say it if you ever *met* a lady here." Richard let his face go sour. "You'd sooner meet a fucking Chinaman."

"You *are* a fucking Chinaman."

"A real one, I mean." Richard made emphasis by shoving his mask back on.

"I'm sorry." Milo took his arm. "I owe you a big one. Listen, though, since you're not busy right now, be a mensch and help me find the angel, huh?"

Richard said only, "Come on," and threw the door open onto the cacophony in the corridor. They picked their way through unmasked kissing couples on the stairway, a Restoration pair, a vamp with a cowboy and a Trojan with a Bavarian waitress in a dirndl skirt. They got down to the mezzanine over the big room.

"You want the angel?" The mandarin looked impartial, but under the mask Milo knew Richard was laughing. "There she is." Milo felt something turn over inside him, for down in the crowd there were maybe twenty angels, all shimmying in formation to the band's rendition of some jingly waltz, and all looking like they were waving up at him.

The day Milo met Bronia, when moments of injury crossed his visions of glory

Milo had wound up hanging out with the unbeautiful Bronia Chambers one afternoon years before while preoccupied with the following day's Balz bike race. Their paths crossed in the Bistra Café on Mozhay Beach, Milo having just completed a sixty-mile ride. He had showered off the grit but kept the glow the ride had brought. Bronia's utterance of his name broke him out of a daydream in which he was climbing up to the sky on his bike. Vexed, he saw her white silk blouse shot through with red flowers, her silk platinum hair tied up with ribbons to match. She looked like she'd been in a road accident.

His elbow ached with an old injury, warning him that it was an invitation to the Devil to be thinking about accidents. He crossed fingers, but still saw himself sprawled on the road in a tangle of cussing jocks and broken spokes. He looked suspiciously at Bronia's frank stare. Was she hexing him? Whenever he thought anybody was trying to put the dreaded *machas* on him he thought of his otherworldly friend Lucy Ephraim and the stigmata she bore with a smile.

"You're doing what?" Bronia asked him, and as was Milo's way he told her he was attaboying himself up for the race. She made the mistake of saying, "Bike racing sure is… interesting." Milo didn't catch her tone, so bored her rigid talking about it. She just said *uh-huhs* that, it dawned on him later, were just her way of nodding herself awake.

Bronia changed the subject by asking Milo why he and Richard Rat were fighting late Sunday evening in a corner of the Rink. As soon as the question was out, Milo's nose throbbed from one of Richard's lucky punches and then his ear, from another, and goddam it there she was again, reminding him of his moments of injury.

The word was that Milo and Richard had clashed over a liking for cop's daughter Niamh O'Dowd, which heralded a new note in their arguments.

"I thought you were pals," Bronia scolded.

"We are." Milo sensed something other than the question at work. The kids at the Lyceum knew that once Milo and Richard ran out of words they slugged things out, then forgot it almost before it was over.

"So how come he kicked your ass?"

"Pals are allowed to fall out. And anyhow," Milo protested.

"What?"

"I kicked *his* ass."

A crack opened in Milo's perceptions as he sat with Bronia Chambers that day: he was puzzling over the knowledge that there was something in her that knew not only that she wasn't among the ugliest girls in school, and that she was actually good looking in some odd, intense way. He felt the power of her gaze telling him that she despised anybody who said otherwise. It pushed through to him when he tried to change the subject back to bike racing, and heard himself trip out the words, "Hey, Bronia, when I'm riding out there tomorrow, getting up those hills, I'll think of you." A spark took the glaze out of her eyes. "That is, you know, if you want me to."

He knew what he meant, which was that he was having a time with her that day despite the injuries, and would be happy to think of it next day and, went the script he was making up, maybe the day after too; he was schmoozing her, he realized, on the verge of blushing. He didn't know what his words had woken inside her. "Uh," he petered out to the silence she stared at him. "Who knows?"

51

Bronia's face was impenetrable for a second and then her gaze became a glare. Milo saw red infuse her cheeks as she formed the words, "Not me. Niamh O'Dowd knows, maybe." With the whole of the Mozhay Beach cool set looking on, she got up and walked, leaving him looking at the big glass of soda he'd bought her.

So how, a reader might be thinking, do *I* know all this for sure? Firstly, I got Milo to tell me his side of it years later when we married. But secondly, and more pertinently, I *was* that same pint-size Minnehaha, that same top-five ugly duckling, Bronia Chambers. Milo was right: I knew I was beautiful, but not till that moment he too realized it. It gave me an inkling of the power of beauty, which would allow me to turn any boy away on a whim. It had to be Milo because he was there. I was also simmering at him fighting over my occasional pal Niamh O'Dowd. It was eating me up inside, and I lashed out and caught Milo with the full force of my hurt.

His face warming, Milo sat and watched the bubbles in the soda till they calmed. He found himself thinking of Niamh, and how he'd sucked the mountain air out of her mouth and kissed her on the lips and on the tit and how she obviously hadn't kept her side of their pact to kiss and not to tell. Niamh's secret lovelorn admirer Richard had found out; that had been bad enough, but now the whole damn town obviously knew. In that case, though, he didn't have to care. Next day, he thought, getting back to the lines of the road that coursed along the map in his mind, he'd stand on the podium in the Rink and pull on the sky-blue fastest climber's jersey. He'd raise a bouquet of flowers, and by doing that would extend to all those Mozhay Beach phonies around him that same long finger he'd managed, briefly, to stick up Niamh O'Dowd.

When Richard and Milo were six, the fight that changed their faces and their lives

The first time Richard Rat punched Milo was when they were at elementary school. They were being kept after school for some misdemeanor. Miss Kodaly swished in wearing one of her big flowery skirts, cryptic smile on her face as she leaned down and shook her sweet scent over them and gave them something to write. Then, like they knew she would, she stepped to the piano. Most kids were happy when it was her overseeing detention and not Miss Ostrovska, who sat and watched kids over her mustache the whole time to make sure they did what she gave them to write before making a drama of dumping it in the trash. For Miss Ostrovska then, Milo used to write about the farm picture, for instance *It is a frigging farm. It has a green frigging door. It has frigging flowers at the frigging windows. There is a frigging cow in the frigging yard and some frigging chickens pecking at the frigging ground.* He told me once that if he could go back in time he'd appendix it with *It doesn't frigging look like any frigging farm anyfriggingplace around Balz.*

That afternoon, Richard ran across and pulled the piano stool out for Miss Kodaly. She said, "Why, thank you, Richard," in her dark European contralto. She didn't know that what Richard did as she sat was tug her skirt up at the back with his long, light fingers and fix it to the handles on the sides of the stool to, just about, show her panties.

Milo didn't mind seeing her panties. So what was he thinking of as he put his hand up? He would never know. Maybe he just couldn't face the melancholy of separation from the fading afternoon outside. It wouldn't be the first or last time he would commit to an idea before thinking through its consequences. Richard made noises forming whispers promising he'd kick Milo's butt, bust his head, break his arms. All the while Miss Kodaly played something languid. As she had her back to them, Milo had to say, "Hey, Miss Kodaly? You know what Richard just did with your skirt? Just hiked it up at the back so we can see your white panties with little yellow flowers? Ma'am?"

Miss Kodaly kept up a left-hand arpeggio, but moved her right hand around her back to her skirt, which she pushed down. The phrase she was playing fizzled out. Richard sat in porphyry agony. Miss Kodaly let the lid of the piano down carefully. She walked over to Richard, looked him in the eyes for a second then got one of his long ears and twisted it till he was going, "Ow, Miss Kodaly, that *hurts*."

She led him to the door, saying, "I know that, Richard. And I'll tell you something, which is that I got a stick all covered in dust because I never used it before in my life. I'm going to use it today, though, right now, and that's going to hurt even more." At the door she paused with her burden. She turned to Milo and said, "Get out of here."

Milo walked through the yard and out into the street, puzzled at what he'd done. He walked out to the cliff over Glass Beach then along Ascension Avenue past the old mansion, then home. He got the feeling that people were looking at him. He lay on his bed and tried to read, but couldn't. In the bathroom he splashed the heat from his face. He was thinking of Miss Kodaly's panties, but thinking even more of Richard, and his rat's ear all red.

He couldn't make out what time did. None passed, then hours. Time was all it needed for the revelation that what Richard did in the classroom he had done for Milo.

Milo's bedroom door opened and Richard Rat sidled in, shutting the door behind him in a way that reminded both of them of Miss Kodaly's attention to the piano lid. Then he picked his way respectfully through the junk and toys on the floor.

Milo found out later that Richard told Mrs Galitzka he was a friend and please could he come see Milo about something to do with school? "Nice boy," Milo's mom said as she swabbed the cuts on Milo's face and yellowed them with iodine and probed in his mouth to see if the tooth Richard knocked out had left any roots. "Cute face. At least, it was cute when he came in. Didn't look so cute with his nose bleeding all down his front. I don't know what you could have quarreled over in two minutes, Milo, but I'm sure you'll be best of friends tomorrow."

It occurred to Milo to tell his mom, "I can't see out my right eye." That made her let out a long breath and get their coats. She took him to the BG to find Richard with *his* mom in the waiting room, about to have fragments of nasal bone and cartilage straightened out. Years later when I was nursing I often passed in and out of that room and saw bruised and bloodied little boys with tight-lipped moms. I can't help but picture them all as Milo and Richard.

Milo's eye never looked quite the same again, its iris a shade darker than its companion, but he saw out of it perfectly. Richard's nose acquired a slight hump, but he was eventually able to blow it without its bubbling blood, and it kind of suited him, somehow. They were indeed best of friends next day. They still went on fighting over the stupidest things though, at the fort elementary, then at the Lyceum.

"You had to have liked her a lot," Richard said out of the blue to Milo years later as they sat on the wall of the fort.

Milo said, "Who?"

"Miss Kodaly." Richard vamped on an invisible piano. "You asshole."

"No doubt." Milo wondered what she was doing and thinking right then, and what color underwear she had on. "I must have." The realization was shocking, and funny. "But not till you showed me her panties."

Me age four, the day I knew I'd be saved by a heroic boy bugler

People said the school in the fort was haunted by the ghosts of the men who got stood against its walls and shot, back in the unforgiving past. I was glad I didn't have to sit behind its bullet-pocked walls. I remember

Miss Kodaly all the same. Struck by her bearing and the way she swung that ass in those skirts, I watched her lead a panting crocodile of pygmy kids up that hill the bright afternoon my mom dragged me to see the old Zacharov mansion.

A straggler scuffed past, a kid with agreeable eyes, like a goat's. It was the kid with the loud voice I saw at church and in the library: Milo Galitzki.

I loved him. I didn't know why. I didn't have the parts in me then to swell up and prompt me even to *know* that. I made big eyes at him till my mom tugged me back into the matter she had in mind.

Our visit to the mansion was in the cause of a brew of nostalgia and revenge. I wasn't to know that at the time, being maybe four, maybe five, but I knew that mansion already.

I somehow knew it when Balz people called it the big house and touched their caps when its owners, the Zacharov family, were chauffeured in and out by flunkies rigid as statues. The Zacharovs were money. It was they who started the factories that filled Balz's air with the filth that turned the frost brown and caved in the lungs of its citizens and who paid those citizens a sustenance wage to bust their guts in those industrial hells. It was the Zacharovs who blew all their dough to the sound of jazz and the taste of highballs then watched it go up in smoke on the Stock Market, who slunk out the gates one last time and didn't come back.

My great granny scrubbed its floors when it was the big house, and as Mom hushed me through the hallway I made an effort not to see great granny on her knees.

"Now we've got the money." I was startled at the echo that followed Mom's voice. That was how she crowned tales like these, to erase the image of great granny's back bent over the business of those who lived cramped into the servant quarters. "Dirty business," she felt driven to explain, though it was left to me to imagine the dirty work. I was meant to feel proud at the mention of our money, but I couldn't. I looked at the dust covering my patent maryjane shoes and felt sad without knowing exactly why. "Why, we could just buy this old place now." Mom's voice echoed its way up the staircase and around the mezzanine. "Lock, stock, barrel."

"There aren't any locks," it occurred to me to say, but only later. I was slow, remember, kids at school going, "Doh," into my face when I got things wrong. "That's how we got *in* here. No stocks either, Mom, whatever they are. And not even empty barrels."

"We've got the money now." Mom was stuck on stocks and shares, maybe. "We've got the nice place to live. We've got the name. We're citizens."

She was tracing the family history for me, how my great granny came from Kazakhstan with other frostbitten Kazakhs and got dumped next to the railroad. "What railroad?" they asked. Fat overseers went, "Doh," into their faces. There was no railroad till the men got off their asses to the piles of tracks and slats and built it, with the women supplying the food and the laundering and the, ahem, comfort. Great granny married a fellow-Kazakh called, for want of a little imagination, Kazakhian but her daughter, my granny, wound up marrying a Polak from Lviv, name of Oborski. He was a fine man who looked after her and my mom till he got killed in an accident on that same railroad. When Mom said we'd gotten the name, it was her way of assuring me that she'd married the Kazakhians and Oborskis out of immigrant stock and that nobody would place us in tents that stank of rancid butter on the Central Asian steppes, nor in famine-haunted settlements. No, with a name like my dad's – Chambers – people would picture us in more genteel places.

Us being citizens, we got to rub shoulders with other good citizens, like my dad's swell friends. An early memory is of hearing them talking about somebody who owed them money. "He is fucked." This was said by Theodore House, a big guy in a shiny suit and a silk necktie with sunflowers on. They let out laughter. "His wife is fucked," Mr House intoned. "His kids?" They all let rip with the only answer. That laughter had an edge to it like no laughter I'd heard before. "His place?" the show scratched on. "His car? His help, even? Fucked. A waiter who was polite to him? Some guy who smiled at him one time on the street, raised a hat and said, 'Good morning?' He's fucked, too. He's *very* fucked. His dog. His cat. His little fucking yellow fucking canary in its little fucking cage. Fucked." I looked from one face to another and tried to laugh too. My dad grinned like a baboon and joined the chorus when it was time to.

These people, now *they* were money. Their laughter was the sound of slot machines. Their eyes shone out silver dollars, and their skin was the shade of grubby dollar bills. I hid my eyes. I scrubbed my skin. I wasn't crazy about it being kind of yellow, but I didn't want it to go green. I didn't want to be money.

Mom busied herself in the kitchen and helped the help.

"Now we employ the help," she was saying as she led me out of the mansion. I knew that. Would the ghosts of the Zacharovs give even the hint of a goddam? Mom guided us out into the last of the sun. I thought of Zosia, our help, and how I heard her crying one time in the closet Mom had given her out back of the house. Years later I found out she was jagging her way through that time of tears because a guest in our house, one of those swell friends of Dad's, played the *monsieur* on her, and hushed her with fifty lousy bucks.

There was a vulgar party on to celebrate some deal or other and it was going on under my room. It kept leaking into the dream I was trying to have, of me and Milo Galitzki levitating above the fort to watch the lights of Balz wink on. I got up and went to a spare room on the other side of the house, hoping it'd be quieter and I could get back to sleep. When I opened the door I threw light on a couple. The girl was on the bed, her skirt around her waist and her legs around the neck of a guy whose face I couldn't see, as it was buried in her snatch. I saw this odalisk's view for maybe twenty fascinated seconds till the girl fixed the whites of her eyes on me and I couldn't bear their scrutiny. Mom and Dad swore I'd had a nightmare. Dad looked me in the face as he rearranged my memory for me. Mom sat there mortified. I know now she was busy thinking, 'This is going on in front of my own daughter, in the middle of the dream I bought into', and not having a clue what to do about that. So she kept on spending the money; nothing else for her to do.

From the grounds of the mansion that day of our visit I looked up the hill to the ochre brickwork of the fort. I saw a little boy caught in the slit window of a tower. I caught my breath, and with excitement knew he was watching for warring Tatar horsemen from the Asian steppes. When he saw them coming he would draw his breath up from his boots and force it into his bugle to blast out a warning that meant *In an instant shall the marauder be upon us.* He'd be diverted by the sight of an arrow in the air. It would hang there graceful and glinting, a second before it pierced his throat. The bugle would slip from his fingers and then the only sound it would make would be a lonely clatter down the walls.

I pulled at Mom's arm in my agitation till she had to break her spiel to snap out a line of *whats.* With a finger I drew the picture in my head of the little bugler on his back on the ground, his short life playing before his eyes and rushing out of his throat as he thrashed around, head going side-to-side. Mom followed my finger and said, *"What,* honey – what on *Earth?"* but he was gone.

That was Milo Galitzki. I knew it was a time of miracles, when magic boy buglers died, their throats torn out by steel but their good work done, and right there and then rose to Heaven to live among angels.

I didn't know then I'd marry him – well of course I didn't. Mom didn't know, either. A couple of years would make it clear that she had in mind for me some Mozhay Beach kid whose name would be suffixed with *Junior* or an ordinal number, to let us know he was the product of his proud dad. Mom had dreams too, lived in her own time of miracles. She wasn't to know her dreams were jinxed. I'm glad I knew her before all she was good for was being ashamed.

I didn't know any of that then. I looked over our little town, my eyes full of lights, my chest full of air. I was thrilled to think of those machines coming to life down there to fill rooms with yellow pastel, and music, or news from the world that lay outside and festered in its madness. My face fell when I thought of the laughing, violent men who stalked that world scattering money and who, wearing the brightest of neckties, saw to it that people got truly fucked, and fucked again. Then I felt relieved to be in Balz in the care of a heroic bugle boy who would tell us of the coming of men like that, even if it killed him.

The Balz Lyceum's feisty girls and their secrets and miseries

The Mozhay Beach set might have looked down on Milo and his crowd, but not to their faces. When they had any contact, which was often in a town like Balz with only one decent school, a cold, mocking politeness prevailed.

Milo got away with knowing the things he knew because he didn't let them make him into a smartass. Not content just to take time out of school whenever he wanted, he would also sit in class the whole semester and neither say nor do a thing, but he wound up with above average grades. Nobody respected that in itself, but it couldn't be argued with.

First year of high school it was the girls from Milo's crowd who set about brewing trouble, bullies like hoity toity Illona Peterlejtner. People said the rooms over Peterlejtner's store had to be full of potatoes and that was why she and her brother had to share a room way into their teens. We snickered that Illona and Axel would just have to get married some day, though never in their hearing. I watched Illona square up to big strong Kasia Krantz one time over some imagined slight; when she said she'd break Kasia's face for her, there was a terrible certainty to it. A silence hung heavy till Kasia backed down, black tears in her eyes because she knew it was a moment of reputation lost for keeps. What made me sore was that Illona was Milo's friend. I thought, 'What does he want being friends with a loudmouth tramp like that?' And it was like she saw me thinking that, because she picked me out of the crowd to say, "Hey – *you*. Go nurse your ugly face before it bites you."

Niamh O'Dowd was the only one who moved between our side and theirs. She had learned from her dad, Balz's biggest toughest grimmest cop Gerard O'Dowd, not to be fazed by anybody. She said that when she went camping on Craw Mountain with Milo and his friends she saw Illona and Eurydice Armentiere in a sleeping bag together, arms around each other. "Like a boy and a girl," she giggled. This didn't stop the Mozhay Beach boys falling in love with Eurydice anyhow. Football players and basketball dudes carried torches for her and hoped nobody would notice their moon faces. They did tryouts for the school fencing team, of which Eurydice was turning into the rising star, a cabaret that used to make coach Leshchinski – a man not only with a mission but with the worst of tempers – very mad.

Eurydice always affected a fixed expression, eyes unmoving, bowed lips barely changing their set. She rarely betrayed any hint of either humor, interest or compassion when in conversation with anybody other than Milo and the others. She was tall on perfect legs and had ass-length light brown hair that her mom brushed fifty times before school each morning. Consequently, an aura of static electricity followed her in the classroom. It crackled on kids' fingers the whole of first class and was utilized for making paper figures stand on end and do magic dances.

Miss Kodaly alerted Eurydice's parents to something odd in their perfect daughter: she went into a trance then emerged from it without drama and resumed whatever she'd been doing. The teacher described it as Eurydice switching off. It wasn't wanton, Miss Kodaly asserted, but she didn't know what it was, and she felt she ought to. Benny and Felice Armentiere maintained a stony silence until out of earshot of Miss Kodaly, when they dismissed her as an interfering witch. There couldn't possibly be anything wrong with kids who got whatever they hollered for, got new everything when it was fresh out, and got bored with it the same day. There were rooms in the Armentiere house, it was rumored, full of junk they'd used once then abandoned, filled with clothes, bicycles, musical instruments, toys, books, games, wrapping paper discarded next to them. It was like Macy's department store in there, people claimed, and all for Eurydice and her brother Benny.

Eurydice was of course a long way from perfect. She wasn't *good* at anything, and wouldn't be till she took up stabbing people later with her fencing. It didn't matter at elementary school, but began to show at junior high. Milo, Mila, Moby, Richard, Orville Charleroi, even Loretta Churchyard, wore out the world's welcome with the enthusiasms they'd developed, no matter how crazy. Eurydice was simply deemed to be beautiful. I guess she had no disagreement with that, but even at an early age I felt she'd one day need to stop being decorative, and *do* something – anything.

She remained the coolest creature in the universe, there was no doubt, until the *grand mal* of her epilepsy took her by the tongue and thrashed her around on the ground, limbs out of sync as she grazed her knees and elbows and pissed her pants and got dirt in that beautiful hair of hers. I sometimes caught the hunted feeling in her features, knowing that the *grand mal* would catch her up again.

What nobody knew was that her dad, used car supremo Benny Armentiere Senior, whose smiling gray cut-out face appeared each week in ads in our local rag the Balz Bugle, used to screw her two or three times a week from when she was little till after she got married. He was destined to climb into his prize de Soto saloon, drink a bottle of bourbon then gas himself years later on publication of Eurydice's book on the subject, *Used Goods*. That was the sum of her ruined life, she said in the book, secret shame and the grandest of *mals* shadowing her through school and college and the ruins of her marriage. I couldn't help but think of the arrogant creature with electric hair and bright teeth all the same, who hung on Milo's arm as they walked up the hill home from school.

The manic artist who pictured the world at any cost to anybody, even himself

Milo and the fort school crowd straightened out early on the idea that their outsider status would be exploited in any way. "You only have to have *one* fight at school." Milo explained the boy-logic to me. "Just make sure people remember it and keep away from you." His was not with Richard, but with Eurydice's hapless brother Benny who, tired of being invisible in his sister's perfect shadow, disdained the fort school crowd and aspired to cross the divide to the Mozhay Beach set, thinking his having *things* would be enough – it never was, of course. Milo couldn't remember how the fight with Benny started, but it probably had something to do with Eurydice. It kept Benny out of school for days and out of Milo's way seemingly forever.

In the first week of the first semester at the Lyceum, Richard Rat broke the wrist and several ribs of a guy called Rollo Vasilevski. Richard was suspended at once, not managing to convince Mr Leeward the principal that he was provoked. He surely was, because once Rollo recovered his parts and his pride he jocked his way through school as an overbearing asshole, but not at Richard or at anybody Richard knew. That wasn't the full stop to Richard's fighting career at school, as there were always guys like Rollo wanting to step up and try their luck, giving the lie to Milo's one big fight theory. I don't know if people like Richard are fearless, as such. Stupid, more like. He brought a scary kind of do-or-die to such matters. His being Milo's avowed best pal made me see both of them in different lights. It didn't stop me thinking Richard was a manic moron, though.

It was the same with Moby Krzeski, whose insanely-priced paintings now hang in big-deal galleries around the world to testify to his sensitive soul. Everybody said it was Milo and Richard who beat the crap out of big Wolfgang Zenn, another Mozhay Beach muscle about town, over some business stirred up, possibly, by the Peterlejtner twins. He was in the Balz General for a week, and him the star quarterback of the Lyceum football team. Coach Leshchinski went ape at Milo over that and barred him from the gym. That hurt Milo and made him produce an alibi. Two bikers roared onto the campus and dismounted from their machines on the front lawn, nobody wanting to appraise them of school regulations about motorized vehicles and designated areas. They found the coach and assured him, more or less politely, that Milo was at the roadhouse at the time in question, tinkering with their bikes in his little engineer's zeal. "Same as a note from my mom," Milo claimed.

The finger for the Wolfgang Zenn assault wavered over Richard still. He gave it the finger back and dared it to halt over him. Wolfgang Zenn's last words till they unwired his jaw were, "What do you clowns want?" Appropriate, because the pair who beat him up were dressed as circus clowns. It was in that detail that it finally dawned on everybody that it had to have been Moby and his brother Selby; that was their ridiculous style down to a t.

I thought Moby was a heathen and a nutcase but he was Milo's friend, so I took the opportunity to make eyes at him once in a moment during recess. "Hi," I said to him. "What can you do with this weather, huh?" It was snowing; still that was no excuse for such a Balz storekeeper thing to say. Even as I said it, I was watching a put-down tickertape across Moby's eyes.

He had the round face of a farm boy, hair that aped strands of brass wire, eyes like chestnuts and freckles like paint splashes across his nose. He made my Asian eyes right back at me, made my teeth the way they stuck out before I got them corrected, made like the artist he was, reflecting life.

All he said was my name. He stretched it out, said it the way my girlfriends called to me, half-playful, half-mocking. He reached over and picked up one of my pigtails. "Your hair's nice," he began. I didn't wait to listen to any more.

Most people agreed that Moby's finest hours in Balz were when he painted the Holy Apostles cathedral with God and Jesus and a stunning eastern Virgin, saints and angels and vanquished devils, gave them all splendor and movement on its walls. However, what people really liked was that the year he was fifteen he painted the mayor, corrupt and pompous Doctor Hoffman, twice life-size on the back wall of the movie theater. He left the mayor with his trademark derby hat and his sash of office, but otherwise pictured him in the full glory of his pale, chubby nakedness. Dead of night, Moby at work with his paints and his rags and his sense of balance and caricature. Balz was a town that slunk indoors to die each night, so he was counting on not being seen by a soul.

It was just his luck that Lucy Ephraim had been dropped off on the highway at that hour after a stint on the road with the circus, and was on her way home. She saw a figure busy on a ladder where a ladder just looked *wrong,* and abided by the law and told the first officer she met that there was a guy robbing the movie theater. Moby had just finished his *magnum opus* when he got helped down by officer Gerard O'Dowd. He got slung in jail but wasn't booked. Instead the mayor, not normally the kind of guy to get involved in arguments about art, personally kicked the living daylights out of Moby for five minutes. Maybe it was this low act that made it slip the mind of officer O'Dowd that he had to detail some men to clean the picture off. By the time that got through his mind, half the town had seen it, ensuring Moby's rise to living legend.

The other thing Moby got out of it was his own week in the BG. The rest of us got a well-deserved break from the self-absorbed little creep.

These were all signs that Moby was the type who would stop at nothing to make his point. Critics say artists want to show life, but they don't; they want to show only their view of it. If they know nothing but bitterness and badness then it doesn't matter what they want to depict. They can turn a thing of beauty into something ugly. People like that are dangerous and, when the world lauds them and lets them, they bring misery and tears and harm that can't be wiped clean with white spirit.

Milo at fifteen, in thrall to the lost songs of saviors

Though Milo wouldn't forget Lucy Ephraim's rescue of him from the salt flats off Reformatory Beach, he didn't see a lot of her as he grew up. When Lucy attended the tea party after getting Milo back she told inquirers that she'd finished her schooling but no, she wasn't going to go work in some factory; she'd try something different. It took a few years to become common knowledge that she performed acrobatics in the circus that traveled as the Udino Brothers' Extravaganza. Balz people talked about that like it was some awful kind of slavery.

"I'm a tumbler," Lucy harked back through centuries of circus tradition to tell anybody who got it wrong. "Not an acrobat." Acrobats had no sense of humor, she claimed, no love of life nor people. They were too hung up on their perfect bodies to be anything but vain and in turn bitter at the emptiness that lay at the end of vanity.

Just before the Christmas Mila got banned from white sisterhood she ran into Lucy in town. Lucy asked Mila how her brother was doing. "He's a bike nut," Lucy checked. "Isn't he?" She was having a problem with her unicycle, and Milo was called down the hill to help.

When Lucy wasn't on the road she lived in a little house on the hill down back of the fort. Its yard was full of scary-high climbing frames and poles for Lucy to practise on, and soft mats for her to fall on. They hid the concreted track on which she perfected her unicycling.

Milo had never seen a unicycle before. He scrutinized it, Lucy said, more like it was a *unicorn*. As he worked on it he eyed the bandages on

Lucy's hands, knew what they were hiding. "God's wounds," she seemed happy to confirm. Milo repeated the two words like a fool out of Shakespeare, his face flushed at what a day it was turning out to be.

He put the bike bits down and begged, "Let me see."

With the flair of the performer Lucy was, she called him and Mila into her house and unbandaged her stigmatized hands. Milo slapped his head in little boy's wonder. He had to admit that the stigmata were even more miraculous than the unicycle. There weren't many questions to ask about either, but Milo asked them all. Lucy said, "I don't know a thing about the bike except how to ride it, so kindly attend to it now and your sister will fix coffee and I'll play you a song about Jesus, peace on His head."

In the house Milo picked up a stick Lucy had in a corner of her hallway. It was black with blue and white and yellow mountain flowers on it, their vivid green stalks snaking a graceful way up and down, like on the side of a Gypsy wagon. There was a lot to divert him right then, so he didn't ask Lucy about it. He got to work, while a part of him got lost in the sound of Lucy Ephraim's strange horned fiddle the way it had so many years before on the flats, as she played the lost songs of saviors.

FOUR

Masked Dance Saturday Night, To One Thirty Amid Angels And Figments And The Green Haze Of Vodka

⚜

When Milo and Richard went from the mezzanine into the soup of bodies, the band clanged to a halt to catch everybody in a second of silence. A flame-haired sax player, a tall boy or a short woman, played a melancholy trill. The bandleader raised his cornet and caught the rest of the band's eyes. Then they began a crazy oompah that cranked the room up into a frantic polka.

"Hey." Richard's voice was deadpan in Milo's ear. "That must be your angel." He pointed left and right. "Or maybe that one."

"Hey." Milo seemed not to have heard. There were two angels within stepping distance. Milo nudged Richard. "Those two there. You ask the one on the left, and I'll ask the one on the right."

"Ask her what?"

"Why, you schmo, ask her... Uh..."

"Ask her if she went upstairs with you?" Richard regressed into the boy living on in Milo's dead days, and let out a whoop. "This is the masked dance and all, but, you know, there are still things you shouldn't go asking a girl."

Milo ignored him. He also ignored the angel on the left, too short. The one on the right he greeted with, "Hey, angel."

Arms and legs moving to the music, she slurred, "Ahoy, lieutenant."

"Sergeant." Milo couldn't pass on a correction. "That is... It's me."

"What?" she said. "Who?"

"Milo."

"And but?" She made her polka into a tango and fell, trusting – foolish – into his arms. He supported her, feathers in his face. She stewed him in a fragrance he knew hadn't belonged to his angel, and said up to him, She stewed him in a fragrance he knew hadn't belonged to his angel, and said up to him, "You have a good time, Milo. But, you know, uh... not with *me*. At least," she said as she righted herself and danced on, "not right now."

"Say." Richard was next to him again. "You got a laundry marker on you?"

"No I don't." Milo went to a pocket absently. "I got a pen."

"Not for me. And I said a laundry marker, lover boy, because if you're going to check out all the angels here you'd better mark their robes. Or else how will you know which ones you asked?"

Richard had a point. Milo followed him back onto the dancefloor. They passed a hangman and a high court judge, gave room to hick cowboys, and sidestepped a vampire. An ancient Greek shimmied by wearing a comedy mask and carrying a surveyor's hypotenuse triangle.

"Pythagoras." A puritan streak in Milo made him feel that math was too serious a subject for the dance. "Very funny."

Richard said, "It's probably your old man." That was kind of funny, too. They were still skitting like boys as they got into a circle of five wondrous angels whose wings towered above the crowd.

The angel faces were identical on the latex masks everybody customized using a children's book on sale in town. That was why all the cowboys looked the same, all the vampires, pixies, soldiers, the ballerinas, showgirls, the courtesans and contessas, dentists, doctors, and all the angels, all disturbingly and confusingly the same.

Richard soon got in conversation with an angel. They all made a dance of spread fingers, shuffled feet and shaken backsides. Milo counted out the steps and reached for the tallest and most graceful of them. He followed steps with her a while but it was obvious that she didn't know who he was from Christ, and didn't care.

"That one you talked to, she said what?" he quizzed Richard as they took up places on one side. His eyes were on the wings in the crowd. Richard was right: how was he going to remember which ones they'd spoken to?

"I asked if she knew you," Richard recited. "She said no. I said that was too bad. I asked if she wanted to. And she said did I think she looked *drunk*, or what?"

After a wounded pause Milo said, "She didn't say that."

"Well, maybe not, but her look did."

"On her mask?"

"What she said was she didn't think so, but she said the little fat one might."

"Sure – yeah." Milo tried to make a face. "I'll see if I can fit her in."

That got a roar from Richard. He banged Milo on the shoulder so hard that Milo's first reaction almost manifested itself in a swing at his friend's face. Milo wished he'd go and... wax his mustache or something.

He couldn't blame Richard for not having grasped the urgency of the situation. Couldn't Richard just *see* that it was important to him though, that of all the people there that night, he might have fallen in love? 'No,' he thought, 'of course he can't, because we don't know each other anymore, Richard and me.' Milo had left to do his college stuff, and had grown in a way that Richard, fixed in Balz, hadn't. He wanted to communicate that then couldn't, not at the dance, anyhow. Not ever, he guessed.

"Drink?" Richard got a half pint of green vodka out of a pocket and waved it at Milo who, about to say no out of habit, got a hold of the bottle and took a swig that burned his gums and made him puff out his chest in an effort not to cough.

The vomiting bear had recovered, and was cutting a path through the crowd as he danced the hora with a girl sailor, clapped on by dancers keen to catch their breath. Milo saw Cleopatra among them.

The vodka rose to tickle Milo's throat and he stuck his head in the air and stretched his neck. It stopped there like a barometer reading. As it sank he came to the lucid moment he had at every Balz affair to reveal the thought, 'What the Sam Hill am I *doing* here?' He tried to pick out the music of the angel's words and to feel like a man in love. He surveyed the horde around him, figments of the jeremiad from all corners of Balz and beyond: spiteful freaks with twisted points-of-view disguised, not very cleverly, as twisted freaks with spiteful points-of-view.

I saw them too, knew they were those people from the world outside who fucked you over and over. They were in town, and there was nothing any heroic bugle boy was ever going to do about that. Among them, no doubt, was a guy who was good at getting into people's houses without their knowing. This would be a guy useful with a saw and a paintbrush, the guy who killed Lucy Ephraim with those ordinary implements, killed her as a sop to his sense of humor, jealousy or revenge, and at the same time robbed Balz of its saint a second time.

Milo thought about that guy too, and courtesy maybe of Richard's vodka saw under those masks the well-maintained faces of the smart boys of Balz, evil because of their stolidity and lack of imagination that made room for the Devil. When Lucy died they made careless laughter at tales told of Lucy Ephraim the believer in the power of God to elongate her limbs and lengthen her body. Bastards.

"Unforgivable," Richard thought he heard Milo say. He leaned down to Milo to hear better.

Milo recalled the voices of those Balz girls at their gee-whizzing and oh-my-good-Lording. He wished it was the right thing to do there at the dance to tell them to shut their noise while he had his memory of Lucy.

It was they and their kind that made the jeremiad stay in Balz, he knew. It was them whose futures had been foretold to bring it to our accursed town.

Milo realized, in puzzled horror, that the bottle in his hand was empty. He swiveled his head to look at Richard, who had magicked up another bottle. Richard raised it to him in a gesture of cheer, called, "Your health."

"Jesus Mary," Milo said.

"Hundred years of it."

Killed for the sake of a laugh, poor Lucy. Was that not a sure-fire indication of the Devil abroad in Balz, spinning his stories to be repeated? Milo's vodka vision gave him the urge to follow the vampires at the dance and run a stake through them. The pixies he'd scatter across the flats for pistol practice and the bear he'd bait with that much-used stake. The cowboys he'd scalp. The judge he'd burn in the Rink with his books. Pythagoras would see whether he could work out his hypotenuse with his triangle forced up his butt. And Cleo, a cage full of asps for her; if her alter-ego was yours-very-truly Bronia Fucking Chambers he'd drown her in a vat of soda. The angels he'd send back express to Heaven, except the one who broke her vows with him. They'd forget Heaven, and hold their tongues with each other's teeth, and love.

So she was which one?

Richard was talking to him. "You and me," he was saying. "Got to catch up."

"Yeah." The word sounded hesitant even to Milo.

"Hey, but you've got to catch an angel first."

"Yeah." Milo was astounded again at how much a monosyllable could betray. He turned to Richard, but Richard was making a line over to Cleo.

A winged figure was looming over Milo. He forgot about those people from the world outside and their mission to build headstones in our town. He found his most charming voice and said, "Hey, angel!"

At the dance I remembered the story about little Milo walking out onto Reformatory Beach in search of his angel. I recalled stories of him in that plane over Balz, distracting Michael Sheltz with angels. It had to be in his blood, the urge to seek out angels. I watched him join the angel dances and knew they were only for those ridiculous robed creatures and those trapped in their wings. I knew too that I'd have Milo for myself before the night was out, though, so I kept my cool and stood back and waited for Milo to exhaust himself on flatulent angel talk.

Milo kills the strong men on that bike, till I put a stop to it the year he was sixteen

Milo wasn't going to fly again, but it was in his nature that his feet would never quite want to touch the ground. I was in class one day making a Herculean effort not to appear slow as Mr Runciman our math teacher asked me with the zeal of a secret policeman about the dumb angles in some stupid triangle. I made the mistake of looking around to see if Milo was listening to me being a math hotshot. His seat was taken by Richard Rat's feet. Mr Runciman was sounding only a little sarcastic as he asked if I was going to just leave the poor triangle unfinished in time and space or what. "Sorry," I said. "I got distracted. You know, Mr Runciman, I get very easily... uh..."

On the road that ran past the Lyceum, I saw Milo. He was on his bike in a blue cycling jersey, the only colourful thing amid the backdrop of a gray day. He was in the slipstream of a truck that, I knew from the writing on its side, wheezed up every month from the south and delivered building materials to a Balz company owned by my dad's client Theodore House. It trundled to another town twenty miles on, then came back through Balz. It hit me then that Milo was going to ride behind that truck for forty miles.

"Forty?" That didn't coincide with the figure Mr Runciman was after. It brought the class out in sniggers. It reminded me that Milo really was as obsessive about riding that bike as people said.

Every year in Balz they put on a bike race. Like the baseball series and the tennis tournament, the livestock fair and the storekeepers' ball, the Easter egg hunt and the icon race, it was an affair that set the bristles of pride on end on citizens' necks. Storekeepers hosed down their slabs, gave away stuff they couldn't sell in a millennium and gossiped in gaggles on the sidewalks. Grannies got up early and squeaked along in their Sunday boots that killed them, and sat on the bleachers set up in the Rink. The podium was there for the finish, along with lucky dip booths and boys selling beer and pop and cotton candy. Chefs presided over enormous tureens of goulash, pans of stroganoff and flame grills from which were promised the all-American burger. Everybody put on their best and chugged around the course in cars till the roads got closed, then on foot.

The race covered seventy miles in and outside the town. The course was punctuated by red-and-white kites every five miles and by race officials pompous with all the paraphernalia of time and motion to mark minutes and seconds. It was the spectators who made it an event though, dotting the roads and spraying picnic food and drink out with their yells whenever they caught sight of a rider.

The riders hit the first sprint near Old Balz and went crazy to get over the line first, so it was a good place from which to spectate. First time I stood there I wondered why there were nurses perched starchily behind a table piled with iodine and bandages. The scrum there usually saw off maybe fifteen hopefuls. One minute they were riding fast and low and the

74

next they were on the ground in heaps of twanging metal and wheels spinning forlornly under their own momentum. The competitors weren't just people like Milo, who rode bicycles all the time, nor only athletes good in other fields. They numbered anybody who could beg or steal or borrow anything that looked vaguely like a bike, and included miners and steelworkers who ate nails for breakfast, and a whole lot of maniacs along for the ride and the air and to see how long they could last. Eight miles out of town sat the roadhouse, and if you stood there you saw the casual riders spot the beer-drinkers outside, wobble to a halt and trip over their tongues in a new race to the bar, then that was them home but no longer dry.

By the time the race got to Preacher's Hill, another fifteen miles along the road, there were maybe twenty riders in serious contention, most of them from out of town. That was the real race, and was where Milo shone. He was fourteen the first year he came out of nowhere and passed them all midway up the climb, sailed over it and schussed down the descent. They caught him at the foot of Craw Mountain but then he got away from them again and summitted alone, and as that had the most climbing points they banged their handlebars in frustration and knew he'd clinched the climber's prize. They didn't quite catch him on the descent from there, and he was able to get up Universe Hill and get the rest of his points in peace. They swallowed him up on the flat road back to Balz and he went down the line like a lead sinker. Because of the climb to the town center, he managed to get up with the tail-end of the bunch once it got back to Balz, but he was dead by then, and barely had the energy for the final lap of the Rink.

And for what? A bunch of flowers and a sky blue jersey with an eagle emblazoned on it. Getting that jersey was the best thing that happened to Milo that year. He didn't care who got the red sprinter's jersey with the lightning bolt, or the sickly yellow one for first rider home, just wanted that blue one to show he got up those hills fastest. I couldn't work any of this out all those times I watched the race, just saw guys on bikes frothing at the mouth and steaming like horses and turning those pedals like the winds of Hell were warming their backs.

That was how it went for Milo the next year too and he stood on that podium, pulled on that jersey and got called King of the Climbs again. He didn't get it the following year. He got it all the other years though, right through college, right up to the year he and I left Balz.

He didn't get it the year he was sixteen because I told my Mozhay Beach neighbor Otto Dreyer, who had twice come second to Milo on the climbs, the best way to get up Craw Mountain quickly. That was with a forty two chain ring on the front bracket and an eleven on the back, with a slug of sugar and water in a one-to-five ratio at the foot of the climb, with not being afraid to leave the slipstream of the bunch early as the road slanted and on passing the second of a certain clump of four sycamore trees, with the sky filling the eyes with tears of pure energy.

The only tears Milo wound up with that day were those of frustration. The eyes of the crowd on Otto Dreyer's disbelieving smile, Milo made his tears in a corner of the Rink, his head on Eurydice Armentiere's shoulder, her hand in his wet hair.

Something in me died then, and made me promise God never to make anybody cry again. Not unless I really had to.

Mila at fourteen, seeking joy, and Milo silent to think of God's wounds and a unicycle

When the Galitzkis went up the hill after their first evening at Lucy Ephraim's, Mila had one thing nagging at the back of her mind. She told Milo he didn't ought to tell a soul about having seen Lucy's stigmata. Milo's face fell as he thought about it. Then he knew she was right. "You can talk about her unicycle," Mila prompted him. He was content till he realized nobody would be interested in that.

Balz's bishop Tauber, who never failed to remind people that he had audienced with the Pope in Rome one time, went to Lucy's house in the kind of episcopalian splendor only the church could conjure up. He made a great thing of blessing her yard and kitchen and living room and bedroom. He forgot her hallway. He left in high-church dudgeon though when Lucy made it clear to him that she wasn't about to donate the displaying of her wounds to the church. "What do they want me to do?" she would ask. "Stand inside a glass box on one of the hills here? I got a living to make."

"Hey, Lucy," Milo had asked her on the next visit, "do you think you're going to become, like, a saint, or something?" Lucy laughed, and Mila too. At that moment Milo saw how a new smile made his sister's face beautiful. Lucy was beautiful too. He felt the forces of nature and of God, and how together they enlightened you with beauty just like a snap of fingers.

"I haven't got time to be a saint," Lucy said. "Unfortunately."

Mila said that to be a saint you had to work a miracle. Milo knew that.

"But you don't think it's, like, a call?" he pressed Lucy. "Saying you're going to wind *up* a saint, maybe, or at least doing, you know… good works?"

That got Lucy's arms folded, saying, "What do you think I do every night in that circus, Milo Galitzki? If helping make a bunch of people forget their pain for a time and laugh isn't good works, you'd better tell me what is."

"Point, Milo." Mila enjoyed being able to say that. "Good one, too."

Mila was touched by the way Lucy's joy shone from inside her. It was Lucy who woke Mila up to Jesus again after she'd been bullied out of serving Him with the white sisters. Prompted partly by that dumb comment of Milo's about her getting to be a saint, Lucy said that to her mind if you

77

could bring any joy to the world then you had to; it was your duty. What she did in her nights tumbling in the ring brought smiles to the faces of those stuck in the poverty of the times; whatever was happening to those people, its process was interrupted when they went into the circus tent. "You make somebody happy," Lucy assured them, "then you're putting some good in the world."

Milo liked the sound of that, picked up the unicycle and gave the wheel a spin and declared that he was ready to burn rubber. In the rectangle of light made by Lucy's door, he went round and round and fell on his face and got up and did it all over again, like some mechanized dervish.

"See?" Lucy said. "Look at you making a clown of yourself, Milo. But it's cracking me up. Make somebody happy, I say, and you're on the road to your own happiness. There's no other way."

"That's the road we're on," Milo said as he sat in the dust of Lucy's yard."

He was wrong, though.

"God's cracking up too," Lucy called, as she held hands out for the little bike to show how it was really done. She was sharp, saw a troubled look in Mila's eyes. She made a graceful circuit of the yard and said to Mila, "Honey, God laughs. I see Him in your smile, and your brother's."

"Really?" Mila squinted up. Lucy didn't tell her she was looking in the wrong place.

"Really." She tugged Mila back to attention. "Manifests Himself in us that way. Listen. There's a billion gods in the world." Her own awe at the figure stilled the protest on Mila's lips. "You go to India one day, Mila, and you'll see them all, but only one Who reminds us He's always there for us."

"India?" Mila said.

"For example."

Mila wondered then if it was true what people in town said, that Lucy had belonged to the Gypsies, that lost tribe of God that survived the sword and wandered out of India centuries before. Did they really get all the way to Balz? That was as likely as Mila herself waking up one day in India.

"They'll get inside your head and talk to you, all those gods." Lucy kept her voice low and even. "But there's only one God Jesus belongs to, and you remember that. And remember, Mila, that you belong to Jesus, you and your brother, and that He'll protect you."

Mila remembered Lucy bringing Milo in off Reformatory beach that day long before, both of them dusted with white poison, and saw that God had sent Lucy. She was caught up again in the wonder of it, to the point of that almost sweet feeling of pain you get if you press on your lips from within with your teeth.

"Only thing He can't protect you from," Lucy warned gently, "is yourself. He gave us free will to do that with. *It is your own wickedness that will punish you*, right? But remember, you bring a little joy to the world and it'll come back to you."

How was Mila going to do that? That night she sat on Milo's crossbar, an arm on his shoulder, and let him pedal her up the hill home. She knew she wouldn't be good on a unicycle, nor bad enough to be funny. She wasn't going to join the circus. She wasn't going to go into the movies or be a cabaret MC. She wasn't going to raise the dead. She wasn't going to feed the hungry or clothe the naked or heal the sick or comfort the dying. Then, on the hill with Milo puffing behind her, she thought, 'Hey, but why not?'

The sisters' vow of poverty was easy, she had always sensed. Chastity, she'd always had the cautious feeling, easy. Obedience, if you had any faith at all, easy. Joy, though, had always escaped her no matter what she did to try to get it. Joy: that would be the challenge.

As they pulled into the yard, she gave Milo a hug that pressed the breath out of him. She kissed his forehead and thanked him for the ride. She decided that joy, once she'd gotten into the habit of putting some around, was a thing that would linger and open doors in the fog around her. She resolved to walk through those doors.

Balz's beaches and their acrobats, monsters and supposed saints

Lucy Ephraim was brought up in the house for destitute girls over Reformatory Beach, a green pasteboard palace in the shade of the reformatory itself. Her right to live there was a legacy from her delinquent and long absent mother. Lucy was the kid who played on the beach apart from all the other kids. There was something not exactly right about her: she was wise and dark and kind of *old*-looking – that was it, partly. She had big eyes and oiled hair in jet coils around her head. Nor was her play exactly what it seemed, with a nerveless expertise to it. She juggled apples and oranges into blurs of color under her raised legs and between her clapping hands. She did handstands and walked an awful long way on those hands. More alarmingly, she climbed the flagstaffs and stood on the buttons on top of them, then stood on one hand. Most of the mothers knew who she was, but any who didn't would plead with her to come down, or call the police department. When officers yelled at her to get down, she told them that, if she was doing any harm against God, the Constitution or the people they were welcome to come and get her. She also climbed the lighthouse which, put up in the twenties by an eccentric called Gogarty with money to torch, was pure northern gothic nostalgia. People guessed Gogarty kept his folly in sight as he vanished on the flats nursing a broken heart and a guilty head over the other folly he left behind, namely the remains of Mrs Gogarty, a bullet hole in her forehead.

Lucy would tell Milo and Mila years later that those were happy times. She was wise to people being disdainful of her art because they were jealous of it. She could have gone stealing from the stores on the Rink on her free days like the other destitute girls; she could have done it undetected, too. Out there on the flats one evening though, she said she saw a path leading right to God, and knew He valued gymnastics over petty theft any day.

The best beach was Mozhay Beach, beach bums decreed, because the salt was good and soft, though to me people who wanted to lie around in the sun on salt needed their heads examined. All the silk hats thought it was a good thing anyhow, when they claimed their quarter behind the bars and restaurants on the low cliff overlooking the beach. Their big deal houses defined the streets, their big deal cars clogged the driveways, their big deal dogs fouled the sidewalks. Their big deal women, skin like spicy fried chicken, wore their jewelry to the beach and gawped at the muscles of the meatheads who played volleyball.

Milo liked Glass Beach best. The broken bottle sand that gave the beach its name ensured that there were no spicy fried bimbos or musclebound beefcakes, nor any uptight mothers with squalling babies. There were only the rocks and the soaring cliff on which stood the Zacharov mansion and, at the summit, the old Civil War fort where he learned how to learn. He liked it mainly because you could walk on the flats off it and follow your thoughts to the absolute middle of nowhere. If you tried that on the other beaches the salt crust was liable to give way, and you were up to knees or neck in treacly mud that, if it didn't cover your head and fill your lungs the way it did for Sister Adelheid, tinted your skin and left its odor on you for weeks.

Glass Beach inspired Milo into daydreams and visions. He spied his future on the roads of Europe, at that crazy bike riding, the colors and clamors and the leg-busting progress to the sky in search of ozone and glory, the bike-rider's tan he would get, leaving the imprint of jersey, shorts, socks and gloves, even the premature ageing that crept up on all bike pros. From the junk that got blown around on the beach, Milo was impressed only by the cogwheel he found, that worldly sign of bicycles.

The rest of it he could look at and pick up and turn over and ignore, most of it, anyhow.

Nobody failed to be impressed by the monster, though. One winter day after a storm, a curious kid discovered the tip of a bone the size of a dime, and his dad got a shovel and a friend and a few hours later there it was. It was big as a bus, had crisp gray leather hanging off its frame, four stubby legs and the remains of a tail and a head like an alligator with delicate teeth the length of a little boy's finger. People guessed it had just crouched down there to think for a second about the fearsome signs of its era and couldn't bear to contemplate its extinction any longer, nor the evolution of other species, just died from being thoroughly pissed. People crowded around the monster's last resting place all week. Then it got put in the town museum.

Stuff from the beaches wound up in the museum's three cluttered rooms that smelled of floor polish and dust. Its curator Joyce Augustine wore men's suits and smoked cigars. She had a voice like a man's too and banged the male teachers on the back and brayed out bright howdos when they brought kids along to sketch the monster and learn how to spell *plesiosaurus* properly. I liked the monster alright but what I liked best was a metal nutcracker in the shape of a Tatar's handsome head. I also liked the native trinkets, shards of broken pots and stone beads, a hatchet and a peace pipe and a rug. There were photos of Balz's churches under construction, and a single snap of the guy God sent down to build them, features shaded by a sun hat. There was a wooden model of the Holy Apostles cathedral made by Milo's grandpa Waldemar Petrov, lit from within by Christmas lights.

The most intriguing thing, there was no doubt, was a sailor's snuffbox made of ivory that had a mean-looking octopus in relief on its lid. In that it was nothing to get excited about. People said though that if you opened that lid and looked on the other side that same octopus was engrossed in doing something to a Japanese woman with chopsticks in her hair whose robe was thrown back, whose legs were spread wide, and whose toes were curled in ecstasy. Kids asked Joyce Augustine all the time to take it out of its case and open it up but she'd just look through them and say firmly, "I don't think you want to see that." The only kid with whom she had to personify her kindly advice with a smack on the ear was, nobody was surprised to hear, Moby Krzeski, who asked her how come she thought she had the right to put her fat spoilsport ass in the way of the appreciation of *art*.

Balz's other museum-pieces were the headscarved women in black who dotted Reformatory Beach in sunshine, rain or snow. Mr Galitzki called them the Hagiography. That got Milo laughing but confused Mila, who wondered, "They're saints, already?" Nobody else went there in the winter except road bums, because Balz was at a crossroads of ancient tramping routes. It was because of this that the white sisters set up a soup kitchen and bandied their brand of comfort along with shoes and clothes and meal tickets. That was where Mila first got to know both the sisters and the bums, because even when she was little she knew her dad was never going to include her in the conversations he mapped out down there with Milo.

When Mr Galitzki was spieling, Mila got the habit of talking to those people littering the beach. She saw the shreds of their dignity in the stories they told, and showed it by listening and interrupting with, "What? *No*. Really? *Hey*," and seeing in their eyes their need to tell, satisfied.

The old women noticed neither the bums nor the sisters, never noticed the rain falling, nor the salt blowing, didn't notice Lucy Ephraim cartwheeling around them, nor hear her when she sat at her window soundtracking her moods and theirs with maudlin violin pieces. They sat on deckchairs, dreamed the names of lost countries, of kings long dead and of husbands and family they were no longer sure they ever had.

"I contemplate," the Galitzkis' neighbor Baba Pishchinska used to say, with Mila sat on her lap. "Some of these old babas look like they're contemplating, but they aren't." She did her alarming screech of a laugh. "No sir, they don't even know what century it is. In the line of contemplating, there's me, and me alone."

They chewed their gums, brushed the flies off their eyelids. At least once a month one of them saw the face of God, and was picked up by the white sisters and taken not to the night shelter as usual but away to be buried.

"Why do they *do* that?" everybody asked at least one time in their lives. "Just sit there all day doing nothing?"

Baba Pishchinska would answer, "I asked that question, when I was maybe your age. Don't rightly recall a straight answer. Didn't do me any good if there *was* one."

The day I was sixteen, when Milo's Venus made me red and wet and green

If Milo saw me making the eyes I had for him, he was pretty good at keeping it to himself. If he was aware of the conversational gambits I risked with creeps like Moby and toughs like the Peterlejtners, the dizzying French *hauteur* I got from Eurydice Armentiere and the sparkly eyes I got from Richard Rat because he was deluded enough to think it was him I was interested in, he didn't mention it to me.

Mozhay Beach girls like me were brought up in an elite whose conventions were designed for one thing: that was to protect the money we were going to come into. Only a few were chaperoned by flesh-and-blood nanny figures, who haunted the campus gates around hometime or waited in ugly cars. But in places outside Mozhay Beach we chaperoned one another or were attended by the boys who lived around us, their futures looming in which they'd all have Mozhay Beach wives to perpetuate their parents' mindless lives on the monster kids they'd spawn. It wasn't a thing any of the girls thought to question. Except me, probably around the time I started to wonder about dad's money.

It was always manifested by the thing stuck in my chest for Milo, who infuriated me because in the years since I saw him going up that hill to the school in the fort he didn't see me, seeing him. Then I had to look at him across those gray classrooms in the Lyceum, staring at my leisure because he never glanced my way.

Mrs Kandinska the art teacher was prattling on one day about the mystery of the Mona Lisa, though far as I could see it was just a dark daub of some dame with bad hair. "Anybody know where it is?" Mrs K asked, in an attempt to get us engaged.

Axel Peterlejtner called out, "Why, it's right there," pointing at the slide projection. As ever it was hard to tell whether Axel was trying to be funny or was just being scrupulously literal. Most of us had called a boycott on reactions to the antics of the fort school crowd, so Axel's comment got a snort of solidarity from his sister Illona and a friendly jeer from Richard Rat. Moby was at the back of the room, already more or less exempt from art lessons as such, busy working on something of his own. He was probably drawing Mrs Kandinska minus her clothes.

"Thank you, Axel." Art teachers didn't ever get mad. Mrs Kandinska just ahemmed. "In fact, it hangs in a big museum in Paris, France, called the Louvre." Somebody said a *Jesus Mary* and it went on like this. Mrs Kandinska talked about her visit there and about other stuff in the Louvre. She brought me back into the class with the mention of Venus de Milo. "That's Milo's Venus," she translated for us, wrongly.

I took Milo to be a person, and not a place. I didn't look at the new slide. I looked at Milo. I knew already that Paris was a gloomy idea of a city glimpsed in movies, one that dragged itself across cobbles to the misery of absinthe, of lovers that cheated on one another but never found anything like love. All the same, something ran its way down the bones of my spine as I sensed that, one day in His own time, God was going to place me there with Milo Galitzki. I paced out thoughts of us walking nights into mornings over the grid of Victor Hugo's long-gone city, by the river or up on the hills, eating fancy pastries, drinking coffee out of bowls, then arm-in-arm in the Louvre, staring at that hapless armless Venus and sharing a smile.

Milo lifted his eyes from his math book at the seeming mention of his name and caught the nearest eye, that of Eurydice Armentiere, and asked her, "What?" She moved her shoulders, and resumed doodling on the edge of her pad.

I was thinking how Milo never saw that I was Milo's Venus. I saw him and me on the balcony off our drawing room at home, twilit. The room was full of dad's friends, all blasted, dancing and swearing exuberantly. Milo and I ignored their row and looked at the maples in the yard, the bats dancing among them. I put an arm around Milo's waist without us looking at each other, nor talking. I stood on tiptoe and kissed him, tasted salt on his lips. I led him through the party and up the stairs to my room. On the way I thought of the white airtex panties I'd put on that evening and how I hadn't drunk anything so I wouldn't have to piss so they'd stay clean. Milo wore a white cotton shirt and tan Chinos, Weejun loafers, no socks, and white shorts. I took them all off of him in the dark and let him take my dress off and slip those panties down my legs. We kissed each other all over for a long time then lay on the bed. I urged him on the way people did all those bike riders, *go go go*, and he crossed the line I had down there, meant to preserve me intact for some frat boy. I had a second of pain that jarred but then we made love slowly and sweetly.

That was the day I was sixteen. I was in recess after that art class surrounded by my friends chirping and schnirping about what they were going to wear to my birthday party next day and how they were going to do their hair and oh-my-goodnessing and good-Lording about the boys I'd invited.

Milo was not among them.

I saw him cross the campus with Eurydice, her arm in his. My little fat friend Ortensia Umberta said how I was red in the face, though I wasn't, not deep down; I was a shade of *green*.

I saw Milo around town when we weren't at school, listened for the swish of his bike. I saw him go up Balz's hills almost as fast as if he were on the flat, saw his concentrated eyes and his teeth pulling on one side of his lip. I looked closely at the features discernible in those ludicrous shorts bike riders wear, that make a guy look pleased to see you the whole time.

I watched him at mass in the Holy Apostles, he and Mila dressed in the dowdy Sunday clothes they wore without protest, that got my friends breaking out the laughter of cats. I walked behind him to communion, watched him kneel and stick out his tongue for the host like a lizard feeding on a fly, saw the priests show him beetle brows till he shut his eyes in the presence of Jesus' body. I watched him look up, idly studying the structures of brick and stone with his engineer's eye as the fathers' voices rang around us.

I thought of that tongue of Milo's and wondered what it felt like. I saw it snaking its way up the gooseflesh on my inside thigh, a livid pink, to where I was pink and livid too. I saw him again in my room, embedded in me, my feet kicking on his kidneys, imagined all the people downstairs partying and not knowing what we were doing.

I looked around me in church, saw some of those partygoers. I saw Milo after, mingling with the pilgrims next to the dark pond in the orchard gardens out back of the cathedral with Mila, Illona Peterlejtner and Eurydice Armentiere. They hung on his arm, pointed into the water, said things that made him spark out laughter. I wondered what they were saying, this string of overbearing girls with sensible shoes and terrible clothes and silver laughter, and wished I could be them, wished I didn't have to go back to Mozhay beach and be my daddy's silly little girl.

FIVE

Masked Dance Saturday Night, And An Angel Hour To Two Thirty With The Moon Brought Down And Broken

———◈———

The party was spilling onto Ascension Avenue when Milo left the mansion, and had spread to the little square that drew the eye to the war memorial. Guys sat on steps and sucked on cigarettes and bottles, rattled out spiel that would end in philosophy or fistfights. Girls made secret laughter about things you could only guess at if you weren't a girl, and even if you were. Masks turned to the backs of their heads, they formed pictures with their hands and chirped like excited birds, like their lives were the biggest fun you could have on this night of the masked dance. Maybe they were.

One girl screamed from a group gathered beneath a streetlight orb, hands this way and that to protect her unmasked face; a giant moth bugging her. Her boyfriend broke the streetlight with an expertly-aimed bottle, which dispersed the moths. A silence fell for a second. The light buster took a bow. Milo had to resist the urge to tell him to get the hell back to his own town and break the lights there. Assuming they had electricity out in Hicksville.

What did he care, though? He didn't belong in Balz anymore. That was written in the condensation settling on his brain. He shut his eyes and felt himself go over a mountaintop on a bike, a release almost like that feeling he'd had with the angel the moment their bodies joined.

He saw a white shape slumped against a wall, groaning. It wasn't an angel. They only groaned when you loved them and it hurt. It was a mummy. As Milo passed him he was repeating, "Oh, holy *Hell*."

In the road Milo passed Michael Sheltz, who was dressed as a crooner. He looked more like a bank clerk who'd been in a sheep-shearing accident, white fluff all over his dinner jacket, blood around his nose and upchuck down his front. He carried an empty wine bottle as if in explanation.

"Michael."

The sound of his name got Michael's attention. He stopped, and a smile twitched around his lips.

"Go home." Milo was alarmed at the weariness in his voice.

Michael let out a delighted laugh.

"For *Chrissake*."

Michael didn't need Milo. It was Mila he needed, but she would never hear him over the saints' voices in her head, and was never again going to magic him out of trouble.

"Go home." Milo gave Michael a gentle shove on the shoulder but turned away, tried to forget him and the ill-advised smile he wore.

Milo went on his way. Greetings were called out to him, ahoy this name and that, though it was mostly, "Ahoy, soldier," and the like. Only one made it to his name. The familiarity of it stopped him. It was no angel calling, however, just a little pixie. She sat on the steps of the insurance company offices that marked the corner where the town proper started, or finished, looking appropriately ornamental. Milo didn't say hallo, only, "Hey, did you see an angel?"

"Seen a few." She edged her head in the direction of the mansion. "Milo?" She patted the step next to her and said, "Sit down? You want?" She ignored the shake of his head. "Got some vodka."

Milo couldn't tell if it was question or statement till she patted a pocket. The thought of vodka made him hear Michael Sheltz singing. He looked at the sky and thought he could make out tiny birds caught in the streetlights. He sat abruptly and let his head hang.

"Milo?" The pixie gave him the kind of pat you give a nervous dog.

"Richard," he said thickly – why, he didn't know. "Electricity brings the moon down to us," it occurred to him, that being a real Richard Rat thing to say. "Traps it in glass, helps us see the things we need to see in the dark. And what do they *do*, the... *nincompoops* that... *infest* this town?" He was on the point then of rising, going back and punching out the streetlight breaker's own lights.

"*Nincompoops.*" The pixie savored the music in the word. "I don't know. What *do* they do, the nincompoops that infest this town?"

"Hold it a second, will you. My head's coming off."

"Richard *who*?" she said into his ear.

As she studied the face he had on, he said, "Richard Szczur," and stuck a hand out in a formal howdo that made her laugh sweetly.

"You aren't the rat boy." She slapped him lightly on an arm. "I saw him, already. He's Fu Manchu, or something."

"Fu Man*chu*?"

"Listen. You want some of that vodka?"

"I don't drink," Milo remembered through a green fuzz. *Oh yeah?* a little voice smirked in his head. *Too late, buddy.* He said, "If I ever drink another thing, it'll be a goddam... miracle. But hey, tell me, you saw an angel where?"

"Over there." She tossed her head. The movement seemed to hurt his own. She meant the white shape he had passed down the street.

"That's a *mummy*." He made an impatient pout for himself. "Listen, did you see one come out of the dance? In the last... half-hour, maybe?"

"A mummy?"

"*No*. An angel."

"I don't know." The pixie's voice pitched up a click. "You think I've got nothing else to do but sit and watch for angels?" She sensed him wavering over whether to say *yeah* to that, glad to see him keep a lid on it. "Why don't you go inside and look for your angel?"

Milo got an inkling that she knew he'd already been doing that.

"And anyhow."

"Yeah." Milo stopped himself nodding. "Anyhow what?"

"What's the big deal with angels?"

"Nothing." Milo looked her over: a creature from a child's picture book with an English garden in it with flowers that flustered, weeds that whined. She wore a mask with stupid red cheeks, a stupid turned-up schnoz, stupid big eyelashes. Its mindless smile brought to mind the people of Balz on feast days when they milled around the town center to offer their noise to the mordant wind that blew in off the flats. He thought of them guzzling green vodka and twiddling the knobs on the junk they surrounded themselves with, making finger-tracks in the dust on it and pretending it all worked still. "No big deal."

"No?"

"No."

Not what the angel did, he wanted to tell the pixie, it was what the angel said. Milo's lost liaison flickered through his head like a movie. Then, he didn't know why, he started to relate it to the pixie. To her sometimes importunate questions he stepped out of his raconteur part to remind her about how in movies you saw a kiss and you knew what happened in between that and the next frame, which showed darkness, or maybe the brightness of a next morning, the protagonists on first-name terms. "So what *is* her name?" the pixie cut to the chase and asked. Milo waved the question away and told her about how he'd sought out the angels he and Richard had seen from up on the mezzanine, making his optimist's way through the impossible job he had.

"But who *is* she?" the pixie insisted.

Milo deflected the question this time with a raised hand.

"Well…" The pixie raised her own hand. "Go on."

Back in the mansion, Milo related, Richard busy with his Cleopatra, Milo had made a conspiratorial whisper towards the tallest angel in sight. He had to butt in to a huddle she had going with two disheveled musketeers he knew to be the meathead-about-town Feiffer brothers. "That's you, Milo?" they asked him. "Your professor dad didn't ever tell you not to interrupt people's conversations?" The angel was too tall if anything, and was almost certainly Kasia Krantz, who was just the kind of girl who'd be seen dead with the Feiffers.

"He *did* mention that." Milo had been about to ignore the insult, then thought how you went away to college to set your mind on higher things and come back a frigging graduate, no frigging less, and people still saw you as another kid from high school with an eternal readiness for the same old squabbles. "But only if they've got any conversation worth interrupting," he'd called as he headed away.

He'd tapped another angelic shoulder, saying, "Hey, angel." And she'd turned, eyes gleaming behind her mask. "It's me, Milo," he'd said, and she'd put her hands on his shoulders and led him out onto the dancefloor, spinning him and laughing. "I love you," he'd chanced. "Listen, my angel, that was my first time. You want to come upstairs again?"

"Creep." She'd danced away, left him with the word and the space it left.

Maybe what Milo had needed right then was a sobering experience. He got one. Those dimestore angels let him know they would fly before going upstairs with him even one time. Milo was burning under his mask, on the verge of tears of pure bison vodka. "People are going to remember this tomorrow," he kept telling himself. "I'll never be able to go out the door again. The whole town will go, 'Did you ever hear the nerve of that guy on the night of the dance at the mansion?'" That was why he had to get out of there, and anyhow even without the aid of a laundry marker he thought he had managed to get through all the angels in the ballroom. He was taking some air at a window, had spied a white shape near the square and tripped downstairs and through the hall and out of the grounds to find that dissolute mummy.

"That's what they'll say," he told the pixie. "I'll be… vilified."

"You'll be – what does that even *mean*?"

"Traduced."

"Eh?"

"*Ridiculed*. All those things."

She snuffled a laugh and said, "I guess you will, if they knew it was you. But this is the masked dance, remember? Could have been anybody saying they were you. I mean, you just told me you were Richard Rat."

"Well." Milo pulled his mask off and fanned his face with it. "*You* knew it was me. And she knew it was, too."

"Who?"

"The angel." He told her later he hadn't wanted to sound so mean. "Of course. Who do you think I mean, the frigging first lady?"

The pixie seemed about to rise to the challenge in his tone but said cheerfully, "You cut all your hair off." She rubbed a hand over the half inch of stubble the barber had left.

A doubtful smile appeared on his face. He said, "Hey," which told the pixie that there was something about her gesture that he liked.

"Why did you tell me you were Richard?" she asked.

"I don't know."

"I mean, like, who'd *want* to be Richard Rat, if they weren't him already?"

No laugh from Milo, though he agreed. He remembered Michael, couldn't see him in the road. He recalled Michael's hand: cut, bleeding. A cogwheel stuck in it? How? Jesus Mary, and he hadn't given it a second thought, too busy chasing the hems of angel robes.

"Richard's your pal," the pixie said. Not a question, so Milo said nothing, just reached a hand up to a twinge in his chin where Richard had punched him. "You're sure you don't want a drink?" She patted her pocket again.

"Yeah." He'd necked a half pint of vodka. He almost couldn't believe it, but it was swimming in his veins. He got some gum out and offered the pixie a stick. She took one and stowed it in her pocket, for after she'd drunk her vodka, Milo guessed, and had chucked it up and wanted to get the smell of her bad judgment out of her breath, wanted to kiss some poor sap. "Pretty sure."

The pixie said, "You don't want to go in and dance?"

In answer, Milo clamped his mask back on his face. The look on it told that he'd fallen for an angel and no, he didn't want to go dance with some pixie. He wasn't a dancer in any case, and even if he had been, this wasn't a time for two-stepping. This was a time like the day the angel walked off with his imagination and left him to violin music and a tongue turned to stone, to Mrs Panufnik and the laughter of his little sister, a monument of a moment. He saw all its faces but wound up with Sister Adelheid's, the one from her oval portrait in the intersection of the brass cross put up in her memory on the steps down to Reformatory Beach.

"You don't want?" the pixie said.

He hated that picture. He hadn't known why for many years, till age and intellect formulated for him the thought that, with its sun-faded gray-and-white realism, it had robbed him of the face in his imagination.

"No?" the pixie tried again.

"No." It was then that Milo saw the angel again. It was too far away to say for sure, but it *had* to be his own magic angel floating in the air above the portico of the Zacharov mansion. "There." He tried to be cool about it, but found himself juddering in an ungainly manner to his feet. "That's her."

He went to call a goodbye to the pixie, but she was hurrying out onto Ascension Avenue and along with him, saying, "Oh boy. This I really got to see. Hey Milo, is it too much vodka, or what? I'll tell you one thing."

"Yeah? What?"

"That's no angel. I tell you, that's just something Michael Sheltz sang up for us."

Michael Sheltz's traits, and graduation summer, when he sang death into
a room

Whatever the source of Michael Sheltz's problems, they led him to a bunch of unfortunate traits, and one of the worst of them was the delusion that he could sing. His singing voice was the noise they play in Hades to set sinners' nerves on edge. It was terrifying, though it was obvious that he sounded in his head like a schmaltzy crooner, the kind that arrested him in mid-step when he heard one on the radio and cleared his mind of whatever may have been in it.

Michael always had a sheet of music with him, to let people know he was a singer. I looked at it once, the tattered script to some song as old as the world. Everybody said to him, "Michael, please don't sing. All that happens is that everybody gets mad at you."

Whenever he caught that he said, "Hell they do." He'd point at himself. "Born to sing."

Michael didn't start to sing till he was about sixteen. He brought the ability back from some institution where he was encouraged to express himself. People guessed it was the singing that got him out of there. Back in Balz he lived at the mission of the white sisters for a time. Maybe they didn't throw him out, but they expressed a strong wish that he should return to his family home.

Michael came back from incarceration the summer we graduated from school. He wouldn't in a million years have thought to go sing in the bars in town but due to an ill-conceived wish to find a butt for their jokes, drinkers sought him out, put a beer in his hand and told him to get singing. In Zigismund Zakopan's bar one night that summer a crow flew in as Michael sang and some shitkickers from out of town made a sport of shooting at it as it traced panicked ellipses above their heads. Celebrated Balz barfly Betty Willis, who had started life as Countess Elzbieta Vilanovka, and had dodged revolutionary bullets across Russia, Ukraine and Poland, got half her face blown off as she stood on a chair to see the fun. As the echo of that last unfortunate shot zinged, Michael sang on. Old man Zigismund advanced on him with half a pool cue held up. The drinkers watched, fascinated. Nobody seemed to notice Betty, thrown over a table and too busy dying of shock and mortification to see what else was happening.

"Why didn't you break his goddam jaw?" patrons asked Zigismund three months later when he came out of his bad mood. He didn't know. "I can break yours, easy," he would mention. That put a stop to the questions.

"Don't ever do that singing again, Michael," Michael was told next day as he lay in the BG bandaged up, which was where I saw him. "You drive people nuts."

"World belongs to people who sing," he'd heard someplace. "Born to sing."

96

He wasn't, though. He was born to misery, and the mocking eyes and quick tempers of the people of Balz. What's more, he was born to his dad's sister who, pregnant again, chucked herself off the fort with the shame of it when Michael was a year old and already, it was agreed, a candidate for vile institutions.

It was the fort school teacher Miss Kodaly who kept him out of them initially by treating him as just another kid, and the Galitzkis, who made a friend of him at school. Milo and Mila seemed to have a feeling for boobies like Michael, and like the strange Churchyard kids and the insular Peterlejtners, and had the self-control not to get mad at them. They saw something in them the rest of us couldn't see, but they were probably as mystified as the rest of us as to what that might be.

The year Milo was fifteen, when Miss Adventure struck him dumb

In the summers of their mid-teens, Milo and his crowd went along the highway and cut through a pass called Ghost Valley, clouded sometimes with fat, feisty wasps, then up to the cold lake on Craw Mountain. They fooled around in a boat and tramped and camped up there. When Michael went, he had to bring along his four-year-old half-sister Anaheim, though it was never clear which of them was doing the looking after. Anaheim laughed abrasively at anything, the color of the trees, the shape of a shirtcuff, the angle of a hat, whatever.

"I wish you'd shut up laughing," was all Michael ever seemed to say to her, the utterance learned at home from various Sheltzes.

Milo would go, "Hey, Anaheim," which would be enough to set her off. In between laughs she'd gasp out, "Whut? *Whut?*" and laugh herself into alarming contortions and colors.

"Happiest kid on earth," Milo used to say, but he would look at Anaheim and feel cut up that the world wasn't organized for happy kids, not in Balz, not if they came out of families like the Sheltzes.

What Mr Galitzki predicted was, "That kid will die from laughing." He was more or less right. One day on the lake, Anaheim leaned back to laugh at something and fell out of the boat. That day Milo and Michael were with the Peterlejtners and Eurydice Armentiere, all slightly drunk on the clear air and the pint of bison vodka Illona Peterlejtner had filched from her dad's store. Their voices fell quiet for a second, then into a cacophony with the overlapping syllables of Anaheim's name. All the time Michael kept up a commentary of, "See that?"

Milo was *not* a swimmer. The mere thought of the water stripping his insides of warmth, he got his shirt and pants off. Eurydice tied a rope around his ankle, and he slopped into the lake. He dived into a faceful of vegetation and came up covered in green to take a breath. He went down again and again but always to the same floral nothingness.

Eurydice said there had to be a monster down there that could swallow little kids whole and not even notice. Milo knew that Anaheim had been sucked into the nightmare closet under the shelf made by the shoreline and trapped there by the weeds. As he climbed into the boat, he brought long strands of them with him, a message that the water wanted him too.

They were poleaxed into silence until Michael said again, "See that?" at which Axel leaned over and slapped his face. Michael rubbed his jaw and said carefully, "You didn't ought to have gone and done that," more verbal dexterity learned at home. Illona then slapped Axel, who slapped her back and was slapped in turn by Eurydice, and then Illona turned and slapped Eurydice. The boat rocked. Milo called them to a halt.

He said, "We've got to think about what to do."

They did as he suggested, but there was little to think about and nothing to do.

Axel took after his storekeeper dad in making a virtue out of stating the most obvious things. He looked pleased to tell Michael, "You're in deep shit."

"Uh-uh." Michael bit on his lip and shook his head. Milo thought he saw in Michael's eyes the distant figure of a veiled woman doing a dance like that done on the fringes of a herd of antelope when a predator has drawn close.

"The deepest brownest stinkingest steamiest runniest shit you ever heard of in your life," Axel spelled out helpfully.

"We've got to think about what to do. Remember?" Eurydice thought she'd keep them in the picture, but it revealed nothing. Their heads boiled and their stomachs queased, and for a second they wondered why the melancholy that fell on them was tinged with the pale green of bison grass. It opened up to reveal all the bad things in the world.

Milo picked up one of the paddles and glared at them all. Illona took the other. They pulled for the shore.

Axel started to hum a campfire favorite about feeling so broke up and wanting to go home. Milo was just about to tell him to shut his noise and give him a mini lecture in the form of a slap about what was apt and what wasn't at a time like the one they were stuck with. Then he realized that the tune had mesmerized and quietened Michael and taken the panic out of his eyes.

"You want us to come with you?" Eurydice asked Michael once they were back at the shore and the Peterlejtners' old man's pick-up, but Michael just shook his shoulders irritably. Frustrated, she said to them all, "He doesn't know what's occurred, does he? He just doesn't *know*."

"Anaheim's gone, Michael." Axel slapped his forehead. "Jesus Mary. *Gone*."

All Michael said was a cautious, "Seen that."

Axel drove. The closer they got to town the quieter they became. As they hit the hill to the town center, Milo asked Michael again did he want them to go home with him. Michael said only, "For what?"

When they stopped in the Rink outside the Peterlejtners' place, Milo said to Axel, "Listen, you've got to go with him."

"Whoah no," Axel said. "Not me. *You* go."

"You've got the car." Milo looked out the window as he said it.

"No."

"Listen." Milo grabbed Axel by the shirt collar and spoke into his face. He could see him trying to decide whether he was going to fight back, but Milo had kicked his friend's ass thoroughly enough once or twice to know that wasn't going to happen. "Take him home. Tell them what happened. Somebody's got to."

Illona said, "Point, Ax. Not like Michael's going to be able to suddenly... eloquize, just because Anaheim went and drowned."

"*Eloquize?*" Axel was keen to divert the conversation. "Is that even a *word*?"

"Talk," Illona explained sweetly. "You know – in *phrases*, and all."

Eurydice burst into tears. Illona side-eyed her, only a token reluctance on her face at having been the medium for the terrible truth they faced. Michael pointed and said, "Born to cry."

"Why doesn't *he* go?" Axel stabbed a finger at Milo.

Milo couldn't answer. He wasn't crazy about seeing the looks on the faces of Bible Jack and Hornrim Jane Sheltz when they heard. The main thing though was that it was going to *blast* him to get to the Sheltzes' porch and see Anaheim's little yellow chair there and know that she was never again going to get up and set it rocking in her haste to run to him when he came to see Michael. It was going to kill him; there was no pulling back from that. She was never again going to be there to say, "Open your hand," to kid him into thinking she had something for him only to take it in her own and not let it go. He heard a voice inside him beg Jesus and Mary to tell him this was all happening someplace else to somebody else.

His hands were holding onto Axel's collar, half of it bunched into them. He let go.

"*You* do it." Milo was about to point out again that it would take Axel a second to drive over to Michael's, but he knew that was just a way of avoiding the heart of the task. Instead he said through his teeth, "You take him home, Ax, or I promise you that you are a frigging *dead* man." He jumped out and pulled on Eurydice's hand and she took it and joined Milo in hiding her eyes. They hurried out of the Rink and along Ganser and Weiss Avenue and up the hill toward their homes.

It was maybe a half hour later when Milo, steeped in the trouble he knew was about to fall on all their heads, whispered to Mila what had happened. His stab at discretion was drowned in Mila's outburst of grief. It culminated in the swing she took at his head which, because he was expecting it, missed.

"You shouldn't try to punch anybody standing in front of a mirror," he advised her later after she'd cooled down. She had just had her knuckles stitched in the BG, and was working hard to dismiss the superstition of seven years of bad luck.

Mr Galitzki had taken Mila to the hospital. Milo had gone with his mom to the Sheltzes' to find the Peterlejtner twins there, and Illona's Mozhay Beach pal Niamh O'Dowd with her dad, officer Gerard O'Dowd, plus a gray-faced Eurydice and her mom. As the line of visitors stretched out to the porch, neighbors wandered over and joined it.

The Sheltz household was exhausting itself with Biblical wailing. Michael's attempts to sing and clap and laugh were curtailed by slaps from whoever was passing him at the time. His stepmom, eyes trapped inside the amber rocks she called eyeglasses, kept throwing up. Michael's out-to-lunch granny was lighting cigarettes and forgetting to smoke them, leaving them burning all over the place like foul incense. Jack Sheltz had hold of his Bible and kept pulling the sleeves of whoever was near and trying to recite to them. Michael's remaining half-sister, twelve-year-old Azousa, sat and glared at anybody whose eye she caught, especially Axel's, as he persisted in looking up her skirt. Illona put a strain on her welcome when, with officer O'Dowd having established a moment of calm in which he could write the events in his notebook, she fingered a melancholy intro on the out-of-tune piano in the Sheltzes' parlor that turned quickly into a manic and ill-chosen rendition of *What Shall We Do With A Drunken Sailor*.

It had to be that tune that made officer O'Dowd decide that Axel's eyes were swimming in alcohol. Axel's untimely little belch added to the picture. Illona decided that her bravado ought to desert her for a tearful little-girl act that didn't kid a soul. Once Milo's big mouth had formed the words *green vodka* despite the curled lips, flared-nostrils and frantic head-shaking of the Peterlejtners, that was another angle to be considered.

There was little point in explaining to Michael what had happened, even less in punishing him, but punished he was. He walked around town marked with bruises for weeks following the death of Anaheim. The rest of them weren't popular either. The verdict was death by misadventure, headlined stupidly in the Balz Bugle as *Miss Adventure*. Gerard O'Dowd elaborated. "They were imbibing hard liquor while in charge of a boat and a kid of four," he was quoted as saying in the Bugle, and that was it, put succinctly for the world to judge. "*Stolen* hard liquor," he'd added. They were all grounded for the rest of that summer but worse, got the pointed gazes of citizens wherever they went, plus the occasional whistled reprise of that annoying shanty.

It was in Axel's and Illona's natures not to give a goddam after a while, but Milo and Eurydice felt those gazes keenly. As a result of this they saw only each other when they could sneak out, sat up on Balz's high places and talked the incident over endlessly. "It hurts," Eurydice said. "Every day, hurts. I wake up mornings and see that kid's face and there's no getting away from it."

Anaheim's body was never recovered. The Sheltzes got a brass cross made and had it put in the ground outside their place with Anaheim's name on it, only it was spelled with the e and the i the wrong way round. Azousa, formerly the most level-headed of the Sheltz clan, said she died of shame every time she looked at it. She wouldn't smile again for a long time though, which is one way of dying. That year at Christmas she joined the rest of them in going out of kilter, and sent people she hardly ever spoke to cards from herself and Anaheim.

"Told you you'd be in trouble," Axel managed to say to Michael whenever he could, drawing the wrath of Mila and, on one occasion, that punch that missed Milo. Whether Mila was there to save him from Axel's words or not, a feeling in the air around him, the absence of his laughing shadow, would hint to him sometimes at the terrible truth.

When Milo was sixteen, and asked one question too many of Lucy Ephraim

Mila found a contentment she had sought all her life that new year after the Galitzkis' reacquaintance with Lucy Ephraim. Lucy was on the road again, but she'd left her spirit behind for Mila. When kids at school catcalled her *Sister Mila* she stopped telling them what to sit on and reflected their sass back at them with a look that left them with gargoyle faces and turned their poison to air. What went through her head were the words, *Why not?*

Sister Mila, she sensed by then, waited in her future. If her peers didn't like that, then screw them. She saw the tale told in Lucy's hands and feet, the sad pass the world came to, silent or violent with jeremiads, when it failed the test God set it, and decided to nail its savior to a cross.

Lucy was away a lot of the time with the circus. She didn't make a lot of money at it. She told Milo and Mila it was the life that kept her there. It was the people, first off, not perfect, but her kind. She pulled back the masks of spangled showgirls, haughty magicians, straining strongmen, taciturn acrobats and scary clowns, and showed the Galitzkis real people who lived and breathed and threw tantrums and did shopping and loved one another, like anybody else.

"Where do you go with the circus?" it struck Milo to ask her.

"Anyplace." She thought about it. "*Every* place. North, south, west, east. I've seen this whole great country of ours. Up." She raised a hand and let it fall. "Down."

Milo remembered her mastering height and air, the gulls wheeling past her head as she danced on the flagstaffs on Reformatory Beach.

"Flew over the mountains, Milo." She knew Milo well enough by then to be able to gee him up and get his eyes bright and blinking with thoughts of high places.

"That is so… fantastic." His bike across the yard looked to him now as crude as the first wheel made out of stone.

"Descended every canyon." Lucy was enjoying herself. "Because if you go up a mountain, you've got to come down. Know why?"

"No? Why?"

"Because," she giggled out, catching Mila's laughing eye, "only a schmuck would spend the rest of his life on a mountaintop."

"Jesus came down from the mountaintop," Mila said.

"Left the Devil up there," Lucy reminded them. "To show him who the schmuck was."

The smile left Milo's face as a vision came to him of Moby Krzeski's painting of Christ in the entry hall of the Holy Apostles, His eyes that

104

blazed alive in the happenstance of art, the chaos that imposed itself into the illusion of order in paint and chemicals.

Lucy set about the naming of places and their listing in the roll calls of good, bad, best, worst. She said nothing counted save the road and the crowds, the lights under canvas and around them in the trailers like a guard of honor. Nothing beat the drama and the noise and the nickels and dimes that clinked into the carnival coffers to make it all possible.

Milo knew it didn't matter where Lucy went; it was just the road, and the ring they erected on it. The romance of the road became a thing of wonder in Milo's head. He pictured himself years later rolling around the countries of Europe on his bike, seeing only those same things, the ribbons of road and the circus the racing societies put down at the end of it to give out their jerseys and flowers and trophies and winners' kisses. Maybe he got a flash of himself standing on some European mountaintop. Salt would prick his eyes and the damp would trouble scars on his limbs and the imperfect mends in his one-time broken fingers, collarbone, ribs, elbow, but he would be holding up a first-man bouquet, thinking of Lucy Ephraim and the inspiration she gave him.

The Galitzkis ate at Lucy's, drank pop, played card games, listened to Lucy's radio and to her playing her violin. Lucy painted the palms of Mila's hands with grids of orange henna, pierced her ears with a magic needle that went through without a whisper, washed her hair in lemon juice and coriander leaves and oiled it like her own, plaited it into elaborate patterns, made her look exotic and, kids at the Lyceum had to agree, kind of dangerous. Milo fooled with the unicycle and often fooled too with the stick Lucy kept by the door, using it as a balance and, when he got proficient on the little bike, steadying it on his nose like a performing seal.

"Do they make you feel, like, closer to God?" Milo asked Lucy of her wounds. He had a way of bugging people till they came up with the answer he thought he wanted. "How do you walk on your hands with them?" he asked her. "How do you play that fiddle?"

"Well, how do you think?" The music had come to her before the marks of Jesus, they knew. Lucy smiled. "I *practise*, Milo."

"God gives you the music," Mila said.

"No. Campagnoli does, Paganini, Tartini, Popper, Warshavski." And a whole lot of other people the Galitzkis had never heard of. Lucy had given up on European village airs by then but acknowledged their unknown composers by saying, "And the music handed down through the pogroms and the revolutions and the movement of people. But God gave it to them first." She squeezed Mila's hand.

Mila couldn't help but spread her palm whenever Lucy did that, and look at it. No blood that day. Lucy bled from God's wounds in a cycle that corresponded roughly to that of her menses. "Does that embarrass you, Milo?" Lucy had asked him when she told them this, and he'd gulped out a denial from deep inside a bloom that showed that he only wanted to talk about one kind of cycle. He had gotten over that though, and examined Mila's hand too, reached out and touched it. He felt the scars on Mila's knuckles, heard the distant laughter of a child ring through his head, then let her hand drop.

When they sat at the table to eat they joined hands as Lucy said grace, and Milo could never make out whether some of the God-given energy in Lucy passed over to him, or whether it was just his hunger making him feel centered and focused. If Lucy's spells in town coincided with one of the bike races he'd entered he tried to get to see her the night before and find some pretext to touch those hands of hers. Milo knew she understood his search for speed and height and glory on that bike. Living much of her life under the unremitting glare of lights, she knew the urges that came together to present the spectacle.

"Have you got the heart for it?" Lucy ignored the comically pained face Mila made behind her brother. "This crazy racing of bikes?"

"I guess." He looked at the picture he saw at least one time a day. He was up on some podium, bouquet in hand, a liveried girl each side of him, arms around his waist, and in front of him a crowd, mouths open to let out huzzahs. It wasn't one of the little podiums they had at the end of the crummy courses he raced in the colors of the Balz Lyceum though, was in France, Belgium, Holland, Spain, Italy, was like the famous Field of the Cloth of Gold they set up for a historic meeting of kings one time, and it was festooned with flags and sponsors' banners, around it a riot of breathless people.

He wanted Lucy's blessing in the touch of her hands and, because he sensed she'd find the idea profane, there was always this pussyfooting around it.

"I'm not a bishop." Lucy would look down at her hands.

"Just wish me luck," Milo would ask, and she did, reminded him to keep upright and pretend he was on the Champs Elysées. Did he know where that was? He looked into the wishing face she had on for him and guessed her big eyes had lit a way through his fantasies, as he admitted, "I sure do."

"Hit that road and burn rubber." She pushed him away and laughed. "Imagine the Devil's chasing you," she said.

He got a creepy feeling when she said that, knew he didn't have to imagine it. The Devil was indeed chasing him. He was chasing Lucy too, and Mila as well. He remembered a foolish tale told by ancient Balzers, drunken Balzers, crazy Balzers, about the day the Devil came to Balz. He wondered if he was still there.

"What is it?" Lucy tried to read his expression.

"What?" said Mila. Milo was back from his final practice run and still in shorts. Mila had seen the goosebumps come up ugly on his shaved legs.

"Nothing." He reached down and picked up Lucy's stick and did a strange thing he couldn't explain. He tapped it on the dark wooden beam running across her hallway ceiling. Something prompted him to ask Lucy if she believed in Balz's jeremiad, but the intrusion of the question defeated him. He wanted to ask if she believed in the sight of things already seen, but saw the question vanishing into a fog. It was the knowledge that Lucy was brave enough to set off into fog in search of the unknown that kept the words lodged in his throat.

"Nothing?" Mila said.

"What?" Lucy took the stick from him. "Be careful with that," she said, absently. It was her height, exactly, Milo noticed. She stood there with her hand on top of it. "Listen, Milo, you're going to be fine out there tomorrow. I've got a feeling." She reached her free hand out and pulled briefly on his fingers.

"I've got a feeling, too." Milo looked for Lucifer, tried to grin him away, knew you couldn't do that. When you grinned at the Devil he just grinned right back and kept spinning the tales that people wound up droning out to make up the jeremiad. Milo got the urge to go down on one knee and lift the hem of Lucy's skirt and breathe in its scent. Instead, he put his hand out and touched the top of the stick. "Tell me," he asked. "What's this for?"

The next day, when Milo let the Devil take the hindmost

Some of the races Milo did in velodromes went by the name of Devil-take-the-hindmost, the idea being that every four laps the riders had to sprint hard, and the last guy over the line was out. With no climbing involved, he had never shone, and had almost given up on them.

It was a different story in the District Junior Hopefuls' Cup race. With several tough climbs, the course was made for Milo. He glimmered through the first part of the day and made himself on-the-road favorite. All the same, Milo decided to trade with that Devil who'd wormed his way into Lucy's yard. The Devil could take this race off him too, and be damned with it. Then he'd leave Lucy and his sister be.

Watchers were surprised when Milo sat up and got off his bike halfway up the last climb that, there was no doubt at all, was going to put him two minutes ahead to clinch the jersey and the race. He had a muscle pinging in his thigh, he said, and that was it; nothing he could do. One leg off the ground, he stood at the roadside and watched a group pass him, in the middle of which was the guy who, unable to believe his luck, would take the winner's jersey, the big bouquet, the battered cup, a measly purse of twenty bucks and a yucky matron's kiss from the wife of the race organizer.

The race doctor got out of his car and looked at Milo's leg, shook his head and spread hands. Milo was history already in the doc's eyes and those of the organizer and sponsor, who rode in the car with the doc. They didn't look at him, drummed fingers on the dash and kept the motor running. The doc dished out some needless advice about liniment and a massage then carried on up the mountain to keep an eye on those still racing. Milo sat on a rock to wait for the little truck that brought stragglers back.

He noted coach Leshchinski's face looking longer than ever despite his neighing out, "Did your damnedest, Milo? Well then." The coach was almost cheerful as he loaded Milo's stuff in back of his pick-up. "Always next year, son."

Milo dedicated his loss to the Devil. When he was stricken suddenly with the absence of joy in the thing, he let huge tears course down his cheeks. That wasn't the way to handle the Devil, he realized; the Devil didn't give a shit about some no-account bike race.

"Hey, now." The coach sketched out the wins Milo would take in the future. "Think of all those flowers. Huh? Wow. A whole street full of the things. All those jerseys you're going to have, so many you won't know what to do with them. Hey," he surged. "And how about all those kisses from the dolls at the finish, huh? Take it from me, Milo, one bad day doesn't make for a jeremiad."

The coach was wrong there, though. Just one little whisper, taking only seconds, could make for a jeremiad. Milo had a dread by then raging through him that he was just the man to make that whisper, to bring the array of the Devil's works crashing down on everybody he loved.

SIX

Masked Dance Saturday Night, Two Forty Five And An Angel In Flight

───◆───

"So what's so special about this angel?" the pixie asked. As she and Milo got through the gates of the mansion, they were caught in a crowd in which Milo dragged feet to note the wingtips of several angels. "I mean, anybody can go into the next frame."

"True." Milo was only borrowing the word, the pixie thought.

"And so?"

"Well..." Milo was struck dumb by the question. What the pixie couldn't know, and what Milo himself didn't quite know, was that he was no longer sure what *was* so special about his angel. *Some*thing was; there was something phenomenally *odd* about the whole thing. He felt the tweak of a line of his stuff gone to a crust on his inner thigh to remind him, if he needed it, that she *had* done the deed with him, for sure. Okay, and it had been special. No – spec*tac*ular. What else, though? Right then, if he was honest, he wondered if he was struck by love, or by lack. "She can fly," he managed for the pixie.

All eyes were on the flying angel, and people were waving, calling, whistling. A pantomime cat meowed, "Whoo, angel! Down here on my face!" Milo knew the voice but couldn't place it. He took a look at the cat's long limp tail and wondered if he should give it a tug. He set his face back to the sky. The angel was swinging through an ever-widening arc.

"*She's* not flying." The pixie let out a child's laugh. For a second, slick-haired Anaheim Sheltz, a ribbon of water weed trailing from a nostril,

111

rose from the lake in Milo's memory. "These saps just *think* she's flying." She swept an arm in a circle. "But I know she isn't."

"What?" Milo stopped. "How?"

"I'm not going to be… hypnotized by anybody." Milo imagined that face looking smug as she said, "You can see flying angels all you want."

"You can't *see* her?"

"I didn't say that."

Milo seemed to be seeking more, then said only, "Listen, who *are* you?"

Despite the pixie's silence, Milo sensed a jolt of excitement at his question. She liked the attack on her anonymity, he guessed, fancied her chances in the guessing game. With good reason.

"Tell me your name," he tried, anyhow.

She was not from out of town, he thought. She went to the Balz Lyceum, he sensed; she sounded kind of… *educated,* for want of a better word. She was sharp and sure of herself. From some of the expressions she used, he felt certain her family had some Slav in it.

"You tell *me* my name," she said. "And if you can't do that, then… tell me about this... creature."

Milo turned his face back up, but told the pixie about the things the angel had said to him on the stairs, how she loved him and always had and always would. "It was real," he told the pixie.

"And but?" she prompted him.

Before he was born she loved him, the angelic whisper said, and that had sounded like the rich music angels were bound to make. When he died she would love him, she'd promised – not quite so useful, but still music. He had wanted to ask why but knew that would be *green* of him, so was glad when she asked the question for him. "Should I know why?" Her nails had dug deep into his wrist. "These things just… occur. It's a bad world out there, full of demented people whose lives turn like the pages of dead books. And if you don't have somebody who loves you, you're lost in it. The world turns into Hell." She'd sounded sure of that as she banged the attic door open. "Your life goes to Hell, and your face and your heart and every thought you have. That's what happens if you don't find somebody," she breathed. "Or if they don't find you." They had embraced.

"It happened." He held a hand up against the pixie's gestures.

Their masks banging together, he recalled, a kiss thwarted. The angel was undoing the buttons on the fly of his soldier pants by then. He had gulped and gotten busy with those on his tunic.

"I never did this before," he'd felt driven to confess.

That had made the angel stop and look in his eyes and inside his head. He didn't know how he knew, but something in her changed at that moment and he heard the quickening of her breath.

"Thought about it a long time." His words had spilled out with a will of their own. "I don't want to think about it anymore."

The angel said, "Got to be a first time." Her voice had gone so small Milo had the sensation that it no longer belonged to the sassy creature who'd led him up the stairs.

That first time was the reason most kids went to the masked dance. It wasn't supposed to have anything to do with falling in love, but that happened, to special people. Milo got an inkling of how special he was, the idea his life wasn't just going to hinge on living in a dumb town and building mechanical things and settling for being happy at the way they did their stuff and then broke so he could fix them.

"Wouldn't be any other times." The angel had regained her voice. "Without this one. Just think about them, Milo, all the other times that will follow." He was doing that already. He had gone to take his mask off, but she'd held a hand up and said, "No. Not yet."

"Why?" he'd said.

"This is the way." She'd removed his hands from her robe and, bending like to touch her toes, had taken it by the hem and threw it up behind her shoulders to tangle with her wings.

"It was real," he told the pixie again.

"Hey, Milo." The pixie tugged at his arm to make him stop and look at her.

"What?"

"What you told the angel, that's Gospel?"

"What?"

"Your first time? On the level?"

"First time with an angel," he kind of lied.

Some years before at his first masked dance he had been on the cusp of the whole business with a girl from a folk-singing family called Zelda Kennedy, when she confessed at the last possible moment that she was unclean. That could have meant all kinds of things. By the time he'd made teeth-gritted goodbyes to her he was out of the running for anybody else. "I mean, un*clean*?" he'd commented to Richard Rat, who'd said she ought to ring a warning bell in that case. The next year he'd thought he was about to schtup coarse, well-made Amelia Steeple from school, but she'd decorated his costume with a multicolor splat of the vodka-marinated comfort food she'd fueled up on, and passed out. The year after, he'd been striking sparks with a sweet girl from the next town when he'd seen some asshole fall out the ballroom window. They had wandered over to see that it was Eurydice Armentiere, so he'd spent the greater part of the night with Eurydice in the BG as she got her broken leg plaster-cast. In any case, these scenes blipped through his mind and didn't mean zip anymore, because he was thinking again about what the angel had said to him.

114

"Didn't you love anybody at college?" the pixie asked, moving to the walls of the mansion to allow the crowd to pass them.

"No." Milo had to think about that. "Not... *exactly*."

"You were there long enough."

"Well, I thought I did," he said, then lowered his head bashfully. He dismissed it with the word, "History."

"Hell." The pixie gave him a sturdy, boy's nudge. "If this angel wasn't putting you on, you're having a time. But she's doing *what* up there, exactly, huh? Why isn't she down here with you?"

"What?"

"I mean, why didn't you just follow her, you sap?"

"I was going to." He told the pixie about Richard Rat and Bronia Chambers coming in. She had a lingering laugh at that.

"But Milo," she reasoned, "isn't that just a little... weird? What I mean is, she loved you all your life, she said, hooked up with you upstairs in the mansion and then vamoosed, then appears showing all her particulars in the air?" A tune began to bug the pixie then, but she resisted it and said, "Doesn't that tell you anything at *all*?"

Milo didn't answer, creased his hidden forehead and wondered what it was he was being told. He walked into the crowd, his head up. He watched the angel switching through the sky to the rough-house squawking and barracking of the chimera of which he was a part, a feeling of desertion creeping into his bones.

"*Mademoiselle from Armentieres*," the words came to the pixie, carried in a jaunty song brought back from a European war. "*Cut up her skirts for souvenirs.*" She thought about it, and improvised to herself, "*Showed all the crowd her underwear.*"

"Hey angel, I love you," was slurred up to the angel, but not by Milo. The call became a male voice chorus, robbing him of the three simple words.

"*Itsy-pitsy parlee-vous*," the pixie half-sang. Her pleasure at the song breaking through to its conclusion made her look up and invite Milo into the conspiracy made by the simple music.

Milo said a distant, "What?"

"Hey, Milo?"

"You're still here?" He didn't look at the pixie.

"I know where your angel is, if she's bonafide."

"Where?"

"There." The pixie directed his eye across the rooftops of Balz, made it come to rest on the lit-up bulk of the Holy Apostles cathedral, which sat sedately on its hill. "That's the only place in this town you'll find angels." She patted his cheek with a green paw, and he stood there, unable to do anything for the moment but listen to the quarter of three bells as they pealed across the town.

Years before, the raising of churches, and years later, Moby Krzeski let loose on them

The mysterious old fellow who raised Balz's churches could neither read nor write, and was said to know nothing about architecture, so the story was that there was no architect at all unless you count God. It's pretty hard not to count God, to be honest. It's easy to see how the old man got the labor, because even in these unchristian days, penniless churchgoers pledge muscle to build churches. Who he got to pay for the materials, though, nobody can work out. For a lot of people, who think about money before they think about God, that is the true miracle of Balz's churches. People who were around back then were so old by the time anybody thought of asking, they couldn't even remember their own names.

Whoever he was, God's builder was a guy who knew one good trick, which made the churches all more or less the same. Aside from the cathedral of the Holy Apostles, they're tiny, but they crown Balz's hills giving some direction to the zillion steps forming the town's streets. The Holy Virgin is made of black basalt, but the rest are red brick alternated with layers of white stone. They're all crosses-in-squares topped with shallow domes and all have an entrance hall the width of the building. Some have fragile belfries. The Holy Apostles has an optical illusion of a staircase around its galleries, up and down which hungover pilgrims and penitents go on their knees on the November feast day of drunkards' patron Saint Martin of Tours. Some have side chapels dedicated to saints nobody ever heard of.

That builder obviously knew how to strike a sweet bargain. He took ten years out of his life and built six churches: Christ the Almighty, Christ the All-Seeing, the Holy Wisdom, the Holy Virgin, The Holy Theodosia and the cathedral of the Holy Apostles. Then he left Balz for a weekend in Philadelphia, and never came back.

The Theodosia was the only thing on top of Crook's Hill, and people told God's builder nobody would slog up there when there were all the other fine churches to go to. There was nothing else there because anything built on the hill never stayed upright. People told him that too, but he built the Theodosia anyhow, on a pyramid of bones going back centuries. It was included as one of the churches in Balz's Lent icon race, when groups of kids competed to reach all the churches carrying holy pictures and statuettes, but it never had a priest, nor a congregation, had walls that went out of true till the dome came down, followed by the rest of the roof, then sat on the hill and rotted.

The interiors of the churches filled up gradually by dint of cash-raising drives reeling in an altar here, a pulpit there, a statue or two, gold stuff, silver stuff and decoration begged with the lure of names set in stone and filigree iron. The Holy Virgin had a copy of the icon of the Black

Madonna of Czestochowa that suffered from an attack of proportion and was meant to weep every All Souls' Night. The Holy Wisdom had a copy of the icon of the Virgin Guide of Constantinople and a silver reliquary in which rested a sliver of bone from the wrist of Saint Josaphat of Ukraine, though most people agreed that it looked like a toothpick. The baptistery in the Holy Apostles had a stone font, and Balz children were deemed to be ready to make their first communion when they could reach up and wet a finger in the blessed water in it. In the entry hall of Christ the All-Seeing, citizens were greeted by a fresco of a life-size Jesus whose uncanny bright eyes trapped their own. Christ the Almighty had a wax Holy Infant like the one in Prague, with changes of clothes and crowns.

That was my favorite church, where I got baptized and where I went to elementary school and Sunday school. It was where Mom and dad got hitched and down whose aisle I'd once hoped Milo and I would walk in black and white and flowers. This picture browned with the years till it looked like the postcards in the sunnyside windows of the post office. It was where they got the destitute girls to do the cleaning, and where I saw Lucy Ephraim for the first time. She was cheerfully climbing up the walls to dust the parts other girls, anchored by their diet of pork and potatoes and doughnuts and cigarettes, couldn't get to, and being yelled at to get right down right now by one of those priests she admired so much.

Some of the churches have mosaics on their walls, saintly faces, crazed eyes glittering in the dark. Some have frescos, which are wall paintings done while the plaster's still wet. I don't know why it has to be still wet.

"That's the difference between a painting and a fresco," Moby Krzeski spelled out for Milo. "You can't call it a fresco unless the plaster's wet when you paint it." Moby had a familiar look on his face, like he couldn't quite believe that everybody else wasn't as clever as he was.

It was Moby who redid the frescos in the Holy Apostles when the church council finally gave in to their fears that the originals were about to vanish into the walls. He didn't only redo the existing frescos but splashed a year out of his free time and painted the whole church. He would paint anything, and learn any technique. Once he'd gotten it in his head, he worked fast.

That was why he was unlucky that Lucy Ephraim spotted him doing mayor Hoffman in the raw on the wall out back of the movie theater. Milo could tell Moby's vanity was torn between the accomplishment of the thing and its consequences, the fearsome beating dished out to him by the mayor; it showed in his narrowed eyes and chipped teeth whenever Lucy's name was mentioned.

He said to Milo once about how there was no art without silence. "God didn't make the world in seven days," he said, "with some bastard banging a piano in the background." At the Lyceum he took all the strings out of the music room piano and rolled them up and hid them, because the school musos disturbed him when he was trying to work in recess. That gesture got him barred from the art room till he put the strings back and paid for a tuner to make it melodious again. Everybody knew there would be trouble when he was doing the Holy Apostles frescos, as priests and nuns and monks used to come and watch him work. "Glorious," they chirruped, and "Praise be," and stuff like that, till he got sick of their jubilating one day.

"This doesn't mean shit," he blasted down to them from his scaffold, his voice echoing around the dome, disturbing the prayers and waking the dozers in the pews. "It's just pretty paintings."

Nobody called out, "Don't you mean frescos?" though Milo would have, had he been present. Richard Rat was, and at Moby's outburst he nudged the nearest person and went, "Holy *shit*." That was unfortunate, that person being Father Tigran, who had been our religious instruction teacher at Christ the Almighty. He looked like an overgrown cherub, with kind eyes under an incidental tonsure and a sweet temper, though on this occasion God and anger gave him the strength to haul Richard down the nave by the scruff of the neck and deposit him on his ass outside.

Some people wanted to bump Moby off the project after that, but they didn't want half-done frescos on the walls. He was left alone to work, though he noticed that choir and organ practice had been rescheduled to coincide with his times there. "What'll happen once you've finished," Milo warned him, "is bishop Tauber'll come round and beat the crap out of you."

Initially, Moby traced and sketched what was left of the original frescos. When he got his cleaning stuff out, the Holy Apostles people watched him, worried. It looked like he was cleaning the original images off which, obvious to anybody who knew about frescos, was what he *was* doing, preparatory to spreading a layer of plaster on which to paint. "You want to leave this to me," he threw over his shoulder each time any doubt was expressed, "or do you want to do it?" Soon they found it too unnerving to watch, and left it to God to keep an eye on him.

The frescos Moby came up with, faithful to the originals or not, are close to magical. There's an Oriental-looking Virgin Mary in a medallion over the entrance hall, who sits with her hands raised and apart. On her chest is another medallion with a picture of the Baby Jesus doing the same thing with His hands. Is He winking? To this day, nobody can quite decide. All the apostles are on the walls of a side-chapel, and another chapel is full of determined and scary-looking warrior saints led by a Saint George whose face looks like Richard Rat's. Flanking the arches that lead from columns to dome are the four evangelists, and in the dome itself is a brilliant Christ the Almighty, a mature Jesus from the waist up, His right hand with fingers raised to Heaven, His other hand with the thumb touching the ring finger. Beating them all by a long way though is the fresco in the semi-dome under the dome, which is called the *Anastasis*, the title written in meticulous Greek.

"What does that mean?" people asked Moby brightly. With a snort of artistic temperament he told them it meant *The Harrowing of Hell*, and to that they said, "Uh-huh, right. So... uh... What does... *that* mean?" It's Judgement Day in this picture, and Jesus comes to claim the souls that are His to claim. He pulls Adam and Eve out of caskets because they will get to be first in Paradise again despite their record there, while He exercises the right of the victor by stomping on a Satan in chains.

"How did you *do* that?" people asked Moby continually.

That forced a suffering saint look into his face as he grouched out, "I don't know. I just *did* it."

Milo especially liked what Moby did with the angels. In the darkest part of the inner entrance hallway, which didn't get much light, Moby produced a line of half life-size angels on the wall opposite his cycling Christ. The angels look like regular boring angels at first. Then you notice that one of them is wearing tennis shoes. Another holds a goldfish in a little bag, won at a carnie sideshow. Another carries a red guitar with a pickup on it. Another is swinging a creased bag with *Peterlejtner's Stores* written on it, and a legend that could be read as *No Quality*. Another has a copy of a crime novel stuck in an armpit.

One of them carries not a flaming sword but a fencing foil, and is smiling, which is unusual; angels, all their serious work to do, were never depicted smiling. What's more, his smiling face is that of Eurydice Armentiere. Moby did that, Milo guessed, for all of them from the fort elementary crowd, who hadn't seen Eurydice smile in years.

"You'll be in deep shit when people see them," Milo said to Moby. "No doubt at all."

"Double doubt." Moby would defy anybody, Milo knew, and think about it later, the way he always did. "The people here don't notice things like that. Their whole lives are *trompe l'oeil*, man – a trick of the *glance*. They look and look, see only angels." Milo would remember that, many years later. "Don't see artifice at all. People look hard as they can but don't see anything. Isn't that why they come to church in the first place?"

The summer it was noticed that I was a woman, and God's plans in grainy dreams

In graduation summer I was grabbed by the thought of saying goodbye to the Balz Lyceum and its boys who'd one day find out that good-looking wasn't the same as smart, and its loud girls who'd shut up at last. I was sick of it all and wanted it to finish quickly, without all the talk.

Up over Mozhay Beach I could sense the Babel as the silk hats did the spending demanded of them by fatuous tradition; party invites stacking up on hallway tables, gold-etched promises catching the sun. In town the salons were busting their seams, and the changing rooms in the stores were as packed as the streetcars in the winter, the air thick with *oh-my-goodnesses*. Pennants flew over front yards, and colored bulbs for the night time. The streets above the beach were choked with caterers' station wagons following pick-ups full of monochrome waitresses. At side doors these lurid-faced big-haired women came out to smoke cigarettes and schmooze with the pick-up drivers while inside, inane speeches were delivered by proud dads. That was the admission fee for the cocktails, the champagne and the finger food: proximity to matriarchs and patriarchs whose agendas were playing out in terms of territory and acquisition. That was the only way they knew how to use the energy they had in place of talent or charm.

In the middle of all this, junior graduated, got the pat on the head, the new car and the preppy wardrobe before heading off to swank in it at college. Those sainted sons got their hands on cash from the family coffers too, and went off to the cities at weekends to drink beer and rent women and have sad Mondays that mystified them.

I hardly noticed graduation; I got it from other people. While they put on gowns and collected their diplomas, I was working already, and was in fact at that moment in the morgue breathing its canned air and looking at my dad's face. He was dead but still managing to say, "I got a cherry red Packard. How about that?"

None of it mattered anymore. I was averse to taking the stage at the Lyceum anyhow.

At my dad's funeral there were Mom and me and his lawyer, a sour-faced little guy called Edmund Utz. There were three beach crones who attended all the funerals and compared notes about the clothes and the cars and the grief. There were two gum-chewing mobsters dressed to the tens for the part. They bent heads during the service, but talked throughout in low voices. Afterwards, they shook our hands and held us in their pinprick gazes and promised to be in touch. None of our Mozhay Beach neighbors came. It might have spoiled their party mood.

Once dad was in the ground, Mom stayed home and looked hunted in the eyes. She watched the help dust things, though I sometimes thought a cautious peace had come down on her.

At the same time I knew she hadn't quite grasped yet that Mozhay Beach life was over for us. "You're a woman now," she noticed at last, which meant it wouldn't be long before she was asking me when I was going to concentrate on the parties she would throw that were meant to unearth me my very own worm from the woodwork of those pretty houses that now looked over at ours wondering politely why it was still harboring us. Not one of the primest, fattest worms, I could tell she was thinking sadly, as she looked at the frame I had which, to be honest, hadn't expanded much since I'd hit thirteen, at my skinny legs and flat chest and sketchy smile that never quite managed to do its best under the gaze of the world.

I only suspected this: God had erased my future over Mozhay Beach from His notebook of things to do in Balz, and put it into another. He had no plans for me to walk up the aisle of Christ the Almighty to make marriage vows – certainly not with a Mozhay meatball, nor even with Milo Galitzki.

God knew that one day Milo and I would sit at the windows of a train, to leave Balz for keeps. I would say to Milo, "That was Balz, and it was home all that time. And Milo?" His eyes full of the crescendos that had led us to the railroad, I would pinch his wrist gently before adding, "I'm glad it's over." I would genie up for him the magic hours we would pass under different skies. "Europe," was all we said as the train ate the line up the eastern seaboard to New York. God knew all that. He knew we'd get on a ship and barf up all we'd ever eaten in our lives, stay in our bunks and look out portholes at the patient black ocean, unable to imagine what lay under its vastness. He'd send us to Liverpool, England, a grainy place in some miserable dream between dreams, then to London, gray capital of the world with stores full of things I didn't know the names of and the beef-fat pong from its cheap cafés and its little cars that looked like bush pigs. God knew we'd marry there; He was keeping a spot open for us at the little church of the Friary in Bird in the Bush Road in south London, and our very own crone to spider out her name as witness that it was done and forever.

Even then, probably, Milo would be thinking of getting into bizarre clothes and onto a bike and riding all over London, then right out of London, period. He would be thinking the same thing as me, which was that if you rode a bike too long in England you wound up in France.

Mom's plans might have gone into a limbo of looks and sighs, but other people's went ahead under the force of their own flatulence. Farewells were performed at parties that Mom and I weren't expected to attend, and spilled into the roads. Cars were packed with the Brads and the Henrys, the Barbara-Anns and the Mary-Lous, and with their monogrammed luggage and accessories. Kids I'd thought of as fixtures in Balz weren't around anymore as a focus of my fears or sneers.

Most of Milo's crowd joined the exodus. Moby was feted in the Bugle for getting into some big deal art school in New England, but mainly for getting an eye-wateringly astonishing chunk of sponsorship cash. Milo was in its columns headlined with the words *Engineer Galitzki the Second*, and it was smart-alecked that at least college would keep his two feet on the ground. Orville Charleroi was apprenticed as a chef in some big deal hotel in New York in whose Hellish kitchens he would stuff his face and learn bad habits with fancy food. Unmentioned, Loretta Churchyard got packed off to secretary college. Eurydice Armentiere too was notably absent from the Bugle's puff pages; it seemed her plans were to carry on being enigmatic and beautiful and see what occurred. Illona Peterlejtner swanned off to train as a buyer for some big store in Philadelphia, but she too was not featured in the Bugle. When a reporter called to ask her to say a few words to its readers on the high-flown importance of trade, she was reputed to have said, "Damn this town. I hope it starves and eats rats." That rumor gained a permanence greater than any the Bugle's gray print could have offered it.

Old man Peterlejtner popped a vein too many at some customer and had the first of a World Series of strokes. He was reduced to the role of the ancient relative who, dribbling and farting, was a fixture in a lot of the stores. Axel settled into running the store, bitter with his suspicion that he'd be imprisoned behind that counter all his days like a statue in a church niche.

Once it was all out of the way I saw Michael Sheltz limping around trying to find the music inside him or mooching his days away on his porch. He didn't know about graduation because he'd stay at Balz's special school forever, scrawling his name and doing potato pictures and counting the apples in the box: born to be taught, but never to learn.

I saw Richard Rat brought into casualty with pieces of glass stuck in his head from some puerile business I didn't ask about. "Uh," he tried to illuminate for me, "a little disagreement."

He hadn't heard from Milo since the end of school, and wasn't interested in answering my tortuous questions, too busy saying how about he and I go someplace and do some stuff sometime? I went out with him and tried to get him to tell me things about Milo. "He's a schmuck," Richard said, then blurted out, "but I miss him. Bron, he's the only friend I ever had here, truth be told, only one who talks about things and makes you stop and go, 'Hey.' You know?"

I didn't. "Like what?" I wondered, and Richard told me, but they weren't the things I wanted to know. Quite honestly, I just wanted to say, "I miss him, too," but didn't. I knew no more about Milo, nor about Richard, apart from what I saw and knew already. I looked at Richard's long face, listened to the things he said, and once in a while caught a glimpse of what it was that Milo liked about him. That was one of the mysteries of friendship, though. Richard had charm in his own way, but at heart was still the little boy who liked a scrap.

One dreary Sunday we were over Mozhay Beach in a near-empty coffee house. I had to tell Richard that I didn't care if he put his arm around me, but that even if I liked it, which I did, romance was never going to happen between us.

"It might," he said. "One day."

"What made you such an optimist?" I laughed.

"Milo did. Told me when we were little that we would never tell sad stories, he and I."

"And you believe that?"

"Well... no." Those stories were written into his eyebrows. I don't know what he was thinking about. The time he lost Mila Galitzka's love by helping spread the story about her joining the sisters, maybe. Maybe it was the memory of slutty Csilla Kodaly. He loved her not knowing she loved Moby without knowing that Moby loved only one thing about her, and that was the sure knowledge that he would drill his dick into her and then forget her. This impossible triangle was uncovered by a laughing Milo the All Souls' Day he showed Michael Sheltz the Heavens and the angels. Richard's heart had surely beaten out a pulse at Eurydice too, like that of every other boy in town, and gotten only her sad little French smile in return. There had been Niamh O'Dowd too, invited up Craw Mountain by Richard, but passing the night with Milo. Maybe he was thinking of Anaheim Sheltz and her weight on his shoulders when she got tired and couldn't trek any farther but could still throw out laughter that clattered through his dreams. Richard had loved all his friends and was left with only Milo; now Milo was gone. "But I got to thinking how pessimism isn't a thing to… contemplate."

"*Man naturally desires happiness*," I quoted.

Richard didn't point a finger and say, *Aha, that's from Thomas Aquinas*, said instead, "But frigging *naturally*." Good enough.

In my head I was hearing dirt spatter the top of a casket, a sound that can't be imitated. I defied it with the words, "Happy stories. Neat idea, Richard. But tell me, where do we find them? And who do we tell them to?"

"I never worked that out." He took my hand and held it lightly in his own. That could have been good and I guess it was, till I heard that graveyard dirt rattle again in my head.

Maybe like me he was recalling Lucy Ephraim's funeral the week before, her bright lights and dreams of flight extinguished for keeps by that sound of sods on wood. Like me maybe, he heard the dirges of the little circus orchestra echo around the town to drown out the laughter of the sick in the heart and, maybe, wondered just what it was going to mean to Milo and Mila to have had the Devil sit at their table and add his thoughts to their own.

When I found the sin of pride, and liked it

If the remnants of Milo's crowd looked lost without him, I was going through a similar thing. I still saw girls from school, but for me graduation had marked our break, and I didn't have much to say to them. What made it hard was living among them, our greetings getting neutral, then frosty, our conversations hanging on threads as they looked at me and wondered what I was holding back from saying. I got along with the other nurses at the Balz General Hospital and hung out with them sometimes, but I hated their shoptalk. They were also intent on burning the misery we saw every day out of themselves, and I wasn't up to the pace they set with their boozing and partying. What I wanted was to know my stuff and get good at my job and pass my nursing exams, and that was it.

I didn't only go out with Richard. I gave some of the Mozhay meatballs a spin if they were home from college and at loose ends. That got Mom all excited, but all I ever thought about was seeing if they'd grown any. It was only the rich ones who could afford to come back weekends, and they were like they'd always been, just more so. They had turned into their dads, already. "Look at what I got," was all they had to say to me in one way or another, quickly followed by the suggestion that I let them put a hand up my skirt. I didn't want anything they had, especially not those manicured fingers probing my parts, so we wound up with no more to talk about, car doors slammed, home early from dates.

I sometimes went to sleep thinking how maybe I'd want what they had one day, but by then it would be too late. I'd be older, my hair gone brassy, and maybe I'd be looking at the mothers and babies on the beach and in the park and wanting whatever it was they had, and it would no longer be available for me to have.

I woke up mornings with different ideas, full of a pride that maybe shouldn't be voiced but should be felt, that belongs to people who are needed. I looked at the white sisters about their business, and gave a thought to Missionary Mila Galitzka, who I'd only glimpsed once or twice since the end of school. I looked for her face among the sisters, thought, 'Do you think that, huh, wake up mornings with the same thing?' I knew pride was forbidden to them, but also knew it would be the sin that lay in their hearts to attack them. I knew then why Milo and Richard had told the world about Mila wanting to put her head under that veil: why shouldn't they have been proud?

That was how Mila showed the world the woman inside her, it hit me. She would wear that veil and people would know where she was in her life. Richard reminded the world who he was with those fists of his, and that was why he had never fully grown up. Inside Moby lurked an obnoxious portrayer of souls. Milo crouched over his bike, turned those gears, won races. That was what they were all at. I put on my whites, which said: *This is me, the one who will heal you of your ailments and injuries. Even if you deserve them.* They looked up from their beds or gurneys and saw the uniform and could rest their minds for a while.

I looked down at Lucy Ephraim when they brought her in. I was on ER duty. I didn't say anything to her and nor did the white or the cap or the watch or the other paraphernalia. I wasn't able to heal her, wasn't able to do anything for her other than conjure up her laughter and the joy she brought to others. That wasn't going to do her any good at all.

Milo exited Balz cut up inside, and outside, his forehead neatly stitched after Mila, this time, succeeded in punching him. He left for college grieving, the destiny of others on his mind, that same sound of earth hitting wood ringing in his ears. I didn't see him walk off to the railroad station in black, but something told me he was no longer in town. I didn't seem to think about him that much, just noticed how every time a bike rider came toward me along the road I looked to see if it was him. It never was.

SEVEN

Masked Dance Saturday Night, To Three O'clock With The Artist's Lament For His Friends

<hr/>

It was hard to tell if the airborne angel was dictating her sway over the mansion's lawn, or following it. Her arms, and not her wings, beat with the motions of a moth trapped in a lampshade. As she passed into the light Milo saw gold pumps on her feet and, through the waves made by her robe, the vivid red of her panties.

"That's her, huh?" There was a lilt of derision in the pixie's voice.

Milo responded with a relieved shake of the head. The magic was fading with each squeal of glee, or fear, the angel let loose. The crane from which she was harnessed started its motor and advanced like a nervous mammal.

"Mine wore sandals," Milo said. "And no, uh, underwear."

"And yours would fly really, no doubt?"

"No doubt."

"I'm glad, Milo," the pixie said. "I mean, look at her. She's... what? Shop-soiled? An angel from a fire sale, maybe?"

The pixie was right. Milo cast his eyes down and resisted putting into words how foolish he was starting to feel.

When he looked up again he was taken by the sight of Moby Krzeski, who was got up as a cop except that his uniform was covered in fluorescent green stuff, as well as his hands and the grotesque features painted on his face. He had an arm around the waist of a cowgirl.

"Hey," Milo called. "Officer."

Moby called back, "Help you with something, soldier boy?"

Moby stepped away from the cowgirl, who promptly fell down. He tched then helped her halfway up, and she oscillated her head in that determined way that drunks come to, and waved him off. Moby saw the approaching figments and the oncoming crane, then took the weight of her under the armpits and dragged her, the heels of her boots making tracks in the mud, and sat her on a low wall out of harm's way. She stretched out and lay like she was dead.

That was Ursula Rock, a girl from my class at the Lyceum. She and I had never been close. I would see her leering at me from conversations across the campus and hear her in the jeering chorus whenever I screwed up in class. One time her voice echoed its way down the shower stalls at school to describe me as, and I quote, *an ugly freaking Pekinese.* Even after that she seemed to think I'd help her out if she ran into me in some place over Mozhay Beach because I was on howdo terms with some guy she was swooning over, who wasn't in a million years going to give a damn about her. I was supposed to go, *oh, she's great,* and not tell guys she didn't wash her hands after taking a piss and didn't change her brassiere week in week out. Sure. Still, I felt bad to think of her the way she was that night, kidding herself still if she thought some guy like Moby Krzeski would take care of her.

"Hey, fairy," Moby said in greeting. Tired of playing, the pixie tossed him a glare and looked away. Milo thought she might vamoose then, but she hung around, getting pissed at the people who pushed into her in the wake of the flying angel and the lumbering ghost in her machine. "So you're how?" Moby was asking Milo. "You're well?"

"Uh-huh." Milo sounded unsure. They muddled through their greetings and brought each other up to date in overlapping five-word sequences. There was a time and place for the exchange of news, and that wasn't at the dance. "Know any angels?" Milo asked at last. He heard the pixie let out a comic curse behind him.

"There's one." Moby rolled his eyes. "Flies and all."

"Not... *that* one." Milo's voice was level. "You know any of them? Who they are?"

"I'm on first-name terms with the angels." They were surely thinking of Moby's angels in the Holy Apostles. This made the thought of a straight answer remote. "Hey, but where *is* everybody? You're here alone?"

"Sure I am."

The pixie refrained from a *ha-hmm* and stayed to one side, eyes half on the crowd.

"So." Moby lent the word a little flourish. "Who have you seen?"

"Richard." Milo tucked a finger under his mask and gave his chin a rub. Despite all the vodka, he tasted blood. Richard hadn't needed to punch him *so* hard. He felt a swoosh of anger at the way Richard had brought him back to the regrettable actions of their schooldays.

"The Yellow Peril." Moby nodded. "I saw him, already. You haven't seen any of the others? Really?"

Milo thought about it, said, "Michael. I saw Michael."

Moby just repeated the name. "Eurydice is here," he said. "So I heard. I've not seen her. Illona's here." He accompanied his recall with a click of the teeth. "You didn't see Illona?"

"No." Milo hadn't even thought about her.

"Might be a big shot... store executive, or whatever she is, but she can't keep away from Balz this one night in the year."

"No. Sure."

"Well, she's around someplace – some, like, courtesan kind of thing, time of, I don't know, Mozart?" Moby looked disgruntled at the thought of it. "Barely dropped her fan to blow me a... *pathetic* little kiss. Little night music, my ass."

"*I* saw her," the pixie offered. She was about to recount her glimpse of Illona Peterlejtner smoking some noxious weed with an ugly biker, then reminded herself that Illona was their friend still, after all.

Milo was looking past Moby's shoulder.

"Galitzki?"

"Uh... what?"

"Jesus Mary." Moby's thoughts broke out. "I come back from college to dress up and get surreal and booze and chew the fat for a weekend, and I find what? I come *alone* to this damn place, man." The gesture he made communicated the New York parties he was missing out on, all strobe lights and avant-garde jazz and cocaine and girls with bobs and shades and skintight black sweaters. "No big *news*, no meeting up the way we used to for a stiff one, no parading through town dressed up. Illona gone straight, Ax turned into a frigging storekeeper. And Eurydice? She's what... *hiding* from us? I come alone." He looked at Milo and the pixie in turn. "What's that about, huh?"

Milo was watching wings. They passed. The angels' laughter skittered into the hubbub around him.

"*Galitzki.*" Moby had always liked saying Milo's family name. Most kids at school shunned its scratchy sound. "What's that about, I put to you?"

"Uh... Right."

"Huh?"

"Sure, Moby."

"Hear me?"

"Maybe we've just all… grown up at last," Milo said. That got a snicker out of the pixie. Moby showed her a curled lip till Milo admonished him, "She's right. Look at us." He pulled his mask off, ran a sleeve over his sweaty face and took in some air, took refuge in a sad little *moue*.

Moby touched his shoulder, said only a gentle, "Hey." Milo nodded. For a second it seemed like Milo's head was going to end up on Moby's shoulder. The pixie was impressed, thinking it was a thing true friends could do: conjure up a shared history and speak without words.

"Do you know any of them?" Milo repeated. "The angels?"

"Well, *yeah*." Moby put on an offended I-know-everybody tone. "Ortensia Umberta's one. Heard one speak – no mistaking *that* voice." Milo thought of Ortensia Umberta and her prize fighter body and voice that could wear down diamonds; it wasn't her. "Now there's a girl could do with wearing a mask the whole time." Moby search out Milo's approval. Anyhow, the Umberta was black-haired, not that that meant much, as everybody cut or dyed their hair or did other stuff to it to make it look different for the masked dance. She'd also hated Milo's guts, since the day he socked her brother for bothering Loretta Churchyard and, honestly without meaning to, knocked out one of his gleaming Roman teeth for him. "Kasia Krantz is one too, I think." Milo stopped Moby there; he knew that. "Selby's one." Moby clicked fingers. "How could I forget that?"

"Your *brother*?" It wasn't him; Milo was sure of that. "Got his habitual sense of imagination, I see."

Selby Krzeski was shady, people said. He had a boat, they said, and ran contraband in and out of the Caribbean islands. He had a truck, the same people said, brought reefer down from Canada. Those same people said he had a whore, and kept her in a red-lit cell in New Orleans. Something had to explain the flashy cars in which he drove back to Balz, the fancy suits he wore and the state-of-the-art consumer goods he bestowed on his parents each time he came back. What he did really was

134

devise programs for IBM and their mysterious computers. Because people in our town couldn't conceive of the manic Selby as a pioneer of something so of the future, they had to think up something. After my dad died, Selby Krzeski came up to Mom and me at the house and dipped his head and said he'd heard about our loss and hoped we would accept his condolences. He was the only person in town who did that.

"Angels *are* boys, man." Moby was irked, it was plain, at the misrepresentation around him. Milo remembered Moby telling him that, probably when he was working on the angels in the Holy Apostles. "Girls don't get to be angels. Tough break, but they just don't. Selby's the only true angel here, far as I can see. But anyhow… *Tell* me. This angel – she stole your billfold, or what?"

"What," Milo chose.

"What's the story with angels?" Moby addressed the pixie.

She stated brightly, "This sap's in love with one."

Milo was about to challenge this version of his plight. A movement of his shoulders let Moby know it could pass for the truth.

"In love with an angel." Moby grinned and shook his head. "I like it." He banged Milo on the shoulder. "So you're who?" it occurred to him to ask the pixie.

She threw out, "Guess."

"Easy." Moby had a head for names and faces. He said, "You're that kid lives over the east gate of the fort."

"Oh – I *am*?"

"Never went to senior high." He clicked fingers. "And your dad superintends the park. Am I right?"

"Have I got a name?"

"Used to go out with Benny Armentiere Junior?"

"Have I got a name?"

"Well, sure you do." Moby said that in what was supposed to be her voice. "But I forgot what it *is*, obviously."

"Hmm. Have I got a face?"

"Short brown hair." Milo said. He'd already seen her tuck wisps of it under her stupid pixie hat. He wasn't sure if he liked the conversation drifting away from angels, but Moby was the unfocused type except where his own ruling passions were concerned. 'Slow eyes,' Milo thought as he reeled out a shaky home movie of the times he and his friends used to cut through the flowerbeds in the park just to see if the superintendent could catch them, his little daughter watching from his hut. 'Cute nose, lank brown hair that never got washed, stick-thin knees green from playing on the grass the whole summer and not ever taking a bath, red eyes streaming with the pollen in the air.' "Hay fever red eye," he offered.

The two of them looked down at her and, whatever way she seemed to look back at them from that mask, it made Milo feel sorry he'd said that, especially when she gave him an answer he deserved: a mocking *achoo*.

"Want to go someplace?" Moby didn't care what her name was or what she looked like. He didn't care that Milo had fallen in love or that, behind the dumb GI Joe face he was fixing back on, his friend might be stricken. He focused only on the thought that if Milo was in search of an angel he was obviously ready to discard the pixie. "That is..." Moby gestured at Milo. "If you've, uh, finished your business with Lieutenant Lovesick here?"

"No chance." She got them pondering vehemence in her voice. "But thanks just the same."

She was thinking of Moby at his painting. Expert with color, she remembered, good at framing his work, she knew, cutting and staining and blending frames to fit in with the hues in the works themselves. A man good with a saw, and with sandpaper. She looked from Moby to Milo,

"God gave us this to eat," she dared. Mr Galitzki looked up, thunder-eyed.

"Yea." Loretta chimed in helpfully with a quote: "*Every moving thing that liveth shall be meat for you.*"

Mr Galitzki turned his thunder to lightning and said to Loretta, "Shut your mouth and eat your food."

"*Howl, shepherds,*" Loretta risked. "*Cry aloud.*" She busied herself with her puzzling task.

Milo suffered a vision of the trusting faces of beasts as they were herded shaky-legged onto a walkway. At the end of it stood that big neighbor of theirs giving off his own mixed signals: kindness in his face, knife in his hand.

"Think of those people who are starving, Milo," his mom tried. "Like in India, someplace. Why, they'd *fight* over that there on your plate."

Mila mouthed, "Yeah, asshole." She fixed the gloomy pools of her eyes on the night outside the window, willed her gaze over mountains and seas and across continents, tried to see India.

"Eat it." Mr Galitzki stopped his own meager picking to watch Milo clear that plate. "And you," he commanded Mila, without looking at her, "be careful with your language."

"Sorry, Pa." Mila in turn didn't look at her dad. She said to her mom, "Why are they starving in India?"

Loretta said, "Because they've got no *food*, dimwit."

Mila hardy-hahed that out of the way and placed a kick on Loretta's ankle. It drew a yelp. Mila asked her mom, "So how come they don't all *die*?"

"Because people help them," Mrs Galitzka told her.

"What people?"

"Good people, I guess. Now, Mila."

"What?"

"You eat your dinner, too."

That night Mila thought of places from which the birds and beasts had fled the knives of butchers. That was smart of them, to know about what God had declared about every moving thing that liveth.

In his bed, what Milo thought about was God giving us goulash to eat, and how that was without a doubt mysterious. He remembered that God gave us free will, too, though. He found himself thinking of that smell Mr Churchyard brought into the house – it was death, nothing less. He was sick up from his socks, the fat in the meat having separated itself from all the other glop to seek a way out. "I made that happen," Milo boasted to me years later. True or not, it worked, and he wasn't made to eat meat again.

"All things bright and beautiful." Mila and Loretta sang out the price of his indulgence at Milo in the house, in the yard, in the park, on the beaches and at school, where they got up a little-girl choir to help. *"All creatures great and small."* All that summer they blared that old tune at him. *"All things wise and wonderful."* They punctuated it with merciless giggles. *"We got to eat them all."*

How Loretta stalked Milo with fire and God and wisdom from the prophet Jeremiah

While Milo became an eater of only fish and vegetables, Loretta turned into an unearthly child with skin that reminded me of veined cheese, and unfocused basalt eyes, a glint of mica in them. She had the smallest mouth anybody ever saw, though it let out the most piercing screams if she was disturbed. *Disturbed* being her more or less permanent condition, this was often. She had a shock of yellow telephone cable hair that made her look cute from a distance, though after a while you wanted to get a scissors and chop it all off.

142

Loretta developed an unfortunate talent for setting things on fire. "Isn't my fault," she managed to say before interested parties rounded on her. Her dad was always having to grub around town for stuff to replace things Loretta had destroyed.

Like Mila Galitzka, she carried a Bible. She held it as she preambled to strangers, "*I do not know how to speak. I am only a child*," before they told her to shut the hell up in that case. She seemed to know the whole thing off by heart, and could quote from it whenever the situation demanded it, though mostly whenever it didn't.

At the Lyceum the first act Loretta committed of note was to determine that Balz would have tongues of fire, a visitation from the Holy Ghost; she lit all the Bunsen burners in the science lab in recess. The place glowed, the only spot of heat and color in the winter gloom. Loretta got as far as, "*Some have entertained angels unawares*," before a teacher caught up a fistful of that hair and dragged her off to retribution.

She was close to Milo, but even he took care to stay away from her unless he ran into her outdoors in places like the park, or on the beaches or cliffs, happy to walk with her into the wind. She seemed to like him greeting much of what she said with laughter. She told him once how an angel visited her and carried a sword of fire and left it like a calling card.

"That's Michael the Archangel." Milo only interrupted her occasionally. "That's one important angel whose attention you got."

"He didn't tell me his *name*." She couldn't be bothered to tell Milo that a lot of the angels had flaming swords and fire-raisers' hearts. She said the angel told her lots of stuff she didn't understand, but the important thing was that the answers lay in the flames, which cleansed as they destroyed.

Milo was never sure about Loretta's angel story, just as nobody was ever sure about his. Once she sat there flicking a Zippo and telling him fire was the most beautiful thing anybody could achieve. He said she was wrong; a bicycle was the most beautiful thing in the world. "Yeah, but how

143

do you make a bicycle?" she challenged him. Then he had to think of flames heating up metal to blend and bend it to perfection.

"Your grandpa's *department* store burned down," she said in wonder when she first heard about that historical episode.

"Long time ago." He stared at her.

"A whole big *store*, burning." She shook her head at the... *scale* of it. "A whole big *store* full of *stuff*, up in *flames*. Imagine."

It wasn't something Milo thought about often, unless prompted by the instances of outrage that his mom summoned sometimes.

"Angels did it," Loretta supposed.

"*Oh* yeah – you *think*?" Milo could only laugh. Loretta didn't mind.

They spent evenings in the lighthouse watching the towers at the refinery burn their gases off. The flames turned to smoke and merged with the steam from the cooling towers, and with the cloud vapor, to make shapes miles across the flats. In the middle of blazing sunsets they saw ships, crosses, moons and horses, anvils and anchors, trumpets, towers, stars and the faces of people they loved or would love in the future, transient and distorted. "No bicycles," Loretta used to like to say, but Milo found them anyhow.

Other times he let her bring him out to the fields to watch the laborers burning the stubble. One evening at bird migration time Loretta, without a word, embraced him. The farm workers were tiny figures a way away and the birds weren't going to pause in their thermal-driven journey to watch.

As the fields raged and crackled and blazed them a backdrop that put flames in their eyes, Loretta asked, "What is it that you see?" As she got on top of Milo she answered herself, "*A cauldron, on a fire, fanned by the wind.*"

"*Howl, shepherds.*" Milo entered into the spirit of the thing and laughed up at her, a little scared at this ledge she had forced them onto but unable to stop himself peeking over.

"*And disaster flaring up against all who live in this land.*"

"*Cry aloud,*" Milo gasped, and giggled.

Her hair full of burrs and seeds, she kissed him for what seemed like a long time. He liked it, mostly. On their ride back to town, Loretta on the crossbar of his bike, Milo knew that the kiss was a significant thing, and guessed they'd do it again. She was taken away for special care soon after, though. When she came back three months later, her head full of electric waves and her motor skills slowed down, it became something they could enjoy or be scared of as it took a bite of their pasts.

Milo never told a soul about that kiss, not even Richard, just told me years later. He knew you shouldn't tell about stuff like that, of course, but I have my suspicions that it had more to do with that classic boys' thing of not getting caught dancing with the ugliest girl. Or kissing the craziest, more to the point; Loretta was, it was clear by then, off her head.

"You know how you're going to die?" he said to her as they watched the refinery gases exploding. "You're going to combust spontaneously one day."

She made him spell that out for her. She said, "Goodness – that would be… *wondrous.*"

"*Wondrous?*" A word no other kid in Balz would use.

"Yes. How do you do it?"

When she'd burned a jagged way through her schooling Garrett Churchyard, in an insane move, blew part of his savings on sending her to secretary college, and she nearly burned that down, or so the story went. She certainly came home early with no diploma, but with her face slapped red, her mouth swollen with those quotes she didn't get out on time. Then she went to work in the rubber goods factory and half of that *did* burn down, the liquid stench of road accidents hanging over Balz for a week. Nobody said out loud it was Loretta's fault, but the factory owner Mr Bitkofski, a Democrat who had a seat on the municipal council, came and tried to beat up Garrett Churchyard. Loretta's dad, used to slaughtering anything that stood in his path and squealed, contented himself with the basics of self-defense like a Christian. Mr Bitkofski eventually burst into tears and spent the rest of the evening sitting out front of the Churchyards' place declaiming to passers-by about bankruptcy, and look what you got for trusting screw-ups like Loretta. He never ran on the Democrat ticket after that.

Milo was walking on the salt with Eurydice and the Peterlejtner twins one evening when they saw the lighthouse lit up. They ran up to the light room, where they found Loretta huddled in a corner in her chemise and panties. "I'm not *doing* anything," she protested out of habit as they put out the flames of the little bonfire in the center of the room. Axel said how Loretta was in deep shit. Eurydice and Illona helped her into her clothes.

"They planted legends and visions in my head." Loretta talked about her sojourn among shrinks and quacks for the only time Milo would ever remember. "Things that aren't mine to see. Am I crazy?" she asked them. Milo and Eurydice put warning fingers up at Axel, to stop him saying, *yeah, Loretta, no* doubt, though the words were in all their minds. Eurydice walked over and hugged her and Illona joined them. She looked at them all sadly. "*No help from clamor on the heights,*" she noted as she heard the swelling of a klaxon that was making its way to her, and knew that, pretty soon, somebody was going to be raising hands to her face.

Graduation summer, and the end of a story

There was never any help from clamor on the heights. The first thing I thought about the night they brought Lucy's Ephraim's body into the hospital was how last time I saw her she was with the Galitzkis, taking a Sabbath stroll along Ganser and Weiss Avenue. I passed close to them.

They were eating ice creams, engrossed in laughter and not seeing me in my church gray and Mom in her widow's weeds. I heard their voices again and thought how in all the time I knew her at school I never heard Mila Galitzka laugh the way she did that Sunday.

The science deserted me for a second and I couldn't believe that Lucy wasn't going to laugh again. "Somebody's got to tell the Galitzkis," I said to myself. I knew it had to be me, though the thought of stopping off at that incident of architecture the Galitzkis called a home set my heart rat-a-tatting.

Forgetting Mila, conveniently enough, I was thinking how I'd walk up to Kazimir Street and in the Galitzkis' door and up into Milo's room and say, "I need to speak to you alone." Those words form instant intimacy. When he cried, the way he did when I saw him lose the climber's jersey in the Balz bike race that time to Otto Dreyer, I'd comfort him. I would be firm and professional, and Milo would raise his head thinking, 'She is a girl you need to have around.' I'd say, "How about a drink, you and me, and we'll go talk about it, or about something else?" Then he'd say how neat that was, and we'd do that. We'd walk on the heights and look out on the town and be silent, but settled, and Milo would know I was there for him.

Seeing dead people was a part of hospital life, a test you had to pass. Even though I'd only been at the Balz General a few months to fill out the empty end of the school year before the graduation exams, I'd seen enough of them. It was tough at first. Then it wasn't. You got used to seeing those faces deserted by life and those beds vacated hastily, and you adapted and turned your attention to those who still needed you. Nurses said it got tough seeing faces you knew brought in, but I'd been to i.d. my dad already, passed that next test.

Before I'd heard either a syllable of rumor or the measured opinions of doctors, I knew I was looking at the surprised and at the same time disappointed look I was told I'd see on presentable victims of suicide.

One of the Balz stories about Lucy was that she kept a stick by her door, and what she did with it was measure herself against it to see if she'd gotten any taller than three and a half feet. If she did, people said, then she'd lose her job in the circus. If that happened – so people said – she'd kill herself, because her life in the circus meant more to her than the ability to breathe. It was just a lot of ifs making up a story. I couldn't even remember where I'd heard it.

The remainder of that shift I passed in a semi-trance, thinking about that story. When I finished work I didn't go to Milo's place. I went and saw officer Gerard O'Dowd, the cop who'd been called when Lucy was found. I asked him, "Did you ever hear that story about Lucy and her stick?"

He looked at me across his messy desk, his hunting dog eyes steady, his set lips looking like he was about to whistle. "I heard it," he remembered. He chewed on something minute stuck in his teeth and let out a breath from the canyon he called his lungs.

He was my friend Niamh's dad, I had to remind myself. She said he was fun and gentle and respectful and intelligent and kind and comic and made her mom the happiest woman on the planet. No doubt. He made *me* feel like an irrelevance.

"There was a stick there?" I asked him. "At Lucy's?"

I was treated to more of the strong, silent part. "Hmmm," was all he had to say to that, except it must have lasted all of half a minute. He stood, and took a sharp look at the door, like he'd never noticed till then what a fine door it was. "I'm obliged." He unfolded a hand, showed me that door for myself and purred out, "I'll look into that."

I didn't go home, nor did I go to the Galitzkis. I walked up through the town and sat on the steps of the war memorial feeling fragile-tempered and miserable. The gloom of the day lay in my chest, and my breath fought friction. I ignored the lights of the square and looked at the dark spaces between them as they ran down into streets. I couldn't help but be drawn to images of the cruelty in them.

I knew it was Milo who'd sparked the Chinese whispers that became that story about Lucy. I knew too that retribution of some kind was going to fall on his head. For a while, I wanted it to. It wasn't Milo who'd had to look at Lucy's body and see it sluiced and toe-tagged and placed in a drawer in the morgue ready for the attentions of Doc Erevan, the pathologist.

I kicked around town with it never far from my mind, tried to forget it and sometimes did, till diverted by Lucy's funeral.

From the fort, I watched a lone figure on the flats, knew it was Milo delving into his soul for more parts of the story that would eventually be his to tell or hide. I wanted to walk out there to him, take his arm and keep pace with him, but that didn't happen. Whatever his thoughts were doing, it wasn't for me to interrupt. There was no place for me under the storm of opprobrium gathering over him.

When Lucy gave Milo a story to tell, and the gesture that would haunt him

Out on the flats, Milo was fixed on the same recurring images. They flickered on the blank sky. He remembered that Sunday walk too: the ice creams, the laughter, the last time he was going to see Lucy Ephraim.

He saw himself wheel to a halt on a steep and stony hillside, the Devil steadying him but, essentially, not giving a cuss about his sacrifice.

The night before the District Junior Hopefuls' Cup race, Lucy had twirled the stick and held it straight and stood against it. "It's how high I am," she'd said. "That's all it is, Milo. I grow anymore, then it's byebye circus. It's true." She raised her hand and drew a finger across her throat, a gesture that would never stop haunting the Galitzkis. "Any higher, and I'm out. I've seen it happen." They thought she must be thinking of friends no longer around, who went to seed in nowhere towns and died of nothing to do and no road to travel.

"But you're hardly likely to grow," Milo had blurted. It didn't seem like such a nice thing to blurt and Mila nudged him, but Lucy didn't seem to hear, had her teeth on her lip.

Milo didn't know who he'd told about Lucy's fear of growth: the usual people, he guessed. Faces ran through the sprockets, laughing.

I don't know now just when I first heard it, but it was in Balz, accompanied by the sniggering of booze hounds and idlers. Mila heard it too, asked Milo was that him, telling people about Lucy and her fear of growing? He said it had to be other people telling yet more people. Where was the harm? There were plenty of stories doing the rounds about Lucy. She was a celebrity, wasn't she, just like him in his own little way, and Moby? People had nothing better to do but talk about them. All the same, Mila had a bad feeling about it a long time before its time to come home, sensed it flying around Balz waiting for its moment.

It was only a matter of time before some low son of a bitch put it to the test. People assumed it was somebody from Lucy's neighborhood, who could look out a window and see her walk up to her door and go in. From there they would have to imagine her picking up her stick and measuring herself. People guessed that was her habit. It could have been anybody though, who wielded saw and paint to reduce her stick by an inch.

Witnesses did indeed see Lucy go in, but nobody saw her come out. Two days later she was found hanging from the beam in her hallway when a visitor called to no answer, got up at a window and smelled something bad, sensed something that couldn't be fixed. That visitor was Mila Galitzka, and she lost that new smile she'd taken to wearing and lost her laughter too, and never got it back.

150

EIGHT

Masked Dance Saturday Night, To Three Thirty And Everybody In Search Of The Things Closest To Their Hearts

◄———◈———►

Milo and the pixie followed their noses toward the fire, and soon saw its glow reflected from the Zacharov mansion.

There had been a blaze at the dance two years before. The wound showed as a jigsaw of black bricks around a boarded-up window. It was testimony to Loretta Churchyard's inability to grasp that, if she kept bringing fire and people together, sooner or later somebody would do something more than slap her face. There she'd stood, wild west saloon singer in fire service red, on her lips broken lines from the prophet Jeremiah. She was with a guy from out of town barely acquainted with her, and in for the shock of his life. They got hustled onto the grass and half-stripped and cut by water hoses. Then they were dragged to the war memorial, tied to a rail and pelted with spoiled fruit from the back of Peterlejtner's store.

That night the mob indulged the wish-fulfilment of kids at the Balz Lyceum, and cut off Loretta's hair. Then they scratched her scalp with a cross. Bastards. It was safe to surmise that that would be Loretta's last visit to the dance.

There was an underlying viciousness there, occasionally turning from atmosphere to actions. You felt it in the air, cutting through the music and laughter, and the movements of people dancing. There were always rivalries, for girls, for boys, or related to contentious sports results, for

Chrissake, and to hazily-recalled slights and insults, between kids from Balz and from those out of town, some determined to settle their business even if it wrecked somebody's face. There were spats between kids whose parents or grandparents hailed from old and new empires, places impossible to pinpoint on maps anymore, revenge for outrages and atrocities most of them knew only from aggrieved hearsay. Balz's bikers let it be known that if there was any trouble to be caused at the dance, they would cause it and, in general, kept an eye on proceedings, but they couldn't be everywhere at once. Much of the shouting happened early on before the arrival of the bikers or, with the addition of booze, later, the bikers having by then been sidetracked into girls, drink, drugs, it was rumored, or were occupied by their aching war wounds. The pixie caught the aggression in the figments, and feared that pockets of the night were harboring violence, the feeling that, someplace near, things were getting ugly for somebody.

People said that had Loretta's fire gotten some wind into it the whole place wold have blazed in a second, taking its drapes and tapestries, sheets and blankets, its frilled collars and silk stockings and lace petticoats, its wigs and wings along with it. And byebye to the cream of Balz's youth. When I looked at the slobbering, staggering masses though, I saw the ghosts of the Zacharovs with their arrogant faces from the Austrian-Hungarian Empire, and shame on me maybe but I felt that a good old conflagration might not have been such a terrible thing.

"Poor Loretta," the pixie said. "The sad tomato."

"Yeah." Milo's agreement coincided with a picture of Loretta leaning over to him on their third birthday, putting her warm hand on his cheek and reciting his name in the manner of a psalm. He felt her hot and heavy against him in a closet a year later, smelling of sweat and sugar and piss and milk, as they hid from Mila, playing a game but also wanting to scare and hurt her with their absence. He saw her, years later, pulling her dress over her head. He got a sure sense of that evening in the fallow field, the smell of burning stubble in their noses and those warm-winged birds incessant up above. He recalled one of Loretta's trusting kisses. "Poor Loretta. Jesus Mary."

It hurt Milo, the pixie sensed, to think again of Loretta getting hurt. She tried to conjure something else to say but couldn't.

The pixie had a hand on Milo's arm as they walked under the faces at first floor windows. The pressure of her fingers was strange, and reminded him of Loretta and the way she hooked a hand around his arm to claim sanctuary with him. Eyes fixed on the glow, the turn of a corner of the building made them part of a rubbernecking crowd, faces outlined by a blaze that had once been a little summer pavilion.

Milo remembered it, wormy and rickety and damp, and Amelia Steeple throwing up over him there.

If the firestarter was Loretta, Milo knew they'd kill her this time and hang her body from a lamp post on the edge of town to warn off others. It couldn't be, though. She was gone from Balz, the rumor being that she'd joined a troupe of travelling evangelicals. He felt a little ashamed. Why didn't he know for sure? He imagined her safe someplace with her Bible tickertaping through her head and giving her comfort. He knew it never would, though; he knew it never had because – God strike him dumb – it was just words, and anyhow the only parts of the book Loretta repeated seemed to be the disturbing ones. Maybe her dreams of fire came to her the way his dreams of mountaintop bike race podiums came, and kept her warm. That blotted out the image of her in a locked ward with crazy people. He let slip his anxiety that there should be no more pain for Loretta by telling the pixie then about how he and Loretta were kind of born together.

"And the hospital?"

"The BG." There was only the Balz General to be born in. "Of course."

"No." The pixie sensed Loretta's absence, her safety in distance, and felt safe enough to laugh. "I mean, it didn't burn down?"

They were among a group of out-of-towners in raggy costumes that projected nothing in particular, hats that didn't match costumes, masks or make-up that were last-minute touches. Some of them clowned and whooped, pushed and shoved. Milo and the pixie passed through them to a core of Balzers whose stances, mannerisms and voices Milo recognized. They could tell by the chatter that nobody had gotten hurt or killed in the fire. It also told them that there was no sign of Loretta, though a few sourpusses were trying to whip up a search party for her, and a reward, no less.

Milo picked out a voice expressing a yearning for Loretta's blood. It belonged to a cartoon cowboy who could only be a guy from the Lyceum called Cezar Torunski, whose dad ran a store that sold shoes that wore out before you could wear them in. Cezar owned a car made up of the fronts of two old Chevy Standards welded together, so nobody could tell if he was coming or going. He himself didn't always know, because one day he was so busy yakking out the window to somebody that he backed the car over a little Kazakh boy and manslaughtered him. He got away with it by taking advantage of Balz's central Asian workers hardly being citizens at all, just people abandoned there by the railroad company.

"Torunski," Milo called to the cowboy. "Drive carefully, huh? Watch out for the bumps."

Milo's voice had a shocking animation as it cut through the rhubarb. The pixie knew fighting talk when she heard it. She stopped herself from saying anything. Maybe it was to do with Cezar Torunski being a bully who deserved the consequences in Milo's twitching fingers.

Some of the rubberneckers had gotten interested in the possibility of some impromptu sport. They moved out of the way, eyes glowing at the prospect of people getting hurt, palms up in invitation for Milo to step through and strut the stuff promised in his voice. Most of them stayed in place though, and told Milo to keep cool and mind that he had no call to talk that way. The cowboy called over, "Big shot Captain Asshole," even though he had to know it was Milo. His pals, one in black-face, one a cartoon red Indian, another a harlequin, flanked him in nervy readiness.

The pixie sensed Milo's need to punch somebody – anybody. People hububbed as his hand went to his mask. The pixie knew that if he took the mask off that was it: they were going to fight. Milo, outnumbered, was sure to get a beating. "No," she hissed at him. She pulled his arm. "*No*. Let's go."

She felt Milo's hand on hers. She knew it was no longer at his mask. She heard him breathing heavily as she turned him back into the crowd. She made them spectators, and then there was nothing to look at anymore.

The drama fizzled out in the opinion that, with a fire going and all, somebody should break out some breakfast stores and get some wurst sizzling, some bacon, some toast. A fat guy in straining doublet and hose and a Napoleon hat started pleading, "Eggs over easy," in a desperation that started off plaintive then turned comic when the crowd took up the chant.

The search was on then for the son or daughter of one of Balz's other storekeepers, future heirs of overpriced goods and bland conversation, of little dogs that were bad-tempered because they looked like rats and knew it. They would forget their days of masked dances and lock up their daughters and volunteer quotes for the grouching columns filling the Balz Bugle about how the dance pandered to the *degenerate* youth of Balz – at least until that same youth slouched into their stores next day. Then they'd lean over their counters and see only money clutched in hands. The call of trade would break them out in cheesy smiles to say, "Can I *help* yew?" not knowing that you were saying under your breath, "Yeah. *Die*, why don't you?"

The storekeepers' ball with the eating of frogs and dancing with the ugliest girls

One of the high spots of the Balz social scene was the storekeepers' ball. It was one of those things that had gone on so long nobody could remember the first one. People went not to mix with the town's storekeepers but because the booze was free for the first hour or so, and the entertainment was good in a lame way that appealed to small kids and adults who never got out much. Every year the money behind the bar lasted a shorter time and they said there'd be no free bar the next year, but they were scared nobody would show up, so it stayed.

The storekeepers were a throwback to some trader nation that resented deep down that they weren't haggling with Silk Road merchants in Middle Eastern bazaars or skimming across oceans laden with the riches of the Orient. In their stores, as you discussed the weather and how your mom was and the high prices of things, you were foot-to-foot hopping to get the hell out of there, because even as a kid you recognized something oppressive in those interiors that made your skin pop. You met them at the ball and had to talk about the same old stuff, only the weather didn't matter and your mom could talk for herself. The things whose shocking prices you might have complained about were absent, though if you looked in the storekeepers' eyes you could see goods arrayed in neat lines, new under a layer of storeroom dust, or faded from the sun.

They had the cheapest band in the world, musical pioneers whose scrawny necks popped out of spangly showtime jackets, playing music your grandparents might have shimmied to in the days before they got arthritic and rheumatic and bronchitic. They had a folklore spot from the awful Kennedy Family Singers, which went down a storm because people were so canned by then they'd have clapped a Tatar invasion. They had a buffet full of stuff they hadn't been able to shift during the year, which all the same vanished in conjunction with the free bar: wrinkled gray olives, bendy salted biscuits, nuts resembling the stools of small animals, tiny cucumbers looking like anemic goldfish, pickled walnuts like horse droppings; it all got chucked down people's necks. People even ate the ornaments off the cake, not realizing that the *pastiage* they were made of was just a kind of bakers' concrete.

On the storekeepers' top table there were people who in the stores sat in back and knitted everlasting baby boots or looked up with a Pavlovian jerk of the head whenever the bell chimed. "This is my mother," the storekeepers would say at the ball. "You know her, sure you do." Then you realized that the antique normally parked in a chair next to the detergent really did live and breathe and walk and talk, though often not all at the same time.

The storekeepers were disguised at the ball in dark suits with cummerbunds and frilly-fronted shirts with ties, and shiny shoes, in spangly dresses and silky wraps and gold and silver brooches dull with the salt in the air. The men's faces were shaved ham pink over their chicken necks, the women's eyebrows painted on in grease. They were doing the conventional, formal thing, but in their own way were more bizarre than anything you avoided at the masked dance.

Milo took Illona Peterlejtner once, though it's fairer to say she took him, her dad having an allocation of twenty tickets. He also had deep misgivings when he saw Milo in that role. When they were little, Milo, Moby, Orville Charleroi and Richard Rat used to go into his store at start of orange season and ask if he had any oranges. He'd bellow out, "Fresh in," would march around the counter, paper bag in hand. Then they'd ask for apples, and get him introducing his eyebrows to each other. Richard was barred forever from visiting the twins during opening hours the day a regular customer was showing off her toddler and he said the kid, who wore welfare glasses six times too big for her, looked like a frigging Buick. At that ball Mr Peterlejtner kept his stern eye on Milo until distracted by the banter of his kind, not realizing that it wasn't Milo he ought to be watching. Illona wound up drunk and on the lap of some out-of-town bruiser who would bother her for weeks, sending her flowers and hanging around below her bedroom window. He was a broken-nosed Romeo like Shakespeare never dreamed up, over whose crewcut head Axel eventually broke a bottle. That started a war that ended one evening with officer Gerard O'Dowd kicking a lot of asses including Milo's, Axel's and Richard's.

Another year, Milo took Niamh O'Dowd, officer O'Dowd's daughter, and outside she showed him how to kiss like the French do, but said he couldn't go any further. He did though, later that year when she went camping with Milo's crowd up at Craw Lake. After graduation, Niamh went to Los Angeles to study dressmaking, and never came back. People said she became a whore and a hophead, but they said that about any girl who left Balz and didn't appear for smily gift-laden visits at Christmas and Easter with toothy husband and squawking babies. Milo got a letter from Niamh saying how she was doing costumes for movie studios. He told everybody that, but still they muttered darkly, "Yah, broke her daddy's heart," because it made them feel good to think of her adrift on the Great White Way.

The first year Milo went the boys hung out together. Their hosts kept going, "Now, you boys okay there? Having lots of fun? Got enough pop?" They bellowed out that they sure were and sure did, but Richard kept magicking beers from someplace. Inevitably they got a little merry, surprised in equal measure by hiccoughs, giggles and the contents of their stomachs inching their way up in search of the air.

Michael sang the one song he knew, about depressed, drunken sailors on a boat trip out of a nightmare. Betty Willis played the piano and snickered and made faces at her friends, not knowing the horrible thing that was going to happen to her not so many years later when Michael sang in Zakopan's bar. He had a high, sweet voice in those days, nothing special, and mostly inoffensive.

It was at that one that the boys held a Dance-with-the-Ugliest-Girl competition. They went to the debris-strewn tables seeking out girls that wobbled, girls that might snap if you squeezed them, girls with mustaches, with dopey hair, buck teeth with or without braces, with glasses thick as pebbles, girls with knock knees and two left feet, who sent see-this-huh glances at their prettier friends and sisters; they danced with them all. Niamh O'Dowd, padded in those days in puppy fat that would fall off eventually to reveal a beauty with a touch of the danger of her ass-kicking dad, was among them. Milo thought about that the night he lay in a tent with her up in the hills above Craw Lake, his hand roving inside her shirt, when she sang out to him in the dark, "I know what you're *think*-ing," and he had to sing back, "Oh no you *do*-on't."

I was among them too – of course I was – disguised as I was then as unbeautiful Bronia Chambers. Richard Rat towered over me and held me close, fingers latticed high on my back where I was sweating. My nose in his chest, I couldn't hear a thing he said, just kept going, "Uh-huh," torn between being pleased to be dancing and thinking he was a moron. Milo thought about that too, years later.

The high spot of the ball had to be the frog leg eating contest. Trestle tables were set up on the stage, covered with white cloths. At one side chefs stood at a cauldron, engulfed by steam. The contestants sat down and were given a number and the MC introduced them all. The crowd would whistle and whoop no matter who it was. Bowls of frog legs would be brought on out, with a permitted glass of cheap hock per bowl. With a roll on the drums the MC would get them at it, and would commentate in a *hey-yah* voice blaring out, "*Attaboy*, gid*dap* number seventeen," or, "Ahoy – how *about* that? Hand for number four, second bowl down." It was always men, any dignity they had dissolving into the chemical reactions produced in them by booze and bravado.

It got disgusting anytime after the second bowl, when you could see the weaker ones flagging, their eyes shocked at how difficult it was getting.

159

More bowls would be brought, the MC hurrahing away. Most contestants gave up some way into the third bowl. They'd pull off the napkins tucked into their fronts and chuck them which, like in boxing, was the surrender sign, and the MC would ask for a hip-hip-hooray as they tripped valiantly down the steps trying not to look green in the face.

"Gross," a few people said, but there was always the majority to cheer this celebration of gluttony as the best fun. Maybe it was, as long as you were just watching, and didn't think of the bums outside being fed scraps through the charity of white sisters, who would have killed for one measly frog foot.

It was the year that we were fourteen when a gap in the steam revealed the glowing face of Orville Charleroi under a chef's hat. Some people yelled, "It's that disgusting fat kid," but Orville ignored them. He stood cooking almost imperiously, no showbiz indulgence on his face, only a hint of contempt each time a cheer went up.

I always thought that when God looked down on the world He didn't just tear His hair out at wars and oppression. He put stuff on b-lists of things to do. I thought it was things like the frog leg contest that made him waste Sodom and Gomorrah the way He did, and give its citizens those sad stories to pass on, even as they stood in rows and cheered.

Some years after graduation summer, when God looked after His own

The storekeepers' ball is frozen in its ridiculous, disquieting splendor in a Moby Krzeski oil painting big as the side wall of a house which hangs in the Paris Museum of Modern Art on loan from some zillionaire. A critic with an eye for the highfalutin wrote that the picture was like a big deal hotel whose doors are open through the plush reception and dining rooms to the kitchens, where the squalor puts the grandeur into perspective. Well – *okay*. Maybe I have that same eye though, because that sentence stuck in my mind.

The picture is unsettling in the mystifying fashion art allows. It looks vivid the way a photo spoiled by camera movement does, and presents a paradox: a tableau that moves. The panorama is topped by those tables at which sit masticators of frogs, mantis hands raised to dark maws, chins and shirtcuffs blending to snot-green and blood-red. At tables off to one side sit the storekeepers and their kin in their slackjaw glory, holding onto bowls of flesh-colored food and drinks that look like urine samples. One has pistols flanking his place-setting instead of cutlery, as if on guard against mysterious forces ranged against him and his fellow-capitalists.

To the left of the gluttons a boy sings into a microphone and the brushstrokes over his head show what you know at once, if you're from Balz, the blur of a panicked crow. A woman bangs a piano and shows a horrible smile on the half a face the viewer can see. Again, if you're from our town, you know that half a face is all one-time countess Betty Willis got buried with.

In the foreground, boys arrest the movement by slow dancing with a bestiary of misshapen girls. There is one with twisted pigtails of white wire, mouth open to reveal a glint of metal, slit eyes open on ball bearings. Her fingernails and patent maryjane shoes have a metal sheen to them too: me. I knew for sure then that Moby hated the idea of Milo forever dancing with the ugliest girl.

Articles were generated in the press about Moby being in the vanguard of new art, and how much he spoke for the spirit of the age and the kind of blah blah that critics think people give a rat's ass about. With those daubs representing it, there was also speculation as to the state of Moby's mind. Anybody who grew up in Balz could have slung a perceptive opinion at those armchair analysts on that, but nobody asked.

Moby wouldn't be seen dead with ugly girls. He went through a catwalk of affairs with verifiable glamor-pusses then silenced the chatter by getting hitched to an heiress from some big cheese New England family. She broke the mold: a wild child but no looker, with her granite puritan jaw and far-apart eyes. She had to have personality, gossip columnists catted, in the same measure as the fortune she came into at age twenty one.

Almost as soon as the image of Moby's face was stamped onto the spirit of the age, he threw the art establishment by reverting to the preoccupations of his youth to work on a major religious painting. He had long before junked religious art, critics panted, had taken whatever he'd needed from it – perspective, scope, the beatific expressions and poses of saints, among other tropes. All the same, news had it that he was in Cupertino, Italy, setting up at its church of Saint Joseph.

The painting was commissioned to commemorate however many hundreds of years from the birth of the town's holy man. This was a guy born in a garden shed because his dad had sold the house to pay off debts. He grew up slow, apparently. When I read that I thought I might adopt him as my own saint. To add to his problems he walked pigeon-toed, and drooled and gaped. Reading between the lines you concluded that he was bigger than his impairments and fought them to shine a light that caught the eye of God. Joseph tried for the Capuchin friars but that tight-lipped frat didn't want him, so he went to the Franciscans, who took anybody. When he finally got to be a priest he is supposed to have mailed his underpants back to his mom because, as he wrote her, his habit was all he needed. You had to hope he gave them a wash first.

His life got interesting when he started to levitate. He flew over the altar when he said mass, the hagiography went, and perched on top of columns and crosses. When I read that the hair on the back of my neck turned to bristles as I saw Lucy Ephraim in my head, balanced on those same things to do her cleaning in Balz's Christ the Almighty church. Joseph took his brother priests flying on his back, which must have led them to an exciting mix of alarm and exhilaration. He was surely the coolest priest you ever heard of. The church bigwigs of seventeenth century Italy predictably hated all this and, on the same charges of messiah-wishing the Romans trumped up to get Jesus, threw him in jail.

162

They had to keep moving him around though, as pilgrims formed crowds outside his cell window. All this attention slipped him into a depression that cowed and killed him.

Saint Joseph of Cupertino didn't wind up as the patron saint of the slow, so that had to be a thing between me and him. He got to be mentor to astronauts and pilots and men in balloons, though: those who braved high places, in other words, so he was Milo's saint too. I liked us being able to share him.

It's a matter of record that Moby grouched through his commission in a way familiar to anybody from Balz. Priests, nuns, monks, novices, organists, church pew crones who arranged flowers and small girls suspected of having the power to will statues to bleed, all were treated to Moby's artist's pique. Finally he tarped in the area of his work till he got finished and people, from critics through bishops to crones, hated that and loved it too; no matter what they say, people know having a mystery is always better than not having one, and is in fact even better than solving one.

Part of the mystique surrounding Moby's work in Cupertino was why this art wonder kid was doing it at all, let alone in a place so inaccessible to the lard-assed pundits and chatter-makers of the art world. Questions were also asked as to how the church authorities could justify spending wonder-kid money, and to that they were able to smirk and reply that it wasn't costing a single cent: Moby was doing it out of the goodness of his heart. It was news to anybody who knew him that he even had one, and they said, "What – come *on*. *Why?*"

Moby reverted to the answer guaranteed to annoy peers, teachers and critics and said, "I don't know. I'm just *doing* it."

The painting is not a fresco but was designed to masquerade as one, a fact pointed out by those excitable critics when photos of it as a work-in-progress were released. It takes up one wall of a side-chapel, and it's full of vivid blues and greens. It also features a lot of gold, which some people didn't think was in keeping with a saint who didn't even wear underpants. You can't please everybody, though, and Moby knew not to try.

Michael Sheltz flew only one time in his life, but he did his share of gaping and drooling. He isn't doing any of those things in that painting. He is neat in his crooner's suit, and he clutches a sheet of music for the Lord of the Dance Christmas carol. He is at the edge of a choir of the faithful, and seems to be making an offering of his song to the levitating saint.

Saint Joe takes up the center, hands clasped on his chest, face a picture of unsettling ecstasy. It's got to be my imagination that makes me think he has a look on his face borrowed from one I often wore, saying, "Not so frigging slow *now*, huh?"

The figure at the foot of the saint is Lucy Ephraim. Her head is turned, her shining plaits swinging with the rhythm of the dance she is doing. She wears a Gypsy dress in a living red, the footless hose of acrobats revealing kempt feet, a gold ring on her right big toe.

Lucy is swinging that stick of hers. It is her exact height. It is dull brown in color, but has elements of green in it, and a yellow that turns finally to gold.

The last anybody ever saw of Lucy's measure was when Mila Galitzka tossed it into her grave, made it clatter on the casket before the dirt made Lucy into a memory. Father Vishnevski had paused at this interruption to his proceedings, licked his cracked lips and nodded, went on with his dispatch of Lucy's soul.

I've got a picture of Moby's work-in-progress as it appeared in a five-page spread in Paris-Match. First there's the usual Paris-Match stuff, the artist as man about the world in the passenger seat of his convertible, that ugly heiress of his at the wheel. Then there he is in a local bar after the day's work, having a grappa with the guys who mix the plaster and paint and offer their labor in the traditional way for this agent of God and propagator of His glory. There's the tetchy artist at work laying down plaster with a trowel, paint in his hair. There's the proud local priest, something in his eyes revealing that he has the devil of a job following an act like Saint Joseph. He grins sideways at Moby and it looks a lot like the artist is busy telling him the joke about two nuns in a bath. Behind them is the work itself.

As it's a work-in-progress, things are not the same as in the finished picture. Michael isn't holding any music, for example. The saint's upper torso and head are nothing but bare plaster. Lucy's pigtails have yet to be added.

The stick she is holding is black and has got mountain flowers on it, linked by elegant stalks. I wanted to think about what the picture was telling me, so it took a while for me to show the spread to Milo. He glanced at it, said, "Yeah, it's good. Moby's going places."

"Look at it," I told him.

"Yeah, I am."

"*Look*, though." I let Milo look a little more, then pulled the magazine out of his hands. He stared as I tore the page out then tore around the picture and gave it back. "*Look*, will you?"

"What the – that is, uh, *exactly* what I am doing." His claim was urgent, as it always was when he knew that I was on the point of forcing out frustrated tears to lead him to things that had to be faced. "For Chrissake."

No, Moby didn't know Lucy in any way that would have led to his visiting her at home, there was no doubt in Milo's mind about that. No, he didn't go to her funeral – of course he didn't. "He *saw* her stick, alright – her *measure*," I had to spell out. "*Look* at the frigging thing, and tell me, now, why I'm showing it to you."

Had Moby ever forgiven Lucy for her citizen act of telling on him when he was doing his zap art on the wall back of the movie theater, opening up that door leading to hospital food? We had to guess not.

"Jesus Mary." Milo threw the picture down. "He got the measure of Lucy in a different way."

"He did." We lay on our bed and looked at the ceiling and saw projected there a black-and-white movie of Moby sneaking into Lucy's place and sawing her measure, then replacing the exposed cream of its top with black gloss paint. We held each other and cried about it, wailed, "What are we going to do?"

There was nothing we could do.

"God looks after His own," we had to agree. Okay, so He hadn't been paying attention the night Lucy's bright logic, that empowered her to calculate angles through the air with the precision to guide hands and feet to the right places, was fatally overcome by the superstition in her genes. "God takes care of things." I believed that, believed in the scheme, the *plan*, whatever God had in mind. "He doesn't like it when people try to *play* at God. He makes them fall off planks in high buildings," I whispered. I pictured Moby dropping dead weight from the lofty dome of some cathedral, his pride trailing lighter than the dust, colored by stained glass. "Makes them hit the ground at thirty feet per second."

"Per second per *second*."

"Okay, Einstein."

"Jesus Mary."

I didn't say God helped run cars off the road at ninety miles-per-hour when the people driving them had a pint of bison vodka inside them. That wasn't His work, was it? Just the same, maybe sometimes He busies Himself with other stuff when the Devil wants to get his work done. I get the feeling now that the thought swept through my mind the night a few months later when that convertible of Moby's somersaulted to a halt in a beanfield off route one twenty eight out of Boston. Under the power lines, fifty thousand watts thrumming through them, with the radio on and the scent of pine trees and the cold and the dark, Moby watched stuff trickle through the white of one of his heiress's broken eyes. Maybe the headline *Artist Seen Ugly With Dead Heiress* cut through the tears that rolled down his cheeks to clean the wounds holding pieces of windscreen glass in place. He got an hour in which to think about how maybe they should have stayed as they were in Paris-Match, his heiress behind the wheel. Her shattered Nefertiti head must have looked even more of a sight by the time the rescue services cut him out. They took him from there to a hospital, where they pumped green alcohol out of his stomach and dumped him in an invalid chair in which he grouches even now, I guess.

A monument to petulance and revenge and the folly of playing God, Moby Krzeski slaloms along the hallways of his own mansion, his own masked dance of modern masters frowning at him from its walls. He knows he's never going to get near ninety miles-per-hour again. He also knows now, I presume, that if he's going to change people's lives he's never going to do it again by breaking into their houses and reshaping their totems. He'll have to rely on his art alone and, last I heard, that is the task that will preoccupy him, along with how to say sorry to the creatures God deemed to be special, for the rest of his rolling days.

NINE

Masked Dance Saturday Night Around To Four Fifteen, With The Chef And The Things He Always Wanted To Say

———————◈———————

The pixie led Milo away from the fire-lovers and through the scrub at the back of the mansion to a door leading to what had been kitchens. Lit by oil lamps, kids were slumped and tired on old furniture or animated, smoking and murmuring. The band was taking a powder, but low fiddle music played in the main hall. A stairway led to the mezzanine. Milo stepped to its rail and watched the crowd.

"She's not here," the pixie observed. There were some angels, none of them Milo's, both could tell.

They smelled fire again, a different kind. They followed it. Milo hesitated as they passed the room in which he and the angel had trapped each other. They carried on to the chapel at the top of the house.

"You're hungry?" the pixie checked. "You didn't want to go breakfast with Cezar Torunski?"

"Not so hungry I need a knuckle sandwich."

The Zacharovs' chapel was a rotunda, frescoes barely visible under graffiti. Milo made out Italian-style cherubs, and remembered Moby scoffing at them. At the back of the room was an inferno presided over by Orville Charleroi. He was larger than Milo remembered him, and dwarfed a Chinese couple, small and neat in stature, all of them in stained chefs' whites. Behind them lay piles of gleaming raw steak, a grinder, onions,

herbs, cartons of eggs, jars full of crushed biscuit and bakers' sacks full of
buns. The assistants worked the grinder and chopped onions and herbs,
Orville yelling instructions without looking at them. A few punters waited
for their orders while others stood eating theirs, or perched on church pews
to do so. Milo waited for Orville to serve his last customer, then stepped to
the counter and said a soft, "Hey."

Orville, though busy with nothing in particular, took his time to raise
his eyes. The pixie saw that he had spotted Milo immediately but hadn't,
for whatever reason, wanted to acknowledge him. Refraining from
pointing this out, she let fly a loud tut, extracting a puzzled glance from
Milo.

"Milo." Orville blinked his eyes slowly, a mannered gesture he
perfected as a child, then cast them back to his work, scooping up
carbonized remains and depositing them into the trash behind him. He took
a tug from a glass of beer, watching Milo through it.

"Busy, huh?" Milo nodded at the set up.

"Hundred per cent best ground beef." Orville's voice was low and
rich and had gained the undercurrent of a growl since Milo had last heard
it. "Know how I'm so certain of that?"

"You ground it yourself," Milo said. "I guess."

"No." Orville made an oink of derision. He nodded sideways at his
assistants. "The monkeys do the grinding. No. I killed it myself. I stood in
a field way along up out over yonder at Vlach's farm. I… studied this meat,
on its legs, yes? I looked it in the eye a long time." He had a look of strained
concentration on his face.

"I'm sure he was pleased to see you," Milo said.

"*She*," Orville corrected. "You don't bludgeon a bull." He announced
gravely, "The all-American burger is dead."

"I should frigging hope it's dead," a guy called from behind Milo. "I'm not eating anything that wriggles." His friends burst into laughter.

"Finished." Orville ignored the interruption. "Only here, at the Balz dance, will you find the all-American burger."

"Well, sure." Milo shared a look with the pixie.

Orville's expression never wavered, his fathomless shark eyes and the line of his compressed lips unmoving. His face had always shut everybody out, keeping both friends and enemies at a distance; Orville Charleroi had bamboozled anybody who tried to get close to him.

He turned a tidy profit at the masked dance, he told anybody who asked, and anybody who didn't, captive in front of him gagging for a burger. "It's a need," he'd say. "That's what it's about, this dance we keep perpetrating, the three things people need. That's food, alcohol, and sex. And you know what? Those three things, done to excess, and they always are, they're incompatible. Like if you wanted to make a dish using ice cream, anchovies and limes. Sure, you could do it. But would you want to?"

Milo waited for this spiel, but Orville repeated, "Dead. Circus clowns," he predicted, "will be selling mass-produced burgers all over America. Hey, but what would you care?" Orville let out an abrasive laugh and slapped his forehead. "I recall that you don't partake in the eating of animals, no?" He turned his gaze on Milo. "You were in Alaska a year, I heard – am I right? And you didn't eat any *meat* out there? Moose, you could have had. Bear, if it didn't eat you first. Rarer than fucking rocking horse meat. You really didn't?"

"Plenty of fish in Alaska. And I was just about to ask if you had any."

"Fish?" Orville roared the word out, gave it three syllables. The eaters in the background stopped their talking for a second. "Fish." Orville shook his head sadly, as if equating the eating of fish with starvation.

170

"Fish," the pixie said evenly. "You know, that you tickled to death yourself?"

Neither man looked at her.

A memory lit up Milo's face. He said, "I remember you eating fish, Orville." The pixie joined him in a laugh. "At least one time."

Orville hooked a thumb at the meat piled behind him. "Milo, tonight is the dance." He sounded patient, though both Milo and the pixie caught the hint of a comedy of anger in his voice. "People want blood. Tonight features the last pure hundred-per-cent American flame-grilled burgers this town will ever eat."

"The... *last* ones?" The claim was a new one to Milo. "How come?"

"I'm gone." Orville removed his hat and let his long black forelock flop. He wiped his face with the rags tucked into his apron pockets then replaced his mess of hair under the hat. "Out of this town."

Customers were forming a line behind Milo. He stepped aside and took a cautious look to see if Cezar Torunski and his pals had abandoned their search for a free breakfast and had opted instead for Orville's great American cuisine. Orville's customers were mainly from out of town, he remembered. The boycott on the ventures of the fort school crowd continued, it was plain, which said a lot about the tiny minds of the kids who'd attended the Lyceum, and how they'd not grown any in adulthood. Orville took the orders and barked them out to his assistants, hollering for onions, tomatoes, lettuce. "Chop *chop*," he yelled. "Small *small*, yes? You fucking *monkeys*." The couple grinned up at him and the man saluted, but the pixie noticed how their looks, when he took his eye off them, manifested a promise to skewer him.

"Out of town?" Milo asked. "Where?"

"Anyplace they know how to eat."

A guy in the line who had no doubt started the evening looking dashing in his trashed linen suit greeted this wisdom with a gentle laugh. "Everybody knows how to *eat*, man," he admonished.

"Think so?" Orville answered in a neutral tone. "Paris, France," he told Milo as he worked. "Bordeaux. Perpignan. Monte Carlo, maybe. Where they pay a guy top dollar to cook for them. And when I'm gone, the burgers'll be gone, I kid you not. Not that you'd worry about that," it occurred to him.

"I guess not," Milo had to agree.

"In fact, Milo, you never worried about a single thing, yes?" Orville's tone was conversational. He was occupied with the job, searing burgers and flipping them, flaming the buns, using tongs and spatula to strew them with salad, slipping them into bags, handing them to his customers and taking the money in one motion. "True, Milo?"

"Well... *hardly*." Milo sensed more than banter in Orville's words, and was glad to see the line of punters disperse.

"You were always so tediously... *good* at everything." Orville raised a finger. "Oh yeah. And had everybody fall in love with you all the time."

"Come *on*, Orville." Milo tried to laugh.

"Yeah. Eurydice. Loretta. Illona."

"Illona – *what*?"

"Even Axel. That fucked-up homo could never take his eyes off your ass in those bicycling shorts."

"You're deluded, Orville." Milo tried to laugh again but he was finding it hard to raise even a smile.

"*Oh* yeah. In fact, I wouldn't be surprised if all those bicycle riders weren't purse swingers. No, Milo, but they did – all fell in love with you. Even Richard. See the light shine out of his eyes every time you and he got all... physical together."

172

"Hey Orville, listen to me." Milo reached up again for the spot on his jaw where Richard had punched him.

"Uh-uh," said Orville. "I always had to listen to you." He lowered his voice. "It's not some vile, evil *thing*, Milo. It's love. I'm not putting anybody down, here."

"Sounds like you are." The pixie's observation got a sideways look of contempt from Orville.

"Just saying, Milo. Just… *stating*. You're good at everything you do, and you always were. Oh, for sure." He raised his voice to drown out Milo's protests. "Math, physics, chemistry. Technical drawing, all your little letters and numbers all exactly the right fucking height. Remember that? And parleying the *français*, you were good at that, yes? My mom always at me, 'Hey Orville, you don't even speak your own *language*, and yet that Polak kid comes top in the class?' Not *my* fucking language. I'm American. Belgium is a place smaller than ranches out west."

"I wasn't top in the class," Milo managed.

"You were close enough. People said it was all so you could whisper the language of love into Eurydice's ear."

"Jesus, Orville." Milo threw his hands up. First of all he wanted to point out that Eurydice's French was more or less non-existent, but he couldn't think of a way to put it without sniping. "That's just… grotesque."

"French word," Orville crowed. "See? But Milo, all that… *sportif* shit, *that's* not grotesque? All that homo bicycle racing? You punish your mind with all those numbers. You punish your body with all that exercise. Know what I thought when I saw you in the showers at school? All that muscle and sinew? I thought you looked like a walking fucking… *x-ray*, like one of those anatomy diagrams we had in the biology lab. You know, you open a page, yes? The skin diagram folds back? You see muscles, organs, veins? Huh?"

173

I remembered that diagram, thinking how the man's expression never changed even though torture was happening with each turn of the page. His skin was removed, then muscles, organs, cartilage, blood vessels and nerves. Only on the last page, when he became bone, the jelly of his eyes was finally gone.

Milo looked stung. Maybe he saw some truth in what Orville was telling him, all those people, not just coach Leshchinski at the Lyceum, who pushed Milo to *go go go* for the Balz Lyceum, bring back another cup to shine for a day on the shelves of the trophy cabinet before it gathered dust.

"And you're a... vegetarian." Orville could barely bring himself to say the word. "Which reminds me. I got nothing for you to eat, Milo."

"I think I lost my appetite." Milo indicated the meat. He laughed, inviting Orville to laugh with him. "And anyhow."

"Yes, Milo?"

"I'm no vegetarian. Last time I looked, fish weren't vegetables."

"They're a tiny step on from plankton, Milo. Hey, toasted buns I can give you." Orville almost did laugh then, as he made a quick survey of his wares. "But I guess you must be used to them, all that time you spend with your ass on that bicycle."

Milo liked that, and even the pixie smiled.

"Lettuce I got, but that's just flavored water. And I guess onions are out of the question," Orville went on. "In case you're going to track down the Frog Princess and glue your tongue against hers tonight."

"That's not... *nice*, Orville." Milo frowned. Only the Mozhay Beach girls had called Eurydice Armentiere by that name. Their high-school catcalls echoed on. "But listen. Have you seen Eurydice tonight?"

"She's here." Orville nodded. "Last big night out before she ties the knot."

"Ties the what?"

"You didn't hear, no?" Orville framed his enjoyment in a wide grin. "Our Eurydice is *affianced*."

"To who?"

Eurydice's nights out had attained legend in Milo's absence, he'd heard. They often involved a fleet of cars from her dad's lot, gatherings of her friends, disputes over bar and restaurant bills, the odd fight and the odd arrest for what the cops quaintly called *conduct unbecoming*, the odd bit of bail and the odd spot of jail.

"Some guy." Orville yawned indifference. "From out of town – Delaware, maybe. Some fucking... businessman type. First of many," he advised.

"You've seen her?"

"She's here," Orville insisted, then confessed, "But listen, Milo, she's not going to spin my way tonight. Her tastes are too... refined for burgers, even for burgers as good as mine. Probably the one delicate thing about her is her stomach."

Not true, Milo thought: everything about Eurydice was fragile, from the hair-triggers in her brain poised to set off the mysterious mechanisms of her trances and thrashing to her long limbs, waiting to be broken. The impact needed for the breaking of a femur, strongest bone in the body, was an unbearable thought to Milo.

"Milo." Orville barked out his little laugh. "Remember the dream I had about Eurydice getting her head cut off by a Guillotine?"

"Yeah," said Milo. "Or at least I remember you telling her about it."

"Sure." Orville grinned, triumphant again.

"Repeatedly."

"Hey, what? Guilty, Milo?"

"What?"

"At least I didn't break her delicate heart."

"And I did?" Milo saw Eurydice through all their times together, laughing over nothing, crying over less, hot-tempered, cool as an iceberg, her arm through his, her back shown to him in disdain.

"The fucking jury is back in."

One of the eaters called from the background, "Hey, can the language, Lard Boy. Ladies present." Milo thought it was prudent of them to wait till they'd gotten their grub before they insulted Orville, in the sure knowledge that he couldn't revenge himself on them by any nefarious culinary means.

"*Ladies.*" Orville snickered, tapped the side of his nose, winked at the pixie. "Here – at the dance? Oh yeah. *Sure.*"

"The jury, Orville?" Milo was nonplussed and, the pixie could tell, genuinely puzzled.

"You broke her heart." Orville held a hand up. "Everybody thinks so and, most important, *she* thinks so. So for all intents, purposes and what-have-you, it's true. She is that kind of woman," he assured Milo. "Expects you to know what she… feels, without her having to tell you."

"Oh yeah? And how would you know that?" Milo realized right then that he recognized what Orville was saying. What little hair he had left stiffened. The Eurydice Armentiere in Milo's life had not been a woman, though; she'd been a child, who bitched and cried and wailed one second and the next was content to marvel and coo and be happy with whatever caught her eye, the way any child did.

"And if you don't know how she feels," Orville said almost in a whisper, "then she's your enemy, and forever. She'd give you a second chance, a third, even. But only so that in the end she can tell you how you let her down that one time, broke her heart, failed to… protect her."

"I always protected her." Milo thought hard. Really, fragile and all, Eurydice had been able to take care of herself. He'd protected Loretta Churchyard, sure, and Michael Sheltz, of course – and Orville himself, all the lame, strange kids.

"No," Orville insisted.

Milo would never be sure what his brain went through that night. It had been a disorientating evening. He was fixated on an angel who had always loved him, she said. He had gotten himself laid for the first time too, and had swallowed more alcohol than he had ever drunk. There were the masks all around him, the half-remembered enemies of his youth, the estranged friends. There was that damn pixie.

Milo would not know what Orville had been talking about till a few years later in a café in the Paris suburbs. He would drink coffee after coffee as he read Eurydice's letter to her family, her friends, her teachers, to the whole of Balz, the catalog of her fractured and sad life in that memoir of hers, *Used Goods*.

"How do *you* know what Eurydice thinks?" Milo demanded of Orville again.

"She told me." Orville laughed out his trump. "Fore-warned, Milo," he bragged. "Fore-armed."

"That way you can always be right," said the pixie. "Or seem to be."

Again, Orville refused to look at her but he scored her one with an appreciative gesture of his index finger. He minused it by addressing Milo with the words, "Another smart midget. Just what this town needs, yes?" He used the same finger to a-ha, reminded himself of something and said, with some enthusiasm, "Hey, Milo, I remember how, when one of those… childish homo bicycle races of yours was coming up, if you were carrying five extra pounds, you used to starve yourself for a week. I mean, fuck, that's somebody who hates himself. Not good, Milo. And yet."

"What?"

"Everybody loves you, so you don't need to love yourself. And you're good at everything, Milo, to get back to the subject. But you know what they say?"

"No, Orville." Milo gave his mask a shake to make sure that the sweat had dried on it. His body language told both the pixie and Orville that he was ready to leave. "*What* do they say?"

"Jack of all trades, master of jack shit."

Orville laughed sweatily and uproariously. He wiped a hand on his apron and held it outstretched. "Milo," he said. "Even I love you. You *know* it, yes? You were my pal. You… tolerated me. You talked to me and listened to me. You laughed when I made a lame joke. You never called me names, even when you were mad at me. You stuck up for me. You'd even do it now, yes?"

"Maybe." Milo moved shoulders wearily.

"Sure you would. This is all just my… bluster under the blubber. I'm a freak. I don't care. And I don't hate myself. Because I know one thing if I know nothing else. If I don't love myself, nobody else will."

Orville's voice had for the first time reached an even pitch, the anxiety of combat fading from it. The men stared at each other for seconds. Orville took his hat off and lowered his head a little, as if inviting Milo to punch it. When Milo shook his hand instead, he looked up and smiled, a hundred little droplets breaking on his face.

"Back out to all that for you now, yes?" Orville nodded toward the chapel doorway. Loud music had started up again downstairs, the dance roaring back to life. He tutted, shook his head. "And on an empty stomach. You go well, Milo."

"You too." Milo waved. "See you in Paris, maybe."

A small crowd appeared in the chapel, figments from out of town, removing their masks to reveal hungry faces.

"Not some vile, evil thing, Milo." Orville called. "Remember that."

"Hope he means the food," one of the incoming punters said.

"I love you, Milo. I always will."

Aided by a three-beat rest in the music, the briefest of silences amplified Orville's pledge, Milo and the pixie by then in the middle of the crowd. They avoided engaging with the stares, the laughter on the faces. Orville yelled, "All-American burgers. Get them here. Get them now. One last *time* in this pitiful fucking town."

Water and blood, fish and science, the winter I was fifteen

As I'd been aware of Milo and his circle all my life, Orville Charleroi had always haunted the edge of my vision. He stood out for a number of reasons. His mom was the widow Charleroi. Too hatchet-faced to be good looking, she was starchily well-dressed and formidable at close quarters. She made pennies as a seamstress sewing dresses that sold in fashion houses for hundreds of dollars, but also took in commonplace repairs for the steam cleaner in town.

Orville's dad had been a nefarious thief who'd turned to burning the things he couldn't carry away. After he was murdered he was made to fit the police picture for a number of high-profile arson crimes. The Charlerois were Belgian, and not originating from east of Berlin like most of the families in Balz. This completed their aura as outsiders, with Latin peoples seen as temperamental and secretive, bearers of vendettas and harborers of vampires.

Garance Charleroi fitted the temperamental bill; her tantrums were legendary. She had stand-up rows with both Miss Kodaly and coach Leshchinski when they insisted that Orville took part in PE at school. She spat at a woman who accused Orville of eating all the food at the only birthday party he was ever invited to. Notoriously, she punched Father Vishnevski as he bent to offer her communion, for reasons people could only guess at, albeit knowingly.

Orville's mom was his shadow till he got to his teens. This inhibited him from making friends with kids his own age, and very early on he developed a pedantic, adult way of talking. His mom urged him to play with other kids but stood over them like a nervy dark angel, just in case those kids' faces showed the names they wanted to call him.

Mrs Charleroi made Orville eat every last scrap of the big meals she made. This might have put some kids off food for life, but food became Orville's sole interest. He grew into a vision of an American of the future: a citizen of a country that ate its surplus instead of distributing it.

Milo was intrigued by Orville at the fort elementary school. As if in imitation of Milo, Orville took little part in classes at junior high, and looked superciliously mystified at whatever any teacher might be saying. It was difficult to see why he was included in Milo's clique, because he was unlike the others. He was robust, yet at the same time too lazy to risk anything requiring physical effort. He resembled Milo and Mila, Moby Krzeski, Richard Rat, Eurydice Armentiere, and the Peterlejtner twins in only one way: he was, despite his freakishness, happy in his own skin, as the French say.

Milo, Richard and Moby were forbidden to visit Orville at home after they dragged the furniture out of his bedroom and left it at the bottom of the staircase. Milo couldn't remember why they'd done such a thing, said it was no doubt Moby's idea: anything to get a reaction, any reaction, out of Orville.

Few people could do that. At high school Orville was a lone figure on the campus, a slow-moving target for kids with mischief in mind. The meatheads called him every vile variation on any name ever thought up to torture fat people, slapped him and twisted his annoying dark fringe in their fists. The football eleven hung Orville from a cloakroom hook by his collar once. Bullies stole Orville's books and kicked them around the campus. Richard, having retrieved Orville's *Larousse Gastronomic Encyclopedia*, complained, "Had to be *that* goddam book I had to get back. I swear it's heavier than I am." A few visits to various households from Mrs Charleroi left, so some mothers swore, the imprints of her Latin invective on their walls. Milo and Richard also put a lot of wrongs to right, and the bullies eventually just found it too much trouble to bother Orville.

When Orville did deign to exercise his cut-glass tones, he developed an unsettling habit of glaring at whoever he was talking to, as if to make certain that he was being listened to. Answers, or even those little conversational grunts people offer, would be greeted by a slow blink and a pause in his monolog. I later worked out, years after having last seen him, that his glare was unsettling principally because you couldn't see into his deep, dark eyes, while he could see into yours. I thought he regarded people in the same way he looked at animals, wondering how they'd taste if he cooked them.

Accompanied by the cursing of Balz's housewives, Orville repeatedly won the three-monthly Balz Bugle cookery competition, *A Dish For The Season*. There he was in print, that fringe flopping over his face, with his blinis and latkes, his stroganoff, his Christmas carp, his marinated mussels, his frog legs in garlic. He rubbed his success in with the modest homily, "If you can read, you can cook. And I *can* read," he'd add, maybe just to remind those teachers who swore he never did a stroke. Most of the kids at school, in keeping with their attitude to Milo and his crowd, made derisory noises, but none registered with Orville. By his mid-teens, he was working at all the Balz events needing catering, such as the Easter Day breakfast in the Rink, the bike race, the storekeepers' ball, the baseball tournament and the Fourth of July dinner. You could see why the chefs were glad to have him, as he worked quickly and had a reverence for the food, no matter how plain, and a pride in it that almost brought a smile to his face. By the time

181

he'd graduated, and whenever he came back from his indentured training, he was running the show for the events. He always looked almost resentfully at the recipients of his food, greeting compliments with a glare and silence; it was as if people's enjoyment of it took something away from his own. He pronounced the names of dishes as they were in their language of origin, so made *blyeenyees*, and not blinis, and *gooh-larsh*, and not goulash, and could never stop himself from correcting customers briefly before serving them.

My only non-culinary encounter with Orville took place when I was fourteen, and it was in our science classroom at the Lyceum. I'd left break early because it was my turn to change the water in the classroom goldfish bowl and feed the poor imprisoned beast. It was a filthy wet winter day, rank with the smell of damp kids in steaming clothes that were not washed often enough. Potato chip packets and candy wrappers were stamped into the mud streaks on the floor, and as I approached the shelf bearing the refilled goldfish bowl I skidded on something and grabbed the nearest thing to stop myself falling. That *was* the shelf. My momentum lent me strength enough to pull it off the wall and down it came, the bowl and me with it. I crashed onto the breaking bowl on one knee and, too shocked even to cry out, watched my blood add a startling brightness to the mixture of mud, slimy pebbles, water weed and broken glass. The fish lay at the center of the mess, stunned for a second at the change in its little world. Then it began a half-hearted wriggle.

Orville Charleroi either came in at that moment or had been there all along. He was standing over me. He offered nothing – not even a sneer – and certainly no hand to help me up. He wasn't judging me to be stupid, I could tell, or careless. He wasn't enjoying my misery; he was just observing two creatures in distress.

Meantime, I was bleeding. It didn't make me squeamish, exactly. I'd already decided to be a nurse, and knew how blood vessels worked. I knew there was no big artery on my knee that would drain my life out of it. I was fretting more about some horrible disease getting in through the cut, as I hadn't got to that part of my book yet.

I also had the fish to worry about. I sent a look of exasperation to Orville, who was still calmly staring. He was so close I could smell him, that same wet wool stink and a reek of something else, salami of some kind. I reached out carefully for the fish, trying all the while not to put my other knee on the floor, and goddam it if I didn't put my hand onto a shard. It pushed into the flesh between my middle and ring fingers, which began to gush blood. I let out a yelp this time. With the other hand I manoeuvred the fish into the palm of my hand, then flopped it into a portion of bowl on its side, a half-inch of water in it.

I got to my feet. I glared at Orville. "Thanks for your help," I told him, then, dripping, headed for the school nurse.

I didn't appreciate that flame-haired jive-talking bitch squeezing the cuts hard to see how deep they were. I also hated her telling me I might never move my fingers again. That got me crying, and she told me not to be such a baby. From all you need to do with your hands, I thought later, all that separates us from every animal except monkeys, I chose to tell her I'd just started learning the guitar. She roared laughing. "Listen now," she explained. "There's a man in France, a Gypsy, okay, and he's the hottest guitar player in the, like, history of the world. And you know what, babe? He's only got two fingers, I swear on the soul of New Orleans. But he plays the sweetest, fastest guitar in the world. So you don't need to worry about that. The guitar is in safe *hands*." I took that to mean that I needn't bother even trying. In any case, I didn't care about some Gypsy guy in France. I was mortified and miserable.

That feeling didn't leave when I got back to class. I found it full of wet kids and an irate Miss Delessena, our biology teacher, one of those born-to-it pedagogs that even the sassiest kids were wary of. It was plain she suspected vandalism. She was holding a deadly quiet inquest into how the classroom shelf had been torn off the wall and the goldfish's little green world sundered into pieces. She let everybody know that she was going to get to the bottom of it before the rest of their lives could even be thought about.

Their mystification told me at once that Orville had not said a word. He'd watched them puzzling, heard accusations and denials fly around the room – again, not enjoying it, I sensed: just indifferent. Miss Delessena had been about to send somebody to follow the trail of blood out the door. When I came in, thirty heads turned and looked at my plasters and bandages. Miss Delessena fixed on me and said, "*Well?*" The rest of the class breathed out and got ready to enjoy the show.

Miss Delessena never suggested I was lying, but there was something in her eyes on these occasions that refused to be placated till she'd unearthed every last banal item of the real story. As I explained, I sent glances toward Orville.

"It was an accident," I said lamely, each time I ran out of things to say.

Miss D disagreed. "It was clumsiness." Her eyes bored the words into me. "It was slapdash. It was… *ungainliness.*"

She looked at me with a kind of pity – not the merciful kind, just the patronizing kind. She wasn't to know that soon I'd be top of the class in biology and would also shine, not quite so brightly it's true, in chemistry and physics. She was unaware too that she and I would be meeting for coffee just a few years later to talk science, and nursing, and the best ways to alleviate pain and assuage people's morbid fear of medicine.

She was unhappy with my explanation, but satisfied with it too, and dispatched a kid to get the janitor to come clean up the mess. She clapped her hands, regained everybody's attention and was just about to command us to open our books when she stopped. Once more she beamed her gaze across the room, saying, "Hold *on* a second here. *You*," she hollered at me. "Stand up." I did so. "Where's the *fish?*" she asked me. A good question.

"I remember that," Milo told me, years later. "Orville ate the fish."

I hadn't said that to Miss Delessena, but her question had prompted me to drag Orville into it. For a little while she got sidetracked into addressing Orville's silence but knew, like most of the teachers, that there was nothing in that for her. All Orville said, in his deadpan way, was, "Maybe it's gone to a better place."

"I guess almost anyplace had to be better than that classroom," Milo joked, all those years on. I was mad at Milo. After all, I was at the center of the tale, bloodied and bandaged, sorry for myself and my broken nerve-endings that threatened to silence my music, convinced that *ungainly* would be the only word to describe me forever. And what? He didn't remember me at all, just the rumor that Orville had eaten the classroom goldfish.

"I don't think I'd describe anybody's digestive system as a better place," I jested back, though I was still mad.

"All protein to Orville."

In Paris, Milo sometimes ran his hand over the blue scar on my knee, which really should have been stitched up by that jazz-addled nurse. He was fascinated by it, and the way it almost matched one of his own, which had retained road grit in it from an evening when he got back from a bike race bloodied from a fall and was so tired he'd fallen into bed without having the wound tended.

Milo and I never saw Orville Charleroi in Paris, if he was ever there. Maybe we never frequented any restaurants fancy enough. Maybe he'd moved on to Monte Carlo by the time we got there.

Most of us in Balz could be described as lost Soviet citizens who became American, but Orville was the opposite. His eventual destination was revealed as Moscow. He was never a communist, we were sure, and certainly never one of the *proletariat*. He moved easily, we assumed, among the *nomenklatury* and mass-murderers, as he fed them on the all-

American burger. *With* them, I thought, unlike Milo and the bikers, and *of* them, too. Who knew what appealed to regally-named Orville Charleroi about a death-haunted society like the USSR? We imagined him observing the trials, the disappearances and the lines for food and shoes, nothing on his face.

Orville rose to become head chef at the Kremlin kitchens. It was rumored that he expressed his masters' disdain of both democracy and goulash by poisoning the Hungarian ambassador. He founded the Kremlin kitchen band, and there exists a snatch from a newsreel of them in pristine chefs' whites playing in Red Square, Orville on the trombone, that honking, farting instrument that expressed him so well. He became the personal chef of Georgy Malenkov, party purger, exiler of rivals, onetime favorite of Stalin, Secretary to the Central Committee of the murderous bastards in the Politburo and then, after Stalin died, Premier. Malenkov was a man who knew how to eat, so it looked like a good match. Orville even looked uncannily like him.

Moby Krzeski did a painting of Orville and Malenkov, known as *Two Fat Men in a Bath*, but actually called *Ice Cream Pisces*. They sit in a tub, their thick hair and fat faces, porcine black eyes almost identical, one feeding the other with ice cream, anchovies and limes, rumored to be Malenkov's favorite dish. Was it a comment about consorting with killers? The little freaking hypocrite. Milo and I looked at it a long time on its wall in Paris's Museum of Modern Art and remembered Orville, and Moby, and remembered the people we'd all been, back in Balz.

That same year, and Mila Galitzka getting too close to one of her heroes

Gossips in Balz catted that Father Ignatz Vishnevski had what appeared to be a time-consuming interest in saving Orville Charleroi's young soul. That explained why he spent so much time at the Charleroi house. He was a visitor for a number of years nobody could ever quite remember. None of the visits seemed to touch Orville; his demeanor in church or anyplace else remained much the same.

The priest and Garance Charleroi were big pals, though they were only seen in public together wherever you might expect to see them, only momentarily, and very properly, like at mass on Sundays, or church socials or Balz's big events. They looked similar, I thought, both tall and lampstand-thin and dark-haired, a yellowish tint to their skin, both in black garments that matched, he in his cassock and she in long dresses that brushed the ground. Even their heads looked strangely alike, she with her hair rolled back around her head in a complicated plait, he with his flat, round-brimmed hat.

Father Vishnevski had a dynamo that kept him awake for most of the hours of the day. He said first mass at six in the morning and, at the other end of the day, helped the white sisters as they set up their midnight soup kitchens, then roamed the bars of Balz collecting money for church causes from drinkers at a stage of exuberance and magnanimity. They often slipped him a vodka or two on his rounds, and admired how he could hold it.

He couldn't always hold it, though. This was revealed to Mila Galitzka one day on one of her walks outside the town, during what she came to think of as her time of troubles.

Mila had entered a phase of solitude not long after she was ridiculed for her wish to join the sisters. At school she said and did the bare minimum. She couldn't stand being among people, she told me, years later, not even her mom, and especially not her dad. The only company she sought was Milo's; it seemed cruel and troubling to her, but he had no time for her. He was just doing the things any boy did, so she didn't blame him, exactly. She resented him, all the same.

One blustery weekday afternoon in fall, Mila cut school and walked through the town to the valley and crossed the railroad. Then she tramped up the hillside. In those days it had only a few houses arranged haphazardly, and only a few animal tracks that led to a rise overlooking Balz.

At the top, she was startled to see a figure seated on a low rock. At first she thought it was Orville Charleroi's mom, then saw that it was Father Vishnevski. Mila knew he was aware of her, though his gaze didn't waver from its fixation across the valley. For a few seconds she was afraid to move, then stepped forward, and said, "Father?"

"What?" Father Vishnevski's eyes moved only slightly. He had an air about him that she recognized as off-duty, the way her mom acted when people dared mention library business when she was out shopping or strolling.

"I'm... Mila Galitzka." Mila didn't know what else to say. It was crazy to introduce yourself to somebody you knew.

"I know who you *are*." Father Vishnevski's tone suggested his agreement.

He knew every citizen who went to church in Balz. He also took our religious instruction class three or four times a term. Maybe most of all, Father Vishnevski knew well who Mila was because he had been to intercede with her mom and dad when they'd made their opposition to her joining the sisters so vehement. The venture had been a failure, she knew, but she hadn't had the chance to thank him.

"You met with my dad," Mila said. There was something weird about the man before her that day. It was more than a sense that he was off duty. Mila had never thought of priests as being anything other than paragons, which stopped her realizing in time that she was looking at Ignatz Vishnevski, just some guy dressed as a member of the clergy. "Thank you, Father."

The priest laughed to himself, then said, "Does your father ever talk about your friends?" He turned his face, still not quite looking at her.

"My friends?"

"Yeah."

"What friends?" It sounded petulant, but it was Mila's belief that she had no friends and also that she didn't want any. She had always been edged out between Milo and the fort elementary crowd. It had never been deliberate, she realized, just happened that way. Loretta Churchyard and Milo formed a bond as babies, but there had been no... *rapport* between her and insular Dominic Churchyard. And later Mila was always part of the gang, but, simply, with it; not *of* it.

"Your... *friends*." Father Vishnevski made an impatient gesture. "Does he ever talk *to* them?"

"Who?"

"Well, that... odious Moby kid? Richard Szczur? Loretta the Bible-Bugle?"

"They're not my friends." It was a long time since Mila had felt friendship for any of them. She wondered how they'd upset Father Vishnevski, or Richard and Loretta, anyhow – Moby's contempt of the priests was evident as soon as any of them looked at him. "They're *Milo's* friends."

"How about Orville Charleroi?"

Vishnevski's stumble over the rolling syllables of Orville's names alerted Mila to the fact that the man in front of her had been drinking. There was something about him that reminded her of the early stages of the state Loretta's dad used to get into. "What about him?" she said.

"Does your father ever talk to him?"

"No. Why would he?"

"He never... comments on them? Any of them?"

189

"He tells them to quit making so much noise sometimes," Mila recalled. "If they're up in Milo's room. Or outside on the porch. That's about all. Father, you know Orville?"

"Orville – yeah. What?"

"Does he have a... troubled soul?"

Father Vishnevski laughed, surprised, it seemed to Mila. He said, "I don't know if it's his soul that's troubled. There's no... *love* in his life, Mila."

"What?" Mila wasn't sure if she liked this turn to the conversation. She looked closely, and frankly, at the priest.

"Is there love in yours?" he asked.

"I love my brother," Mila declared. "I love my family. I love Jesus."

Father Vishnevski roared out another laugh. Mila was confused, but raised a doubtful smile in answer. "Oh yeah." He nodded over some private joke. "We *all* love Jesus in this town, huh?"

Mila saw that he had a slow burn of anger on. He wasn't wearing his clerical collar, wore an open-necked gray shirt under his cassock. He ran a hand through his short, wiry hair, made a silver line through it that faded after a second. She pointed across the valley to Balz at the churches, she supposed, didn't know what she wanted to say, but he read her mind anyhow.

"Faith isn't about having a bunch of churches full of plaster and paint and colored glass," he said, almost to himself. "It isn't about *babushki* singing hymns and lighting candles. It's not about turning up Sundays in your best duds and your new hat." He joined Mila in pointing. "These people, they live in sin – they're... *immersed* in it – then come back from the dead, full of their sin and what it's done to them, seeking God's shelter, again and again. Only Jesus could come back from the dead. It's not about statues of saints and angels. You think Saint Paul gave a single, solitary...

cuss about all that? The early Orthodox people, the Constantinople Greeks, they had the right idea about that… junk."

"Junk, Father?"

"They broke the statues, smashed the icons, till they got persuaded out of it. And by who? Statue builders and icon makers. Storekeepers." He made a money gesture with fingers that, Mila saw, were bleeding. She realized he'd been punching trees, looked back at the birches flagging their way. "The Jews," Father Vishnevski went on, "the Mussulmen, they don't hold with graven images. Their faith is in their heads, in their… learning. In their culture. *Yeah*. Don't need pretty pictures. Don't have plaster saints. They have Holy men walk among them all the time, Holy men you can buttonhole on the street, ask for guidance. And they give it, in all humility. Their faith is all around them, wherever they are."

"Father," Mila stammered. "I… don't know what to say."

"Then say nothing," he snapped. He pulled a half-pint of bison vodka out of a pocket, uncorked it and drank. "Wait till you have something to say, Mila." He held the bottle out to her, waited for her shake of the head then took another swig. "Then I'll listen to you." He turned away from her. "I'll always listen to you."

"Father." Mila looked keenly at him, looked stern. "You're not going to…"

"What, Mila? Not going to what?"

"You're not going to smash the statues?"

"No," he said gently. "Don't worry. Those… gaudy gewgaws and *chatchkas* are safe."

Mila's first reaction was to let out a nervous laugh.

"I have one plan only, at the moment."

"That's what, Father?"

"Kill this bottle. Hey, you want?" Again, he offered the bottle. Mila again shook her head. He took a long drink and pointed away from the town, to Crook's Hill, and the wreck of the Theodosia. "That's my favorite church," he said. "Hey, Mila G."

"What, Father?"

"You want to come up there with me now?"

Mila considered it. She said, "Why?"

"Why not? I'll show you something."

Mila waited, then said, "What?"

The priest remained tight-lipped, looked away from her.

"What?" she repeated.

He shook his head. He took another swig, then, caught by second thoughts, drained it. He aimed it at the town, threw it and walked away. "You want God, huh?" he aimed back at Mila.

"*Yes*," she said.

The priest dismissed this with a wave. He said over his shoulder, "There," and pointed again at the Theodosia. "You want Him, God's over there. No statues, no relics, just God." A cloud came down and engulfed him, and he disappeared, very abruptly, from her sight.

TEN

Dawn At The Masked Dance, With Pixies And Bikers, Violinists And Angels, Pale Ghosts, And Essential Revelations And Ephiphanies

"Orville Charleroi says your name all the time, Milo." The pixie sounded so convincingly impish that Milo took a close, puzzled look at her. "He must really love you." She giggled. "That's one sure sign."

"Fun-*nee*," he seemed to agree.

She followed him down to the ballroom. The brass band grotesques were on again, playing crazily fast, whipping the dancers into a frenzy. Among the dancers, masks were back on, exchanged haphazardly, it was plain, or just found abandoned, and reused. They raised steam and heated the place up.

Dancing was a ridiculous thing to do, it hit Milo. He would never do it again.

"Orville didn't mean it in some... *weird* way," Milo said "Hey." He hesitated, as if an idea had just occurred to him for the first time. "Do you think bike racing... *is* kind of homo?"

"Well... no." The pixie made a slight nod all the same. "But so what if it is?"

"Well it *isn't*."

"Says you," she said, but promised, "I believe you." Still laughing, she led him around the dancers and through the main doorway.

One thought illuminating Milo's mind was that he was at his last masked dance. Another was that it was time the pixie took a hike. Then he could sort through the boxes in his head in peace, chuck stuff away to reveal whatever he needed to keep. He said to the pixie, "Hey, listen."

"To what?" She flexed her green fingers on his arm. "I'm listening."

He wanted to ask what she was doing there with him. He wanted to ask why she didn't just go have some fun, do whatever kids like her came to the masked dance to do. She didn't have to tell him that the dance was just a bunch of sad sacks whose thoughts were at dead ends. The conversations, the laughter, the dancing – all ways of ending the night in oblivion. She sensed that Milo's own thoughts were there too. She shook her head.

He said, "What about your friends?" It was odd that in the time they had spent together not a soul had sung out a *hallo* or a *hey* at her.

"What friends?"

"You've got to have *some* friends."

"I do, I guess." She had to think about that. "But I told you already, they're assholes, like yours. So what about them?"

If they were truly assholes, he might have asked, why weren't they there? He clicked his tongue and puffed out air and, not really meaning to scan the outdoors for angels, saw one nearly at once. She was twenty feet away and one of her wings was hanging down, broken. She was big and tall and had her mask off and a square yard of brown hair flowing free. She swigged from a bottle, then passed it to a biker known as Rages.

"Hey, Rages," Milo called.

"Ahoy, Joe College." Rages waved and held a great hunk of hand out for Milo to shake. It was only this that woke Milo up to the fact that he had gotten near enough to be able to peer at the angel, whose mouth looked like it had been smeared onto her face. She glanced through him with gray eyes that were beautiful but found more often on girls in drawers in morgues than on girls in warm rooms who sat astride college boys after promising to love them. Her voice was like pig iron in your breakfast when she said, "*You* again," to let Milo know they had met that night already under less congenial circumstances.

Milo knew what his angel wasn't. He also had the sickening feeling that he was forgetting what she *was*, how she'd looked and felt and smelled. He sensed her fading into the night.

"So you're doing how, Milo?" Rages was presenting Milo with the bottle. Milo took a polite look at it and said he was okay. Rages shot a look past him, said, "Hey, fairy," and, like a wine waiter at the Ritz, offered the pixie the courtesy of the bottle too.

"Pixie," she corrected him.

"There's a difference?"

"Like between vodka and gin," she said. Rages liked that, and whaled out a great belly laugh.

Milo took a look back at the mansion and at the shadows of the moving figures in there streaking the ceilings. For the first time that night he felt bushed. He wasn't going to go back in and make a fool of himself with angels all over again. He saw then that Rages was laughing the baritone bark of a dog and waving at him once more, and that the pixie was leading him away. "Like I said, all your friends are assholes," she was whispering. "Good outfit, though. Looks exactly like a biker."

"That's what he *is*." Milo was already laughing as she nudged him to tell him she knew *that*. "He isn't a friend." He didn't know why he felt driven to correct her. "He's just somebody I know. I used to work on his bike." He put hands up to make cowhorn handlebars. "That's all."

What Milo liked about the bikers was that they lived outside the ugly society around them. They were guys who'd gotten drafted or sweet-talked into wasting their young lives fighting a war to preserve that society, but knew its rules for the tricks they were. They couldn't ride away from it but did their damnedest, even if that meant they had to make up their own rules. Milo saw that it was worth a try, and he was glad that, with the tinkering he'd done on their bikes to get them to burn holes in the night, he'd helped them do what a lot of people didn't have the imagination for.

"That guy killed forty Japanese soldiers all at once," Milo thought out loud. "Or so I heard."

"Ouch." The pixie stopped. "That must've taken it out of him."

"No. He... uh, he used a flamethrower." Milo wished he hadn't brought the thought out. "I know. It's kind of... *horrible*."

"Forty barbecued *Japs*? *Kind* of? For Chrissake, Milo."

"Yeah."

"Hey, listen." The pixie stopped again.

"To what?"

"You hear?" There was a tension in her that tickled the backs of Milo's ears for seconds, but it was only music she was talking about, indistinct, lonely. They were too far now from the mansion to hear the band. Somebody nearby was playing a violin.

"I hear it." Milo went to walk on.

"That isn't the band." The pixie arrested him, one foot in the air, poised. "That's, like, magic, Milo, magic music from nowhere." She dared the suggestion up at him then remembered, as she saw a projection in her head of Sister Adelheid squelching into honorary hagiography, that Lucy Ephraim's violin had soundtracked many of the significant parts of Milo's life, and that she should have swallowed her words.

"It's no magic." Milo turned to her. "It's... Melodia Kennedy, from the Kennedy Folklore crowd. She always wanders round the dance this time of night, drunk as hell, sawing at that... misery board."

"So it is." The pixie went on hastily, "I... *like* music."

"Oh yeah?" Milo looked like he was thinking how that was just what the world needed, more damn music, when he had an angel to catch and wanted to hear only the music angels could make out of dumb old words. "Well, that's just… great."

"You really want to find her?" The pixie kept Milo at a standstill.

"Who?" he stalled.

"The angel," she quoted at him. "Think I mean the frigging first lady?"

"Sure I do." He stopped, searched the crowd and the sky.

He pictured his angel seeking him through the debris of the dance, heard Elysian masses of violins, as he and the angel met and raised masks and kissed and held each other. "So it *was* real," he and the angel would congratulate each other. "I *knew* it was." If he didn't find her, he would never know. The pixie gathered all this from his face, but saw something else in it too, saw it frazzled and fooled and marked by fears.

Milo almost told the pixie then about how nobody had ever said they loved him, not with such instant proof. Loving somebody wasn't a big deal, people thought, but when it happened you knew you'd been living up to then only with other people's ideas about what love was. He reflected on how he had a father who devoted all his energy to ideas that would never mean zip, and a mother who never once said she was interested in a single thing he did. He had a sister who refused to look at him, like he was something that lived under a rock.

He almost told the pixie all these things and then, as they picked their way through the grounds to the front of the mansion, he *did* tell her. "You don't know what it means," he said, "to have somebody tell you all that out of the blue." *Out of all this*, he tried to gesture, *this thing around us, this doomed dance, this gloomy town that tangos to its own jeremiac dirge.*

"Oh yeah?" She seemed to be on the point of correcting him on that score then kept on track and said, "Well, your dad *is* weird. He prowls

197

around on your roof and throws potatoes at people, for Chrissake. But that doesn't mean he doesn't love you."

"I know *that*." Milo couldn't be bothered to tell the pixie that it was actually tomatoes. And not from the top roof but from the flat roof over the porch and it was only one time. Nor was it at people, only at Father Vishnevski, the day he decided to talk to Balz's wisest guy about Mila wanting to join the sisters. "It doesn't mean he *does*, though."

"And your mom. I haven't seen her in a long time." The pixie laughed nervously. "Hey, but *that* doesn't mean she doesn't love you. What about your sister?"

"What about her?"

"What's wrong with her?"

"Nothing." Milo pictured Mila, her down-turned look as she swept past him in the house – territory that became hers during his years away at college – and showed him her back. "She's okay," he said, too brightly. "Hey," he was prompted to ask, "do you know her?"

"Yeah." He couldn't see the pixie's face but knew she was exasperated, like she wanted to say, *Milo, the whole freaking* town *knows your sister, thanks to you.* She said only, "Sure I do."

"So who *are* you?" Milo wasn't sure if he cared or not. When she told him one more time to guess, he wanted to tell her to go sit on a mushroom.

"You don't know my voice?" He concentrated on that sample. It was familiar, though everybody spoke with the same twang in Balz; the same inflections, the formal English o sound and the languid a, the liquid r and disappearing Polish l. That was the same anyplace, he guessed; you put a mask on and the parameters changed and you didn't know who was who nor what was what. Milo might have been starting to get curious about the pixie, had he not started to follow a figure at the periphery of his vision, one that streaked a white trail across his eyes.

"What would you say, Milo?" the pixie said. It was only later that he was touched by something in her voice that betrayed her energy subsiding, her lights dimming. "If I told you I was the angel you were looking for?"

"Too small," was his first reaction. It wasn't going to get much past that. "My angel was tall."

She was already looking down with him at the figure making her winged way across Glass Beach. This angel wasn't falling over walls or showing her underwear from a crane, nor swigging out of bottles with lowlifes. They knew it was his angel.

"Like that one." Milo breathed the words out in a rush. "Exactly like that one right there. Hey!" Milo's voice resumed its standing as the loudest one in town. "Angel!"

On the beach, the angel stopped and looked up. She shimmered for a second, made an ethereal photo, one she must have known Milo would remember all his life. He forgot to breathe out as she raised a hand to shoulder height in what could have been a wave.

"That's her." He grabbed the pixie's wrist in his excitement, drew her to the edge of the cliff and hailed the angel again.

"No kidding." The pixie was trying to ignore the vision down there of Michael Sheltz tied to the signpost that warned against falling rocks. He had balloons fixed to him, but in the improvised loincloth he wore, he looked for all the world like Saint Sebastian. She caught a side-on impression of store mannequins placed to make a triumphal Roman way into the fog coming down. She turned her attention back to the angel. "Oh boy," she said. "Hey, well, Milo, you'd better get down there after your angel, before she disappears again, eh?"

If he hadn't been in such a blinded hurry Milo might have stopped to think about the green little tones in the pixie's voice, and to reason that they weren't part of her costume. By then he was busy though, surveying the rocks leading down the cliff, wondering whether he could navigate them in the dark without breaking his neck.

When he leaned out, his head wasn't sure for a second what his body was trying to do. A light winked in his brain to warn him that he was about to cross his center of balance and fall. It dimmed and disappeared as it registered that the pixie had grabbed him by the belt of his tunic to bring him upright.

"Oh," he said.

"Hey," she answered.

By the time she'd said his name he was loping along the front rails of the mansion, the unfolding light revealing the debris of the dance and those surrounded by it. For Milo they had about as much substance as the statues scattered across the lawn. Maybe it was this that stopped him seeing the figures keeping pace with but also decreasing the distance between the pixie and him.

"No, Milo." Near the gate into Ascension Avenue the pixie took hold of Milo's belt again and pulled him to a halt that shook him. "Don't go down there."

"Are you kidding?"

They couldn't see the beach from there, just the sleeping town. Out of Milo's sight, they sensed, the angel didn't exist.

"You're... crazy if you go down there." The pixie was aware of people near them but was intent on Milo's angel-haunted face, on the jock smell of him, sweat and aftershave and years of rubbed-in liniment and fear of losing. "There's... danger for you down there. Believe me."

"Danger?" The two syllables demanded all Milo's attention.

"Maybe not." Deserted momentarily by words, the pixie let go his belt and brought her hands together in supplication. "But... unhappiness. There's unhappiness there."

200

"Jesus Mary." Milo was turning, off balance again.

"The danger's right here."

The voice came in a laugh from above. They looked up and took in three musketeers on the stone gateposts, at least one of whom was a cowboy. There was half a second in which Milo and the pixie betrayed their puzzlement with silence and lack of movement. Then they saw the features on masks, a minstrel in black-face, a harlequin, a cigar-store Indian, saw an arm raised and another, as the first missiles burst on their heads and backs and chests and engulfed them in clouds of white. Each had the passing dread of seeing the other engulfed by cartoon explosives. More phantoms edged their way into the action, making a crowd as they swept around the gateway laughing excitedly, and burst two-pound packets of flour on Milo and the pixie, pushed into the nucleus of a little white world in which communication consisted of the single sound, long and drawn-out: "*Groogh!*"

They tried to make other sounds. Milo tried to call out, "*Bastards,*" but choked on the first syllable and couldn't even cough it out. He coughed his guts up instead and bent to seek a breath deep enough to expel the flour from his airways. He tried to rub the stuff out of his eyes, made out breathless, giggling figures, the rustle of clothes, the sight of a silk-sheathed leg, a broken bow on a patent shoe.

The antagonists' laughter rose. Milo glimpsed one of their number who'd messed up his throw, knocked his hat off and covered himself in white: a musketeer all high boots and waisted coat, a fancy rapier in his belt. Milo recognized it, the copper strip on its blade near the handle inscribed with the name of its onetime owner, Eurydice Armentiere. As Milo took a step toward the figure, the musketeer sneezed and the elastic holding the stupid mustachioed face in place snapped to reveal the pink, mortified face of Eurydice's brother Benny. Abandoned by his friends, he was as exposed and foolish as Milo had always remembered him. Milo's desire to step up and raise a fist at him diminished into a sense of futility that had, in the past, put him off his swing; Benny was just too… *poor* a specimen to punch. Milo was in any case sidetracked into a ground-shaking sneeze of his own. Benny Armentiere slunk back through the gate.

When Milo was able to blink the flour out of his watering eyes and spread a little batter down his cheeks, the attackers were gone. There was just the little pale ghost of the pixie.

She had always been there, it came to him. Always hovering, little pale spook, not just that night; always. He saw her pixie face covered in powder, knew that if he got her to take it off, her real one, pink and pristine, would be one he knew. He wanted to ask her to unmask right then, but there were first things that had to come first.

"*Bastards*." That was the very first thing.

"Absolutely no doubt at all."

He looked at the ragged white figure she cut, pale figment, and was about to comment on it, then knew he looked the same.

"Torunski," he said.

"You got to him, Milo," she remembered. "Doesn't that make you feel a whole lot better?"

"Well, yeah." What would make Milo feel even better would be to go down to Torunski's store and kick its big window in and, he promised himself, once this business was out of the way, he would do exactly that. No he wouldn't. He'd grown up, hadn't he, object of an angel's love? Wouldn't he most certainly give Cezar a good *zetz* on the snout though, next time he saw him? No, he guessed not. Yes he would. And next Resurrection Day he would steal a municipal fire wagon, aim its hoses at the Torunski store and wash the whole edifice away down the gutters of the town, fill them with cheap shoes, go ahead then and wash all those damn stores away, leaving standing only his dad's sturdy arches. "I guess."

"Here." The pixie had picked up Milo's mask. She held it out to him. "You should've kept it on. That's what they're for, huh, masks? Protection?"

"Jesus Mary." Milo squirmed, shook himself, banged hands on the wall, kicked it, raised clouds.

"That's exactly what you were saying before." The pixie tried to click fingers, made only dirt, gave up. She danced on the spot a little instead, and shed flour.

"Holy shit." Milo didn't look at her. "Come on." They left a powder trail along Ascension and down the slope to the square, shook it onto the couples sprawled on their route. They scuffed their way down the flight of steps that turned into the walkway to Glass Beach.

"What are you going to do?" the pixie called.

"Take your mask off." Milo was staring out onto the scenes on the beach, each shaded in a monochrome brought by the time of day.

"No."

"Who *are* you?"

"I'm your angel," she said. As they landed on the salt she sat down abruptly, leaving Milo to monolog his way on.

"Uh-uh. No you're not. Oh God," the pixie heard him say. "What a frigging night."

On the beach, party girls persisted in having a blast. Masks on still, costumes raggy under a patina of salt, they picked out dance steps in careful formation. Chumps with guitars and woodwind, plus a bull fiddle player who was proudly butt naked behind his instrument, raised voices in a song that had to be from some abandoned mountain town in the east of Europe.

In royal disdain for all this sideshow stuff, two great dynasties lay side by side: Ming, Milo guessed, though he was sketchy about details like that, and Ptolemian. Richard Rat's mandarin had one arm around Cleopatra and the other raised to point out objects in the sky. They had to be imagining the constellations they were taking turns to name, hidden as they were by the fog. Milo didn't dare disturb Richard again to ask him about angels.

He knew, anyhow: there was no angel down there, and no questions to ask.

A balloon strayed past Milo along the ground and it was this that alerted him again to the sight of Michael Sheltz. He had been untied and dressed in shirt and pants and jacket. Milo guessed that the dicky-bow and cummerbund sported by one of the mannequins had the Sheltz name and address sewn into them. Michael was being guided toward Milo by a dark figure with firm hands on his shoulders.

"Hey, Michael," Milo called, and Michael slowed, found his feet at odds with each other and fell over them. Finding himself on his knees was hardly going to surprise him that night. He looked up and smiled serenely.

Milo took no notice. He faced the long form of Michael's chaperone: there was Mila Galitzka, going through her time-honored part of retrieving Michael. She blinked wary eyes. Milo took a few steps into her path. That made her turn and, after an anxious look around, pull Michael to his feet to hold him in front of her like a shield. Her tongue came out and she licked her lip.

It hit Milo then that he ought to take his mask off, that Mila was giving the evil eye to his toy soldier face. He pulled it off and threw it onto the salt.

"Mila," he said. "Listen."

Mila took a look at the streaks on his face and the crystals of flour in his ears, nostrils and eyelashes. It looked to Milo that a thought was putting itself in her way. For ten long seconds, he saw what she saw: a little boy on Reformatory Beach, face covered in alkali, hand clutched in the white hand of Lucy Ephraim. Mila looking him in the eyes was so unusual that it made him stop breathing all over again. Mila tossed her head to dismiss Milo, shoved Michael past him and walked on.

"You're doing *what* here?" Milo was talking to her back.

"Screw *you*."

They were the first words Mila had said to her brother in four years.

Where Michael had fallen lay a cogwheel, sticky with blood. An eleven, a twelve, maybe. Bicycles out there, Milo remembered, races to ride and win: a different life to live. He picked it up and put it into one of his pockets.

He sat on a rock and watched Mila and Michael diminish into the backdrop of the cliff and the patchy fog, only to reappear again, sometimes sharply defined, taking the steps up. He heard Michael start to sing, the verse curtailed by God only knew what.

"*Feel so break up.*" He finished the verse in Michael's own skew-whiff way. "*I wanna go home.*" Milo didn't have a singing voice, but it didn't matter. He had a soldier's haircut. He had a bike rider's legs. He had a lover's hands, didn't he? He had the smell of an angel on him.

No angel on the beach, though: no angel, no doubt at all.

"Hey, Milo?" The pixie was standing over him. "You didn't ask your sister if she saw your angel." She let out a silvery little laugh. Milo made a humoring ha-ha with the bones in his jaw. "Not a good moment, huh?"

"I guess."

"Why, I bet that angel of yours is up in the atmosphere by now, watching us and laughing her saintly ass off."

"Sure."

Milo got up and faltered into a walk. He swept his eyes along the beach and up and down the rocks that made the cliff, up to the cliff road from which he had seen the angel. His eyes followed the path leading up the other end of the cliff just before the fog claimed it. He consoled himself with the thought that she *had* to have flown – really – to have gotten away from there so quickly; she had been a real angel after all. Whatever, she hadn't waited, had foregone all she'd said to him, all she'd done with him those few hours before when his life was about to change.

"Shown a bone," he said, mostly to himself and, about to make a big deal out of saying *what*, the pixie followed the thread of the words and kept schtum. "Got given a stone. I'm that little dog. Not Richard."

"Tell me, Milo." She was talking low now. "Answer my question. Hey, Milo?" She touched his arm lightly, got him to halt. "Listen."

He was listening, but he was crying, too, not like a man with a college degree and too much booze in him, but more like the little boy who'd sat on the beaches years before, seeing angels yet. The pixie reached up and got one of his tears on her finger. She put it to the lips of her mask, took away a line of flour and brought their color back. "Salt," she said. "Hey, do you think that's how the beaches got made? Out of all the tears from guys who lost angels? Listen, Milo, and tell me. What if I *were* that angel you were looking for?"

He didn't say anything. He knew that people were funny when they were crying but trying to talk, and he saw that the pixie knew that too. He trapped his teeth in his lips.

Behind them, the dancers kept made their circle into a grand oval that spread closer. All they were good for, Milo thought: footprints in sand. He tested his voice out, said, "I wish they'd *stop* that."

He followed the pixie down the beach. "You're no angel," he answered at last. "I mean, you're a pixie." They laughed at that. Milo took the opportunity to wipe the snot off the end of his little boy's nose.

"Angels come and go." The pixie sounded like she'd had experience with God's whimsical creatures. "They come down, pull their angel stunts, then disappear. Not fair, huh? Who can catch creatures that size who've got wings? Hey, Milo. Look at me."

It wasn't as if he could help that. By then she had his face in her hard little hands. "It's occurred to you already that she was lying, Milo." She nodded them hurriedly through that. Both knew that had he said *no* she would have been *very* disappointed. "Having some angel joke. I mean, people do stuff like that at the masked dance. That's what masked dances are *for*, you sap. You think it's all so boys can get lucky enough to schtup girls' brains out? Not at all. Joy and pain is what this thing's about. That's what this whole town's about, this whole life they got for us here."

"I know that." Milo was lying: he hadn't known it till she said. He'd had a boy's belief in the simple view that looked good in dreams and on the resumé a boy wrote in his mind then told his asshole friends about.

The pixie let go of his face, and for a second he felt himself poised once more on the edge of a cliff, the gyros spinning lopsidedly in his center. Atlantic light was filtering through from distant Delaware Bay. Milo looked up. Men in balloons up there, he guessed, green showers of frogs safe in whirlwinds from eaters of frog leg and loving the ride. There were birds racing the night dust out of their wings, singing it on out of their lungs. There were swarms of moths split between the moon and the sun but, he knew, not a single angel.

"Joy and pain." The pixie was no longer holding onto his hand. "You get one, you know the other's someplace near, and there isn't a lot you can do about that except be ready for it. Hey."

"What?" Milo turned and saw that the pixie was undressing in a spray of flour dust. Her boots were off, and her chest was bare, little tits gone stiff in the cold, her ribs like a washboard, her belly rounded and peaked by a back-to-front navel. She pulled her pants down. All the while her pixie face leered up at him, its lips vivid and red.

"Come on," I told Milo. "Take that stupid uniform off."

"Jesus Mary."

Milo seemed to be thinking about it, though he wasn't. He undid his tunic with a vestige of military elegance, then lost his cool at his shirt and popped the buttons off all down the front.

"You're going to take that stupid face off?" he called.

By the time he looked up at me I was throwing it away already; my pixie life was over, and I was never going to need it again.

"Done, already." I wore a smile that alarmed Milo and, for a second, hurt him. "So now how about you?"

ELEVEN

The Day After The Masked Dance, When I Hid From The World All Dressed In My Best

⊷———◈———⊶

If tradition allowed you to act how you wanted at the dance, it was the opposite the day after, with a long list of rules to be observed. What was magic in the night didn't stand up to the scrutiny of daylight. Next day you got up and washed off the dirt, got something good down you, got into your best threads and promenaded the town and ate ice creams and cookies and drank shakes and coffee on ice. It was like you were trying to kid yourself that you weren't the delinquent who got up to whatever you'd managed behind a mask the night before. You walked in the park or on the flats off Glass Beach, went to an open-air piano recital, maybe, watched crooners and jugglers in the Rink and gave your change to the bums.

It didn't matter if you'd hooked up with a sweetheart or not, because you could do all this stuff with your friends. I was more or less out of friends, so it had to be Milo I would be meeting. I was happy about that; I got out of bed and cartwheeled across my room, in any case. I ate breakfast and rode out Mom's questions and silences, and took a bath, glad I'd put in for the whole day off when other nurses were nursing monster headaches as well as patients.

I walked into noon with the memory I'd pictured the whole morning: Milo holding me and pushing in and out of me, and the noises we'd made. If nothing else worked out with him, I told myself in a small voice, there would always be that, what we did the night of the dance.

I saw the stone seat near the bank where I watched Mom paint her lips one time, mirror in her hand, vamping her red smile till it looked right. How come I remembered that? I spied the little store where a wheezing fat lady with black teeth and hair in a bun sold buttons and ribbons and gave Zamoysky cookies to kids if she liked the look of them. Long in the ground, I realized. I remembered how her eyes were always anxious, studying every face. Why did I remember that?

Little girl with her own money in that same store one time, little violin case in her hand, on tippytoe to pay the lady for costume braid, little girl with an old face, poor Lucy Ephraim.

On the corner of the Rink I passed the battered tin sign for Peterlejtner's store that claimed to have *Quality You Really Can Afford*. I saw the recess around which I saw a crowd one day, watching what turned out to be Eurydice Armentiere in a *grand mal*, and Mom telling me I would have nightmares if I watched.

All this wavered in black-and-white. I thought of Milo, and the town in my past was gone on the wind.

So we'd go where that day as we stepped into my future? We'd do what? Would we go someplace quiet and do it again, that thing we did on the beach – where? I asked the birds, stepped through the streets of Balz in my new white shoes and my new blue dress thinking the world a strange and terrifying place full of storms in which you had to seek out the harbors, and thought I had found one. I stood in the Rink and waited under the arches for Milo. It was only by chance that I looked up and saw a name on a little plate, a long-gone year, and the words *Engineer, Galitzki*. I thought that was a good omen.

I watched the blades and belles of Balz mooching by or purring along in their daddy's cars. I saw the friends I'd had once, looked at them with what I can only call an arrogant pity. I saw Illona Peterlejtner getting leggily out of some guy's convertible, saw Eurydice Armentiere drift past in white, her hair full of sun in a halo barely keeping pace with her head, saw Moby Krzeski in the clinches of a lah-di-dah city girl with a voice to cut cheese with. I saw Richard Rat and his Cleo, a sassy girl from school called Yanka Navratilova. I even saw Michael Sheltz.

I didn't see Milo. After a while, I found myself hiding behind an arch. A foolish look took over my face, and heat rose from my collar. I looked at my shoes and didn't like them anymore. I wanted to kick them off and leave them, tear my dress off and leave the shreds behind.

Something happened with the sun and the clouds, and the day colored itself like one of those Dutch paintings, no longer looked real, which told me it was time to go. I didn't appreciate the trudge through town and up the hill, nor Mrs Galitzka telling me that Milo was out.

"*Out?*" The way I felt would double me over at Mrs Galitzka's feet if I wasn't careful, wracked by tears of anger. I paused at the edge of this moment of injury as it passed through me. I was still standing upright. "Where, out?"

She didn't know. She gave me a look of weary sympathy. A voice from inside asked who was there; Engineer Galitzki. Mrs Galitzka said, "That nice albino Indian girl, for Milo."

That banged some gong with him. It got him out anyhow, an anorexic figure with unkempt hair, a beard to his breastbone and grimy feet with yellowed bird's toes. He had his pants on, just about, was pulling suspenders over the shoulders of his white union suit as he came out. "She's no Indian," he had to have heard.

"One of my great grannies was from Kazakhstan." I didn't look at Mrs Galitzka, in case she might think I was reproaching her. "And I'm no albino, either."

They took this in, and peered at my eyes. Mr Galitzki said, "Interesting." He showed his headstone teeth and went to on to say something about hey but did I know the American Indians *came* maybe

211

from Kazakhstan, long before my great granny, just upped and walked across the frozen sea on the Bering Straits and put up their tents and got on with the stuff they did?

"*Interesting,*" I returned.

It was then that I spied Mila behind the screen door. I caught her eyes in mine. Hers widened for a second till she went back in.

"Hey," Mr Galitzki said, "you were a blonde, I thought?"

I said, "Where is he?"

"He's out." He showed me a place on the porch where there was nothing. "Took his bike." I thought then I could hear puzzlement in his voice. They were sizing me up with a view to determine, I guessed miserably, just how much self-respect I fancied I had if, dressed to be killed-for, I'd allowed myself to make that trek to their door. Mr Galitzki said gently, "Listen, child."

I don't know what else he said. I looked down at where the bike lived. I remembered Milo telling me a long time before that, for him, being on a bike was like being in a place between the places that hemmed him in. I don't know why I thought of that then as I stood there wanting only to slap him and see an x-ray of my fingers come up on his face. I tried to make out that the heat in my cheeks wasn't there and said what was meant to be the coolest of thank-yous. The pitying look on Mrs Galitzka's face registered, though, and I was in mid-utterance as I turned. I walked down the hill and into town, back through the lovers of Balz, head held high but wishing, absurdly, that I had my pixie mask on so I could cover my face.

Some weeks after the dance, when Richard Rat got me singing, and
wondering

Angels came to Balz, stole the hearts of saps and could do whatever they wanted with them. From that I took bitter consolation. No girl was going to be an angel forever; Milo would find that out. That was going to be the big let-down with angels, how they couldn't live up to the props, couldn't fly for all the grandness of their wings that brushed attic ceilings.

If I cared, nobody knew. Not even me, till I got to the ends of days facing the walls of my room and the thoughts that troubled me into sleep. By day I was my same old self. But I didn't look out for Milo around Balz anymore, and tried not to think about him as that guy I'd coveted for nearly my whole goddam life. All the same, the future wasn't in color anymore, and seemed to have no sound.

I was in one of the packed-out little bars near the hospital with a couple of girls off shift when I ran into Richard Rat. He bought us all a beer.

"You dyed your hair and cut it off." He looked almost hurt. "Why did you go and do that?"

"*Her hair's nice,*" I quoted at him. "*Pity she looks like a gook.* Did you ever hear that at school, Richard, huh? Did you ever say that? Doesn't matter if you did. I just got sick of being a blonde, you know? And sick of parting my hair at the back and having pigtails. Pigtails look good on... *pigs*, maybe."

And I remembered how it was my first masked dance, and how I'd wanted to do it properly. More than that, I'd wanted to be able to stand back from the girl with brown hair who got into costume and let some guy inside her and, if I had to, claim that girl had nothing to do with me.

"Blondes are cool," Richard said.

"So are polar bears," I kind of agreed. We talked in the disconnected way we had fallen to, that of friends, I thought. Almost.

Richard was tired of his job, whatever it was at that time. He'd had enough too of the wasters and losers he had drifted into befriending, and had signed papers to join the Marines.

"*My boy will have his big white horse,*" I said.

He said, "What?"

"*His epaulettes, his nice sharp sword and his shiny leather boots.*" I trilled, "*My boy will ride off to war.*"

"Uh, right." He showed me a face bestowed on people who have just reached defining moments of craziness.

"Don't you remember that song?" I asked him. "We learned it in first year of junior high."

"No doubt." He nodded without agreement, almost diverted. "Well, we've got no war, but we will have."

"We will?" The thought was sobering. "With who?"

"The Soviets, maybe." Richard made a self-conscious frown. "Maybe all those little communist countries in Europe. I don't know."

I said, "Some of those little communist countries are not so little." I thought of Poland – wasn't Poland huge? "And they can't send you to a war with Poland, Richard, for example. You're a Polak." I laughed, because we just *couldn't* have a war with Poland, land of polkas and memories, grannies and ancestors, songs and sausages and synagogues, death camps and mass-murder and refugees; Poland had had more than its fair share of war.

"Korea?" Richard was trying to resist a barely contained sense of excitement. "Some other place out that way. *Ah.*" He dismissed it. "Can't think. Anyhow, there sure as hell isn't anything here." I felt uneasy at the look that stole the light out of his eyes. "Nothing here for man nor woman nor child." He swept an arm up to take in the people in our backdrop, steaming and sweating and downing their vodka.

"Nor polar bear," I finished for him. He almost raised a smile. Maybe Richard was seeing himself as a future denizen of bars in which men bragged about nothing and argued and fought over nothing while their livers went to hell inside them. I caught his potential for that part, sure

214

enough and, just as I was about to opine that putting on a Marine's uniform was a desperate thing to do, I told him why not. "Hey, *semper fi*. Stick with what you're good at already."

I tried not to think of Milo in his uniform, but there he came, *attaboy*, struggling out of it.

"You never feel you're growing out of this place?" Richard asked me. I said you had to be someplace. He nodded, said, "Did you hear Eurydice was going to get married to some schmo in the advertising business?"

"Why should I have heard that?" I said, though of course I had.

"The schmo son of some schmo her schmo dad deals with? Like an arranged marriage like they have in Arabia or someplace like that?"

"Well." I made a barf gesture. "At least they'll get a swell automobile to leave the church in."

"Sure." It wasn't a big deal, but I was glad I'd brought a smile to Richard's face. Almost together, we said, "And maybe even at a discount," because Benny Armentiere Senior, for all the money he made selling that American dream of cars, was known as a tightwad of some notoriety. That was nothing, of course, to what he was going to get known as just a few years later, once Eurydice's book about him was on the stands.

It wasn't to do with Eurydice Armentiere, anyhow. "Moby'll never come back." Richard was doing a roll call of his friends in Balz. "Illona's rising like a storm in whatever the hell she does. Orville is fixing to go cook fancy-pantsy food, in Paris, France. Ax has turned into his dad already, and now so has Milo."

"Right." I stopped in mid-nod. "Huh – and Milo *what*?"

"Gone nuts." Richard looked violent for a second. "Sits in his room, does nothing, says nothing, sees nobody, thinks *what*, I have no idea."

215

"Probably turning into a bike." I said that only to distract Richard from the look forming on my face. "Did you ask him?"

"If he was turning into a *bike*?"

"What he's *thinking* about?"

"Sure I did." Hands sketched out his frustration. "It was *what* to me, he said. 'I'm your buddy, damn it,' I told him, and, hey, he just looked at me and he was, like, 'And but well, so leave me alone, then.' He has got something on his mind that I can't… fathom."

"No doubt." I looked like I was getting the call from my colleagues, though they were happy to leave me to Richard if that was what I wanted. Instead, I drank up and left Richard to them, heard him making his hey-how-are-we-all-doing noises as I got my cape and left.

The same night, when I made a district nurse house call

"He'll see me," I told Milo's mom. She squinted at me and stepped back and let me into the house. In the doorway to the lounge old man Galitzki was pulling up his suspenders. I thought, 'Doesn't that guy *ever* get dressed?' I sent him a nod he ignored.

"What happened?" he said to Mrs Galitzka. She looked from me to him.

"He's there?" I asked her. She waved me toward the staircase and said to keep going till I saw the light under Milo's door.

"What happened?" I heard Mr Galitzki say again. "She is a frigging *nurse*," he spelled out.

"Uh, nurse?" Mrs Galitzka called, but I was winding up that staircase by then.

Milo was lying on his bed wearing only a pair of cycling shorts. He looked like a jock's sarcophagus. He moved his eyes at me when I came in and I saw a whole movie flicker through them. I guessed it was the most surprising thing he'd seen since I'd gotten out of my things in front of him on the night of the dance. I was way off the mark there.

"Something happened to you, Milo," I said quietly. "And you're going to tell me what, eh? So I don't go around thinking I've got the plague or something?"

"The... what?" He sat up.

"What did she do to you, Milo?"

"Who?"

He looked me in the eyes for the first time when I said, "The frigging first lady. Who do you think?" I allowed him a second of silence, and spelled out, "The angel."

Around the room lay crumpled clothes, books, magazines, and the mounds of scribbled-on paper that make up college notes. There were little mechanical models mounted on and housed in wood and metal, plus tools and parts, I guessed, from bikes: cogwheels, brake and gear cables, front forks, spokes, wheel rims, saddles cut into cross-section. I saw Milo's winner's jerseys, some in frames on walls, some in a heap in a corner, his baseball jacket with the Balz Lyceum logo, his framed picture of silk-hatted engineer Isambard Kingdom Brunel, his chipped statue of Saint Theodosia, red-robed, cowled in black, a rose in one hand, a cycling cap hanging off the other.

Out of this chaos, though, only one thing drew my eye. It was a pair of angel wings made with gull feathers, and, it looked like, human hair, looking strangely real, like a dead thing discarded after a hunt. I stepped toward them, then thought better of it. "Found her." I pointed. Milo followed my finger, and hid his lips. "You're going to... *tell* me about her, Milo?" I asked him. "Or am I just going to find out, like, by... *osmosis* or something?"

"Osmosis?"

"For example."

217

"It isn't easy," was all he could get out after thirty seconds' deliberation.

I said, "What happened? Tell me."

"I can't."

"Sure you can."

"I can't."

I stood over him, said we were going out. "Go wash your face," I suggested. "In fact," I couldn't help but notice, "you stink." I said it as kindly as I could. "Go wash your everything, why don't you?" He looked up at me. "Oh, so I'm a nurse, is what you're thinking?" I cracked. "Want me to give you a bedbath, huh?" He didn't even attempt half a smile at that. I said, "At home I got a new dress." I pictured it in the closet, where it had hung since the day after the dance. "Nice light blue with a faint white chalk stripe, mother-of-pearl buttons down the front to halfway, a round collar and short turned-up sleeves with a lot of room to them, very European convent girl."

"Convent girl?" That seemed to grab him.

"Convent girl. It's made of delicate cotton, and cost me all but a week's pay from Maybelle's on the Rink. At home also I've got new white shoes, pointy toes with a strap across that buttons at the side. Not a big heel."

"*Convent* girl?"

"Imagine my embarrassment," I let out, "to be standing in the Rink waiting for you that day two weeks ago dressed in all this stuff and the world and its aunt not too busy with each other to notice me there looking like a spare part."

"Jesus *Mary*." His hand flew to his mouth. "Oh *God*." I saw that he was thinking about that date of ours for the first time since we'd made it. "I'm sorry."

"Imagine my irritation when I drag all the way up this frigging hill to see you only to find *what*? Mr Bike Racer's burning rubber on his wheels, hubba *hubba*. You're sorry for that, Milo? Okay, well, I forgive you. And but, Milo?"

"I can't tell you."

"You kissed me." I sat down next to him. "Remember? And then we went into that next frame."

"Jesus Mary."

"Yeah."

"I'm sorry."

"We made *love*, Milo." I felt my back arch again, my insides shifting as Milo moved inside me, felt his lips cover mine then share them and leave them and move down to my neck, my shoulders, collarbones, where they tickled, my nipples, his hands on my spine, my knees up his back as I trusted him to hold me and not let me go till our business soared us into the light.

"I'm sorry."

"Milo, that wasn't a complaint." I had decided that blackmail wasn't going to do anything for us. "I liked it. Why don't you kiss me all over again?"

"I can't."

I looked at him and knew that was true; I don't know how I knew, but it was, and he couldn't. Once that stuck out so plainly there was nothing for it but to get up and pick my way through the obstacle course on his floor and leave. I was going to tell him I hoped things worked out and all and whatever people say, but didn't trust myself to speak at all.

I lost Milo in the minute it took me to get down to the hallway. His mom took a hold of my arm and pulled me under the staircase and whispered, "You spoke to him?" I said I had. "What's wrong with him?"

"I spoke to *him*." I couldn't hear my voice the way Mrs Galitzka was hearing it, just felt it filter through the snot defying gravity up my nose. "Doesn't mean he spoke to *me*. Listen – you ask me? *Nothing's* wrong with him and, I tell you, there's nothing a nurse hates more than a hypochondriac."

"You came next day." There was a warpath tone in Mrs Galitzka's voice. "The day after that sinful dance. Did you go to it?" Her eyes searched mine. I stared back. "Covering your faces with masks like sinful fools ashamed of the faces God gave you. I say that isn't right. You know about how people used to do that back in the villages where we all came from? You know that?" Her voice was as near to a shout as a whisper can get, and I had a pain in my arm where she was holding it. "Used to do that back when they thought dressing up and parading around would make phony gods put healthy children in their bellies and send them a decent harvest. All for the magnate who owned them and their labor and the stuff they grew. Know what happened to those children? Dead by age three of malnutrition, so they had to ruin themselves with more and more children. Blind ignorance is what the masks covered up."

She was right: those who risked body and soul at masked dances would risk always doing the dance and, to some extent, always wearing the mask. I couldn't argue with her about that. I told her she was hurting my arm, and she let go.

"I begged him not to go." The veins in her temples moved in a pattern, and settled. "Every year I beg him, and every year something bad happens. That's where it started, whatever it is. He barely speaks a word. Comes out of his room only at night, like some damn... creature."

"Who else came that day?" I asked her.

"Who else?"

"Who else came to see him, that day after the dance?"

"Why, nobody." She set her features to work on the question. "Just you. But he wasn't here by then."

"I know *that*." Only God knew exactly how much I remembered that. "Is he eating?" I summoned up my nursing persona and asked.

"He eats, but not so much. You're a nurse," I'd reminded her.

"A frigging nurse," I updated her.

"Can't you take a look at him?" she resumed with some dignity.

"At his what?" I said. "I'm a nurse, not a doctor."

"I begged him not to go." She made her eyes luminous. "And *she* went this year too."

"Who?" For a second I thought she meant Mila. I was about to laugh lightly, and reassure her that Missionary Mila would never have joined the sinners, not even for a night.

"My daughter," she spelled out for the face I'd put on. I thought I might put Mrs Galitzka straight on that score, but she went on, "Caught her coming in at five in the morning. I thought it was Milo and I got up to make sure he wasn't so stinking drunk he'd do himself a damage or leave the door wide open. And it was her. I don't understand them anymore. I really don't."

"Mila went to get Michael," I remembered. "That was all."

"Michael." Mrs Galitzka bit her bottom lip and pondered the name, the sadness it conjured up.

"That was all," I assured her, and imagined I saw the bite on her lip ease.

"Tell me," she said. "What did he say to you, nurse?" She raised her eyes. "Exactly?"

"I told you." I stepped away from her, into the hallway. "He said nothing. I've got no idea what's on his mind. Maybe he doesn't, either.

Mrs Galitzka, tell him from me, will you? Tell him I'm only a nurse when I'm at the hospital. Tell him people who need nurses the whole time are *sick* people."

The same night, when I promised to climb mountains

It was twilight, time of doubts or revelations, for the putting on of sad private faces, time of bats and biting flies. I stood on Kazimir Street, scratched at the pit a mosquito had started on the back of my hand and looked at the tower I had just left. I recalled the times I saw it across the rooftops, imagining being in it, naked and asleep in a bed in there, my arms tight around Milo, his arms tight around me, the two of us dreaming the same dream of safety and valleys, fruit and music and levitation and love.

I said to myself, "You are crazy is what you are to be doing this over some guy with an angel fixation who what's more is turning into a bike, or at least has about as much to say as one." I told myself I didn't give two cusses if Milo Galitzki left his room or talked or walked or did the cha-cha or what. Then I decided, since I wasn't stomping down the hill on my way home, that I obviously did. Maybe all this meant was that I was crazier even than Milo. All the same my breath kept holding itself, and my heart clattered while a voice inside me was willing Milo to come out.

I thought about the bike, and what a fixture I'd look if Milo sailed out on it and left me standing. I crept back over to the Galitzkis' and up the steps to the porch. I pulled back the tarp and saw the bike. I thought of hiding it someplace, then guessed I'd better not let it out of my sight. I could have pricked one of the tires, but maybe that would just have made Milo tear his hair out. Or even mine. A *eureka* sign fizzed in my mind to tell me that the obvious thing was to up and ride it.

Astonished at how light it was, I picked it up by the crossbar and dangled it briefly from the palm of my hand. I remembered a time I heard Milo telling Eurydice Armentiere and Loretta Churchyard how he'd build it to take him so high up mountains he'd get to kiss God on the eye.

If Milo wanted to expand his knowledge of what wasn't easy, me getting up on his bike wasn't, though once up there I felt committed to some kind of rhythm, with my feet fixed in the stirrups. *Nurse on bicycle*, I thought, *district nurse*, and that was exactly what people who came across me would see. They'd also see my uniform riding up my ass. I didn't think I ought to go down the hill; I'd never be able to get back up in any kind of hurry. I messed with the gears and scrunched up the gradient to the top of Kazimir Street. It struck me that it might have been easier to carry the thing. I looked down at Milo's room, and saw its light still on. There was no traffic. I rode in ungainly ellipses.

I thought I might give it another quarter hour, tops. I saw the door open to light up the porch a few minutes later. The bellow Milo made was like that of some anguished animal in a trap. I knew I ought to get down there quick before he died of that anguish. By the time I did he would have been rushing angrily out the gate, except that he was doing a clacking duckwalk on his stiff-soled cycling shoes.

"Now doesn't that just slow you down enough to make you think," I called. "Huh?" He sent me the broadest of smiles, or at least sent it to his bike.

Next thing I was rolling down to him. I'd forgotten that my feet were trapped in the stirrups, and it was a good thing he stopped me, one arm around me, one hand on the bike. "Hey, Milo, I got your lousy bike back for you," I adlibbed cautiously into his ear as he helped me off. "So I'm insisting that you owe me a walk. *Insisting.*" I didn't give him time to think about this. "You go put some sensible shoes on." I drowned out the noises he was making. "And maybe some pants." I regretted having to say that, his ass looking so... defined in those odd shorts. "And Milo?"

"What?" He turned and stood in the light on his porch, looking hurt and confused, sure, but tall and strong too. I knew then that things were going to work out; I don't know how – I just did.

I forgot whatever it was I'd been going to say and said, "Listen. There was one thing I didn't tell you that night of the dance."

"What?" He rolled the bike onto the porch and faced me.

"I was scared to say it." My voice was high and loud in the quiet street.

"Say what?" His eyes were beautiful. I knew they had nothing in them but me.

At the door behind him his mom and dad appeared, faces a blur. I took a big breath, called, "Milo, it was me who wanted to say all those things she said to you. And Milo? Those mountains you want to climb?"

Mr Galitzki shook his head and went back in, but Milo's mom stayed, hand at her chin. A little smile crept across her face.

"I'll climb them with you," I promised Milo. "I'll climb them too."

That very same night, when the world became a different place

"It's good to smile," I said to Milo. "See? The world's different when you smile." I forget what I did to make him do that; something I said, some face I made, maybe some gesture. We were on the walls of the fort. As we passed over the west gate I reached up and kissed his face and he stopped like I had hit him. I passed hands around to his back and he put his arms around me and his head on my shoulder, and shook something gently out of himself.

"Still can't tell me, huh?" I asked him. He kept the question out by not opening his eyes. I made the only decision there was, and said, "I'll say this once. If it's more important for you to keep it to yourself than it is to tell me, then do that. That's your prerogative. But for the love of Christ let's talk about *some*thing, huh? This is our first date, after all."

"It is?" He made a snot-nosed laugh.

"It is." I liked the lilt in my voice. I said it again, stamped my feet with the pleasure of it. "Maybe on our fifteenth date we can sit here stargazing, but you owe me this date, remember? I told you already – my dress, my shoes and so forth? And Milo, we already did the business people think of under the patter on dates. So you don't need to wonder what that might be like. Say something. Impress me."

"Impress you?" Milo picked through the junk in his mind, which had to be even more cluttered than his room, and recounted how the military got the scrub cleared on the hill so they could build the fort. I guess they were at a crucial stage of the murder of native Indians or something, because they couldn't spare soldiers to do it. What they did was get all the settlers of Balz to gather there with axes and sickles and wheelbarrows. They stood and scratched their heads, made jokes about the dumb soldiers wanting them to harvest the weeds on the hilltop. When they were all in place, officers dropped coins of small denominations all over the hill from air balloons. That got the settlers to work and at one another's throats, and had the hill cleared in a day. All for nickels and dimes. "That's the people of Balz." Milo shook his head.

"Us?" I said.

"Children," he despaired. "Fooled by the things that shine the brightest." I saw that he was talking about the angel in his own way. I was going to say that but I'd promised I wouldn't mention her again. I resisted too the temptation to look up to check she wasn't hovering above us.

"Listen, college was how?" I asked instead.

"I learned stuff." He looked at me in surprise. "I wanted to finish quick as I could, so I took six courses each semester. I sat in libraries, read a lot of books, worked on projects. Got a name as a nerd." The face he made told me that was nothing to him. "I played chess with other nerds. I did a lot of running. I rode varsity team on my bike." Maybe it was years of the look I was offering this that stopped talk of moves, jumps, podiums, jerseys, bunches of flowers. Maybe it was something else. "I got a first, *summa cum laude*, got to be Engineer Galitzki the Second."

Years before in the Bistra Café over Mozhay Beach, he'd told me all about bikes, their stupid wheels and gears and how a rider ought to breathe on the stupid climbs, what stupid drink a rider ought to drink on his way up and how, night before a race, a rider shouldn't stand if he could sit, nor sit if he could lie down. Why had that made me so mad? I'd liked Milo an awful long time by then, but could think only of Niamh O'Dowd the day before, telling us about Eurydice and Illona coiled around each other in their tent up by Craw Lake. But what was her answer to the breathless question somebody thought to ask, as to how if she wasn't sleeping in the girls' tent, just where *was* she sleeping? She'd made a smile that started small but got overwhelmed finally by her big white teeth, her cheeks red as apples. The circle let out a whoosh of, "What, with Galitzki?" and prompted Niamh into the kind of denial that meant the opposite. I was still seeing red and green when I met Milo next day. Deep down I still wanted to talk about going up Craw Mountain with him, sleeping in a tent with him like Niamh O'Dowd did, getting out of my clothes and into a sleeping bag with him and being able to smile about it the way Niamh did, my cheeks suffused with blood like hers. I wanted to talk earnestly at him about getting up early and watching the sun come up, and meantime there he was gassing about goddam bikes.

There was another idea that hit me that day: where, I was thinking, would it go if I went out with him then? Milo was sixteen. I was fifteen. It would have been one of those callow teen things that kids did, badly, got out of the way then went on to somebody better. Milo was too precious to me for that; it would have been the anticlimax of my entire life.

I was teen enough to be thinking of a flirtation with Otto Dreyer at the time, for what reason I can't think now. Otto was a breath away from a convertible, had a bright future and a face unaware of its underlying arrogance. The only thing that wiped its smirk away was coming second on the climbs to Milo in Balz's bike race. I fretted for a while at the memory of how when I ran into Otto I told him all Milo had said about what gears to use and what to drink and when to break for the attack; I told him it was magic how I knew, even as I cringed at the words.

"Why?" Milo asked, and I hung my head. I thought he'd broken into it and read my shameful memory that would tell him why he didn't pick up the king climber's jersey the year he was sixteen and why Otto did, but then remembered that I had asked him about college. I remembered why I'd asked.

"There was a girl, though?" It was bugging me, the thing he said on the night of the dance about the angel being his first time. What I was thinking was how no guy went away to college and didn't have a girl. That was one of the things kids went away to college *for*.

"Kind of." There was another story in Milo's tone. I pinched his wrist, made him look at me. He said, "Yeah, sure."

"And but?"

"And but nothing."

"But Milo, every girl has to amount to *some*thing."

He was serious with her through his second year at college. She had corn-colored hair in bunches, and freckles, and blue eyes, wore bright dresses and American tan stockings, thought fuck-me shoes were shoes that pinched your toes. She was very *haimisha*, good at cooking and tidying up the kitchen after. "Good at shopping," Milo recalled, "for Chrissake." Her name was Letty Quinn, and she sounded like tinned fruit and double cream in wedding present dishes only used when the priest came to visit. There had to be more to her than that, and Milo said of course there *was…* but he kept getting the creeping feeling that she was so goddam nice she verged on awful.

But he'd liked the certainty of Letty, liked her being there where no girl had been before, and the way she sheltered him from the asshole things

227

the boy in him still sometimes wanted to do. She was on the face of it his perfect kind of girl; he was able to persuade her into bike riding, hiking, canoeing, nineteenth century French novels – whatever, all the things he thought everybody ought to try.

The one thing he couldn't persuade her into was screwing, though. She told him they'd be married before they got into that kind of thing. Milo put his all into the assault on Letty's ramparts but one day had to own up that the challenge was all there was; the day he schtupped Letty, that would be the end of things with her. He saw how unhealthy that thought was making him. He pole-vaulted out of bed one morning and went around to her room to say the big byebye, a thing she agreed to with indecent haste. That was the end of his second summer semester. He blanked out Letty's memory with thoughts of the coming year, to be spent at an engineering faculty in some bleak Alaskan town where all the women had mustaches or were married or both.

It became clear to me then that the angel, as she led Milo up those mansion stairs, had come bearing not just love but all those certainties Letty had loaned him. She was about to schtup his brains out for him too. "Oh," I said, "hey," and I saw the angel in Milo's eyes.

I knew then that I would always see her in Balz. I'd stand behind her in lines in stores, feel her elbows in my ribs on streetcars and pass her in the shopping crowds on Ganser and Weiss.

"The angel, Milo?" She snuck herself into my voice, and Milo's face went into the shadows I'd drawn over his mind. I remembered my promise, and put my own face into shadow.

"No," he warned me. I knew he was about to get lost again, not just from my sight but from his own, if I went back on my word.

"I told you they were bad news," I couldn't resist.

"You don't *know*."

I pulled him to me and kissed his wet face and swore I would never make him cry again. "You don't *know*," he said over and over. That was true – I didn't, but I would: I'd know, I'd find out and I'd know, use the force of my will and would *know*. It came to me that my will was the strongest thing on that structure on which we stood, that were I to raise a hand and decree it, I could set the whole thing tumbling with the force of my will alone. I looked at the skies, full of the ghosts of men in balloons, full of angels, showers of frogs and flies, heavy with the unkind weather on its way. We wouldn't see it, it hit me, wouldn't see the seasons pass anymore in Balz. I'd wheel us in and out of the clouds that threatened to fall on us, no plane, no strings, no wires, no tricks, just that will of mine. I would make Milo soar out of his jeremiad on wings strong as steel, and would hang onto him with those fierce fingers of mine and bring him to the ground so gently it would be like he'd fallen asleep and woken up in a new life, one in which the unhappy stories had no place at all.

TWELVE

Three Years After Milo's Last Masked Dance, When I Took Up A Challenge To Travel

———◇———

I saw Mila Galitzka's prudent mouth and felt the gaze of her fresco eyes from behind a screen. I saw Mila on Balz beaches in a series of pictures from when God-deserted Sister Adelheid smiled a vocation at her to the night of the masked dance, giving Michael Sheltz the benefit of that vocation and Milo the business end of her vocabulary.

Mr Galitzki was a wise guy, and not a wise man. I'd never gotten to know Mrs Galitzka, but I felt that her wisdom lay in avoiding knowing too much. My dear Milo was clever, not wise. There was only one in the family who was truly wise: Mila.

If anybody knew about Milo's angel, she did. "Yes you do," I finally told her. I had worked my way to those words over a long time, never far from them. "Sure you do." I called the masked angel back into Mila's life with those words, and she couldn't find a corner dark enough to hide her from them.

A second of protest ignited sparks in her eyes. I looked at the powerful figure she cut, and at her big callused hands. "Now listen," she warned me.

That made me put my head on one side and say, "I'm listening." I kept on listening.

"You're wasted as a nurse," she told me eventually. "You ought maybe to be a detective."

To that I said, "Hell no. People's stupid crimes bore me shitless."

She guessed it hadn't taken a Sherlock Holmes to work out the scenario I'd drawn. What impressed her was my tenacity, my insistence on removing masks from faces that nobody would want to look on. "Your sense of, uh, vocation," she said. I treated her to some of it.

"Milo had no visitors the morning after the dance," I reminded her. "Had none all day, had just one, later that afternoon."

After a pause, she recalled, "You."

"I saw you." I gestured a frame. "You stood behind the screen that afternoon and watched me."

Mila had gotten my letter addressed to her at the Balz mission and had finally opened it two months after I sent it, once it had been forwarded across the world to her. It's not mine anymore, I guess, but I know it off by heart as it said only, *You remember me, sure you do. This finds you well, I pray. I heard you finally joined the angels. I want to talk to you about that and if you agree and write me, I'll come home and see you. I may come anyhow even if you don't write. Milo is well and I am too. We're living here outside Paris. I'm still nursing, a specialist now in oncology, and Milo is making a living riding that bike. Best wishes.*

Mila read through those lines and tried to forget them then one night watched herself guide pen across paper. She had nothing to hide. A long time before she'd gotten all on her chest off to God through His earthly agent Father Vishnevski, so what did she have to fear from me? She sent a scrawl that suggested all that, and mentioned that if I were ever in the Delhi area she'd be happy to see me.

I thought, 'Huh, in the Delhi area in*deed*.' I went and had a cognac on the square at Pantin, the suburb north-east of Paris that Milo and I had called home since he broke into the pack-horse life of a full-time rider of bikes. I drank up, then left and walked and saw my face reflected in the window of the travel agency. I went in and learned that the airfare to Delhi was astronomical, and I asked the agent if we were going via the goddam moon, but I had some money saved. What was I going to do with it? Buy some dumb thing that would make a noise or sit there and frown at me if I didn't dust it regularly?

Milo recuperating was enough. This was maybe a month after his fall in what would be his only stab at the Tour de France. It didn't matter that he'd raced his amateur ass off all around France and Belgium to get his pro racing license, nor that the cycling pundits had been cautiously proclaiming him as one of the climbers of the future. It didn't matter that he had grabbed a mountain stage of the Tour of Spain earlier that year and had gotten to make that Cheshire cat winner's photo that, blown up to life size, graces a wall now in the Balz museum. "It may not be the *Tour dee France*," curator Joyce Augustine is reputed to tell visitors. "But it's closer than anybody else in this town is going to get."

It meant zip, once Milo came off his bike on the descent of the Col de la Madeleine peak in the Savoie Alps and smashed his femur. His collarbone was also broken, along with some ribs and teeth, but it was the femur he fixed on as he lay in a heap of frame, forks and baby fir trees; it meant that, had he been a horse, they'd have shot him, and not had medics winching their way down to retrieve him.

Milo was high as a kite in more ways than just his location on a mountain. He could never remember how much of a shot he'd received in the team hotel that morning to keep him going at full tilt ten days into a punishing race. The team doctors kept the makeup of their concoctions secret, just had the riders pull down their shorts and offer their asses to the hypodermic. Milo had gotten a little higher on the resin his fall released when he scattered those pine needles, and had seen a vision of Eurydice Armentiere. She lifted her head from her typewriter and smiled sadly. He was reminded how she too fractured her femur and how that one time was enough to stop her picking up a foil, donning a breastplate and protecting her face with a fencing mesh again.

232

He also got a flashback to the clown driving the car that had closed the road to him on the descent to leave him with an inch of gravel and the sole option of the empty space below. It looked like a Pathé news car but there was no cameraman sticking out the top, just the driver, hunched over his wheel but looking uncannily like Eurydice's brother, Benny. Milo had been aware of Benny round the competitive cycling scene in Belgium, France and the Netherlands, but had managed not to run into him.

Benny Armentiere worked for a doctor, it was said, which meant he was a drug dealer. All the riders were on the sauce. Only a few years later a champion, asked about drugs in his sport, would snap out something on the lines of how they were expected to pull off superhuman feats of endurance in all weathers and – what – did people think they did it on *mineral water*? It created a not-exactly-legal world that shadowed all the tours.

There had never been any love lost between Milo and Benny Armentiere. Benny had always been Eurydice's stupid big brother: dull to her sharp, ugly to her beautiful, inarticulate to her eloquent. Milo, Richard and Moby, at their most puerile, had let him know this with tedious frequency. Milo remembered Orville Charleroi recounting Eurydice's tale of how Milo had broken her heart, and the unforgiving nature behind whatever she felt for him. Benny had evidently nurtured his own unforgiving streak.

Milo was at home, on basic pay till the end of the season, but fretting about his future. There was no good moment to tell him about my travel plans. I paced around, smiling at the puzzled faces he pulled. "Delhi," I confessed to him eventually. "I've got to go to Delhi."

"The one in… *India*?" he exploded. "Are you out of your mind?"

I guess I was. I hadn't been going to tell him Delhi at all, had been going to make it Scandinavia, the only area in Europe he hadn't gotten to know from that obsessive bike racing. Then I thought what if the plane crashed? I'd have been embarrassed in my afterlife, to meet up with Milo having left him thinking I just walked out on him and disappeared someplace up by the Arctic Circle. "It's a conference," I told him. That wasn't a million miles from the truth. "I'm a big shot nurse, remember? I'm… expected to do these things." That was true, albeit having nothing to do with what I was talking about.

"*Delhi.*" Milo tried to make grand gestures without letting go his walking stick. "*India*. Jesus *Mary*." I had to take that as his blessing.

I was there nine days later. From the airport I took a cab as far as I could, then had a bone-threatening rumble in a bicycle taxi. I still had to walk a short way through the crowds in the Shiva Temple district with my map in my hand and my white hair turning heads. By the time I reached the gates of the mission I'd picked up an entourage of a hundred interested souls. I'd also lost a shoe.

They weren't supposed to have visitors at the mission, only by long-time prior arrangement. The first Mila heard of it was the sister superior calling her in to tell her she had one, and that she was family.

"*Family?*" Mila was astonished and excited. She was also bemused at the thought of her mom making her upright way through the quarter, her anxious eyes blinking at all those upon her. She didn't know what the sister superior was grinning at. "How's that, sister?"

"Her name is Bronia Galitzki," she was told "Now you're not telling me anybody else in the world has a name like that, are you?"

The light I shone on Sister Mila at the Delhi mission

I waited in a little room with high windows that looked like a jail cell. Rooms in Delhi had to be that way or else the fearsome sun would flood in and burn your retinas. Sister Mila strode in and made my own eyes at me. Because of that sun, or was it because in her head she was back in Balz and looking at me across a corridor in the Lyceum? I didn't ask, just got up and made my own eyes back. I said, "Hey, sister."

She raised what had the potential to be a smile, swished over and towered over me. Thinking about them carefully, I saw, she eased out the words, "Sister in law." I wondered if she was correcting me just for the sport of it and thought, 'Is it going to be that way? Then this will be hard.' Then she committed to that smile. She reached out and hid my hand in hers and said, "This is, like, *such* a surprise."

"How so?" I let it rest on my lips, that I'd risen to the nose-thumbed challenge at the end of her letter. She looked thoughtful then, was worried maybe about what lies I'd told the sister superior. I let her know they were just little ones courtesy of that good friend omission, who'd helped me out so much with Milo. "I didn't mention an invite," I assured her. "Said I was passing. And, you know, I guess I would have, if I hadn't come right on in."

We giggled a little at that, but I was letting out deep drafts of breath and my knees were shaking. Mila waved me back into my chair and pulled one out for herself. "A lot to talk about," she said. It could have been a question so I said there sure was.

Her eyes were tired, but she had a glow just like Milo's after he'd gotten through a long haul on that saddle; she looked fit and well.

Almost like she was talking to herself, Mila said she didn't believe in Hell on Earth, thought that a fanciful and dangerous idea. "We all suffer on Earth," she said. "But it's nothing compared to Hell. Hell lasts for a time without end, and that's how long sinners suffer down there."

I wanted to remind her that I was a good Catholic girl, and knew all that, thanks, and to spare me the fire and brimstone bit. I said softly, "Mila, don't talk to me about sin in the abstract. I came all this way to talk about concrete sin. I came to talk about *yours*." I had mouthed those words so many times. Now there they were, hovering between our heads to make me think, 'Mila, I'm sorry, I've come here to make you suffer, a little more than you already have.' I said, "I'm not interested in all the other sinners. But there are certain sins have got to come to light."

She whispered that no light mattered to her except the one God threw on everything, and how her sin had already been illuminated. "You've brought part of that light with you," she asked me. "Huh?" I had to accept that she was all square with God.

I was thinking of a different light, though, the one that had lit up Milo's mind ever since that night of his last masked dance, the best night of his life, and the worst, only to be obscured by those terrible angel wings. I found the will to say that she wasn't square with me yet. She may have been Sister Mila of the Destitutes of Delhi, but she was also the key to the angel that screwed my husband and made him turn over in his sleep each night ever since.

"Milo didn't tell you about the angel." She let out a deep breath and gave her head a good long shake.

"You'll tell me." My reminder reddened her cheeks. She made my eyes again, squared her shoulders and brought her hands into two fists under her chin. "*You'll* tell me," I repeated.

A little guy came in without knocking, showed mossy teeth, put two mugs of gray stuff on the table, then left. "This is what, exactly?" I asked Mila. She said it was tea. I didn't want to seem ungrateful, because I could have killed for an *infusion*, but to my mind milk wasn't something you put in tea. Nor was the sugar and spice I tasted when I dared a sip. It was glop. But that was how it came in India, Mila told me, so who was I to just show up and whinge about an entire sub-continent's tea-drinking habits?

As I opened my throat wide and drank, I heard Milo's voice telling the story about how when they were little Mila heard her mom one day saying how she'd die for a drink of tea as she sat down with her feet in a basin of water. Kind Mila brought her some, only it turned out not to be

236

tea but pee, freshly squirted by Mila straight into a fine china cup. She was still at an age when she got her amber liquids all mixed up. Her heart was in the gesture, it was accepted. "Not to mention her amino and peptic acids," Engineer Galitzki opined.

I managed to wipe the story out of my face, though maybe not the engineer himself, because Mila said, "You heard about my pa?"

"Sure."

I saw the little pile of postcards on the bureau in our living room in Pantin, all saying only, *Why did Ulysses do all that stuff?*

I loved each time saying to Milo, "So, *do* you want to go home?" I loved it because to that he could only say, "Hell, no. I want to stay right here with you."

After about the fifteenth card I'd sent one back that said, *Screw Ulysses*, my only written correspondence with my father-in-law. They'd kept on coming just the same, though close on the heels of the last one we got a letter from Milo's mom. It told us that Witold Galitzki was wasting away with cancer of the bowel, and had weeks to go.

A call to Milo's mom had let us in on the sensational information that Mr Galitzki wouldn't see or talk to anybody except Father Ignatz Vishnevski, of all people, with whom he was spending all his waking moments. We wondered if we were hearing things. We refrained from saying anything cynical about atheists petrified at the imminence of God. We prayed for the old man, thankful that he had been brought back from the brink of eternal nothingness. We kept that up till six weeks later when marine sergeant Richard Szczur telephoned to say that Milo's dad was gone, and was about to be buried with due ceremony in the graveyard behind the Holy Apostles.

"But you heard what he did," Mila pushed me.

"Sure." I spoke slowly and loudly, like to a child. "He went back to the church."

"Oh, hey." Mila almost laughed. She said Father Vishnevski might well have brought her dad back to the church, but that he'd opted for the opposite direction. He put the grouchy atheist in the ground with all that Roman ritual then went to the priests' house, dumped his cassock and collar, packed a carpetbag and left Balz without a word. Nobody knew why, though the finger pointed at the bitter old engineer and his persuasive rhetoric.

I had to rein in a laugh at Mr Galitzki receiving last rites and winding up in consecrated ground, the sardonic revenge of the departing believer turned cynic.

I said, "Jesus Mary."

Mila said only, "Yeah."

The trouble with Milo, she started off back on track, was that he was in some ways exactly like their dad. All they did was rooted in science and math and logic, worlds of answers, and there were no other realities. Milo was all intellect, and he paid others the compliment in the first place of assuming they were the same, but in the process had no feeling for the different strands that made them.

"You couldn't see God for logic in that house," Mila said. "I had to look hard for God. When I found Him, I had to hide Him." I knew that. When Romualda's dad Waldemar Petrov was alive, the place was guarded by religious icons and statues. Milo's favorite was the one of Saint Theodosia preserved in his room under dust and junk, while Mila's was the portative icon of suffering Saints Barbara and Katarzyna, which ended up as her only possession.

"That was sin." Mila hesitated. "It was a house full of it." I thought of the house in which I'd been brought up, the gentlemanly oaths sworn on its couches and armchairs and the wishes that got fulfilled in its bedrooms.

I could roll out for Mila a frame or two about houses of sin, but I just nodded, keen to keep her on the subject.

"Milo had no sin in him," she said carefully. "He sinned by mistake – without fail. Do you know how *annoying* that gets after a while?" She made a face I couldn't read. "He always managed to do something bad. And it was always a thing he didn't have to live with."

"Like what?"

Mila started off by getting me to bring to mind a kid called Peter Polkovski, how he came to Balz one summer to stay with an aunt. Peter's dad had lost all his dough, and a lot of other people's, playing the stock markets. He had kept his side of some Faustian bargain by scattering his brains all over a Dow Jones chart with a soft-nosed bullet. Peter's mom, obviously a pragmatist, had junked Peter in order not to get herself distracted out of her glamorous widow part.

Mila met Peter one day when she was struggling up the hill home with groceries on her mule of a bike. He was sitting on his aunt's porch and called over, "Hey, I'll carry that for you, if you want." She was about to call back did she look like she was crippled or what... Instead she caught a glimpse of the pain behind his blinking eyes, and thought, 'Hey, why not?' In any case, he was the first person in a year to say a kind word to her.

"Except for you," she broke off to remember. I knew exactly where and when: I saw us in that Lyceum classroom in recess, saw her breath on the window. I saw Richard Rat in the yard doing the remonstrating he was so good at, saw Milo too, his face hidden in the copper conductors of Loretta Churchyard's hair.

Mila was never in a thousand years going to get serious about Peter. She walked with him around Balz when she was feeling badly used. That was it, though she took the decision not to mention that to him. Peter was cute rather than handsome, would grow out of that into blandness, she guessed. He was never quite there, Mila thought. The reason she liked him was because he didn't know anything about her. As it was the long vacation, they weren't up against the bacterial claustrophobia of school. She didn't tell anybody about him but at the same time didn't risk drawing talk by trying to keep him a secret. I saw them a couple of times in some of the coffee houses in town. Like Mila, I could barely remember what Peter looked like, since he got shunted off to another relative someplace else before fall semester, leaving behind not a memory, but a silhouette.

"I remember Peter," I said just the same. "And but?"

"This isn't about Peter." Mila begged my patience with a raised hand. "It's about Milo."

Milo came across Peter and Mila as they walked up on the cliff one day. He sailed past them on his bike, then turned back and wheeled alongside them. "You know Peter?" Mila asked. Milo said not exactly, but *hi*. They made smalltalk till Milo said he had to be getting along. He did just that.

It wasn't Milo who told Mr Galitzki about Peter and Mila out walking. It was more than likely some lounging storekeeper, those eyes and ears of the town waiting for somebody's business to interfere in. Her dad played the thundering parent, said she was too young to be getting serious with any boy.

"Serious means *what*, Pa?" she asked. He said she knew damn well what it meant, but she had teenage mischief in her enough to want to goad him out of his village elder spiel and say it. She didn't have any ideas about wanting to do the deed with Peter. Other girls our age did that, she knew but, like me, reckoned not as many as said they did. "We weren't all Kasia Krantz," we agreed. Mila's mom joined in and said Mila should wait till she was old enough to make her own mind up. Mila said she was, and she had. Neither parent knew that she still had white sisterhood in her sights.

"God isn't good enough for your little girl, Pa," Mila said to him. "Mammon isn't good enough. In between is what, I don't know."

Later she heard her dad pay a state visit to Milo's room and went and listened at the door. "You knew about this?" she heard the cross-examination begin. Milo said sure he did. And but so what? Mila loved him for that, for a minute. Engineer Galitzki played attorney. What did Mila and Peter do? Milo didn't know. Why should he?

Their dad said, "You know this kid? You know what his old man just did?"

"And but, Pa?" The whole town knew. "Suicide isn't... genetic." His dad told him he'd tell him what was genetic and what wasn't, actually, thank you.

"Remember what I told you all that time ago?" Mr Galitzki said. "About how you've got to take care of your sister?" That was how it stayed for a minute, the voice booming. Mila saw all over again the man with the sadness and the madness of the road in his eyes, the man who nearly ruined her. She stopped her bones shaking. "You do, Milo? Or you don't?"

Silence from Milo, who saw the man's eyes too, and felt the sense of every wrong thing he had ever done coming back to haunt him. "You do?" it went on. "Or you don't?"

"Jesus, Pa."

"Think Jesus can help you, huh?" Mr Galitzki laughed out. "Listen. You know what this kid wants to do to your sister?" Milo said he didn't. "He wants to fuck her." There was a percussion in the word, the suggestion of an accusation. "That's all he wants to do."

"I don't care who fucks her." That was what Milo said. Mila didn't want to listen to any more. She would have a few years of running conversations in her head with Milo during which he wound up assuring her that what he meant by that was how it was her business what she did with her body. She heard them years later, the week of that masked dance, the echoing words of the two men in her life as they argued about what was her choice to make, her thing to do or not do. For then, though, all that was left to her was to go lie in her room in the dark. Even there she found no comfort, stretched out as she was on the bed where their house caller did his stuff with her that awful day back when she was twelve, which made those ill-chosen words of Milo's ring horribly true.

Twelve o'clock at the Delhi mission, and a prayer invoking an angel

"Milo trusted people without question," Mila told me, "like a little dog." He expected them to have the same logic as him, she meant, the same compassion, the same humor, the same little dog's sense of awe. "Is that a good thing?" she said. "It's charming to start with, but in the end you get sick of little dogs, want to shoo them away with a broom. Trust is fine, you know, but it only works if you can trust people who can be trusted."

Why did Milo trust Illona Peterlejtner with the knowledge of what happened to Mila while he went riding French mountains in his head? Once it was put into words, though, that was Milo bowing out, leaving Mila with the first big chunk she had to bite on.

Mila would never forget that day when she found herself watching a man look up from locking the door behind him to open a crescent moon in his face that turned into a smile. He streaked a smell of roads and freight cars across the room to her, took her chin in thumb and finger. He leaned down and kissed her mouth for what seemed an awful long time. Right then, Milo had left her to be the loneliest, most frightened person in the world. The man got hold of her by the ankles and turned her upside down, and the skirt of her dress fell down and hid the world from her blood-filled eyes as he carried her up the stairs. She guessed that was the last glimpse she would ever have of it.

"How do you forgive that," she asked me. "Having to look at your own death?"

Mila had sat in squad cars with officers O'Dowd and Edel and Protzner, kept up a vigil at the railroad yard, near the beaches, anyplace the white sisters were about their business of dishing out soup and cabbage and comfort to bums, but her uninvited visitor never showed. "We'll hang him up by the feet, honey." That was a pledge right from officer Protzner's lady cop heart. "We'll neuter him like a cat." If they did that, though, what was he going to do except squeak and bleed? Were the cops going to shake what he took from her out of him and make him give it back?

"You're disturbing that kid." Sister Jozefa, the sister superior at the Balz mission, had finally said to officer Protzner. "How dare you put revenge in her head?" A kind of philosophical argument took shape then along the lines of how sister Jozefa, pardon officer Protzner's French, didn't know shit and how she ought to watch out in future when she left her station wagon causing an obstruction.

Thanks to Milo, by then Mila couldn't even go to the stores without some beaming asshole sending meaningful *ssh* looks around as he boomed out, "Hey, how are you now, honey?" and passing her free candy to suck on. She was out walking with her mom on the Sunday evening before she was due to go back to school when they passed a group of kids from the Lyceum who sent her the kinds of stares she knew she would have to get used to. It was only one of them had the fool's bravado to howl like a dog, and Mila somehow knew exactly what that meant. She cringed herself into a stupor that evening and didn't go back to school for another week. She had to walk around then with the feeling that the entire town had been up in her room when it happened; not stopping it, just watching.

Sister Jozefa told Mila she knew what was in her heart, and that she understood it, but that forgiving was the only way to get free of it. Even as she said that, Mila felt some of the bad lifting from her bones. "Say you'll try," the sister begged her. Mila nodded herself into the word, then the deed. She forgave the man with the tired eyes.

I would not have done that. I'd have been with Officer Protzner.

Mila went to Milo's room and put an arm around him and forgave him too, got him weeping tears of relief.

It was Milo, though, who brought the words, *poverty, chastity, obedience, joy* to the curled lips of the kids at the Lyceum a couple of years later. Girls even wrote the vows on toilet walls, countered them with the rhyme, *Mila Galitzka just needs a boy*. I watched my friends do that. Once again, the school hummed with rumor about Mila. Once again she had to face it out.

"Milo and I were close." Mila held up thumb and finger squeezed tight. "Closer than that," she said. "And that went in really deep and hurt. I knew him. Why didn't he know *me*? I loved him and would've done anything not to hurt him. So why did it seem like all he ever wanted to do was hurt me? But you know, when people called him names, he could call them worse names. If people punched him, he could punch them back but harder. Nothing touched Milo, nothing hurt him, and so he didn't know how other people could hurt. He had no… sense of it. You know him now." She paused as if to think about the weight of those words, our three lives and the trails that led between us all. "Do you know what hurts him?"

It might have been easier for her to write Milo off as a plain bad kid who enjoyed the chaos he brought and got some kick out of it, but she knew that wasn't true. It might have made things much easier for her later, in the years she harbored her own sins against him, but she was too wise for such tricks.

"Falling off mountains hurts him," I told her.

That brought lines to her forehead, pursed her lips, made her say, "What?" I pictured Milo at home all those miles away, his walking stick next to his chair, his career a question mark. I was about to expand on my remark when Mila said again, "*Nothing* hurts him."

"*You* hurt him."

The words made space around our heads as a bell rang in the building. "The *Angelus*." We both breathed out the name of the twelve o'clock prayer about a thing made known via the message of an angel.

Mila was out of her chair. "Lunch is after," she said, though I could see she was uncomfortable, and that a part of her wanted to stay and address my three words. "Go settle in your room." She seemed to have decided that I wouldn't want to say the *Angelus* with her and her sisters. She was right. "And we'll eat. And then I've got stuff I've got to go and do." With a shoulder, she indicated the building around us, and all of Delhi that lay outside. "But we'll talk again later."

"You bet," I said.

She stopped at the door, said, "Talking's hard."

"Talking hurts." I saw that, the theme of our thoughts right then, the theme of Mila Galitzka's life in Balz, saw it come into her face for a second just before she left and made soft steps on the flags outside.

Remembering Lucy Ephraim, and the day she stopped tumbling

"Lucy," I said. "It all came down to what happened to Lucy Ephraim." Mila and I stood looking out of one of the windows of the clinic the sisters ran. I imagined Lucy tumbling artfully over the rooftops of Delhi, in and out of the radio masts that received signals from a world that would prefer it if the place got swallowed up by the force of its own energy, just the way Lucy herself was. "Didn't it?"

Having dismissed Lucy's fear of growth, what in all the far-flung reaches in his mind made Milo think others would see it in the charmed way he did? "That tiny creature Lucy Ephraim believes she might grow and lose her job in the circus," people related. "And to reassure herself that she hasn't grown, she stands each night against a measure she keeps in her hallway. Did you ever hear the like of that?" Did Milo really not know that the citizens of Balz would hate the thought of Lucy Ephraim going to sleep at night knowing she had her days on the road and her nights in the sawdust to look forward to while they were stuck with futures full of rusting junk and kids who'd grow up as deluded as they were? How could he *not* know that?

The carpenter and painter wanted what? Wanted Lucy to cry, no doubt, like the people in Balz who kicked their dogs to remind them that their lives were even more miserable than their own, who raised cockerels with care right up to the night when they armed them with spikes and set them loose in rings to fight to the death. Milo wanted to be able to tell a good story; it was as banal as that.

"He told it to Moby," I said to Mila. In my mind I hovered over the artist in his invalid chair. I broke him out of the reverie he was conjuring in the attic rooms in his head, tore him from it and made him look up in alarm when I projected to him the words, *yeah,* you, *you little* brute.

"Moby?" Mila's face said, *and but? He told it to everybody.* I knew society mags like Paris-Match never made their way to mission houses in places like Delhi. It must have occurred to Mila, though? That it was Moby? It no longer mattered. Whatever it was the carpenter and painter wanted, you had to believe he didn't want Lucy to hang herself over it; it was a consequence nobody had anticipated.

If Milo was appalled at the consequence, Mila, who felt that she owed the faith surging inside her to Lucy, was shrouded by her grief. She tried not to keep saying it to herself, but because of a chain whose links led back to Milo and his mouth, Lucy was gone, pointlessly and painfully.

"I couldn't look at him anymore," she said.

We surveyed the mission's hall, now overflowing with the afflicted of Delhi, waiting for us to finish setting up at our table. We watched a woman lead a milky-eyed child toward us, and set about our work, our talk a secret from them.

"You know it was me found her?" Mila wasn't even able to think about her brother from then on without seeing Lucy suspended from a beam in her hallway. "You know what I thought? I thought right then what a dumb thing it was for Lucy to have gone out on the flats all those years before to get Milo back. She should've let him walk around out there till his head filled up with salt and antimony and he came to a halt and died. That's what she should've done, and then *she* would've lived. That was my thought. And, you know, you just can't... *harbor* thoughts like that. It's not like you want them. They're there, and they won't go. They stick in your head and it's all you can do to make them stick in your throat so you don't say them out loud. You can't have thoughts like that and kid yourself you're the same person you were before you had them."

That thought of Mila's turned into the sin she was to carry to replace the joy she'd had, to fill her up in exactly the same way. "Sin cripples you," she told me. "Stops you walking the same way, stops you talking, stops you thinking. It's true. You're a good person." She deadpanned her change of tack, looked puzzled at the idea. "I remember you at school. You weren't like your friends. The night of that dance, you walked around after Milo the whole time. I saw you. And I thought then you'd love him and protect him like nobody else. He didn't see that, did he? I did. Meantime," she whispered, "I had already sinned. And you..."

"What?"

I waited. Our patients sensed something other than our visible business passing between us. They looked from me to her with some interest.

"You were the real angel."

"There were *no* angels at that dance," I said cheerfully. "But go on."

"I lost it," Mila said through her teeth as she snapped open a sterile packet and revealed a hollow needle, beautiful in the light. "Just lost it, when officer O'Dowd said to me, what about this stick story, did I know about it? He told me then he'd been to the morgue and measured Lucy against the stick and how it was shorter than her. Whatever it was I had, I lost it then. I knelt down and prayed for Milo's damnation. And you can't pray for things like that and next day get up and go on with the kinds of plans I'd had. I was about to join the sisters. I was old enough. I was prepared. I knew it was no... child's infatuation, no religious hysteria. It was what I'd wanted to do for the longest time. But suddenly I couldn't do it. I was in sin, and I couldn't get out of it."

I loaded a hypodermic and tapped bubbles out of it as Mila swabbed the arm of a child who looked like one of those mummies in Peru. We lost ourselves for a minute in our tasks, but I thought it was the right time to tell Mila about how I'd seen Lucy brought into the Balz General, and how I'd gone down to see officer O'Dowd to talk to him about the stick story. She said nothing to that, but bit on a knuckle for a second. I noted its dull scars, remembered she'd punched a mirror and broken it the night Anaheim Sheltz died. She needn't have bothered; no number of broken mirrors could have explained our town's more than generous share of bad luck.

"Milo said what to all this?" I asked her.

Milo's face said what it always said on those occasions when sorry wasn't going to be enough. He sat on the porch and waited for Mila that dark afternoon after Lucy's funeral. This kind of scene always followed those lines, Milo looking uncomprehending of the world he'd revealed with its clamors and colors. He'd sat there and shaken his head. Mila had stood and said nothing, biting on that same knuckle.

"Jesus Mary," was all Milo could find to say.

"Say what?" Mila was full of exhaustion and aspirin, of the questions of stupid police officers and the platitudes of mourning circus people. She stood in an aura made by her grief.

"Mila?"

248

"Don't say my name." Her finger was raised. "Don't say Jesus's name. Don't say Mary's name. And don't you *ever* breathe Lucy's name to me. It was *you*, damn it," she said softly. "It was you *killed* her, you *ass*hole. It was *you*."

"What?" Milo's eyes flickered, those of a frightened animal.

Mila wanted to step into his head and run through it to point out the tobacco smiles of the Balz storekeepers and the drinkers of Ganser and Weiss and the Rink, and the motormouths at the Lyceum, all repeating that story about Lucy Ephraim and her fear that she might shoot up and grow. She saw then that he was well aware of his part in Lucy's death.

"She didn't say it was a secret." If anything, Milo sounded even unhappier with those words than Mila was. She turned a foot and couldn't tell later whether she had meant to walk away or not. In any event she put her weight on that foot, drew her fist back and hit him over the right eye. She saw him tumble sideways off the porch.

"You *wait*, Milo Galitzki," she called down to him. "You fucking *wait*."

"*Jesus*." Milo was on his knees in the dirt. He rose slowly, a hand over his eye, blood seeping between his fingers. With the other hand he steadied himself on the porch rail. "Wait for *what*?" he groaned up at her.

She swore she really didn't know what she was thinking as she promised him, "I'll give you a secret you'll *never* dare tell."

Evening at the Delhi mission, and Mila with the face of a poor child

Mila's sisters welcomed me with the assumption that I was a new aspirant. I had to keep saying, "*Hell* no. Uh... sorry. That is, not at all. I'm married with Mila's brother."

"Married," a lot of them oo-eed, "with Sister Mila's brother." Only one of them got me thinking rather than grinning stupidly back, a short

Mediterranean-looking girl with the premature face of a schoolmarm. She said in cheese-cutting English, "Sister Mila has never said that she has a brother."

Dinner got them good-humored. Me being their guest from the world outside, they wanted to know how the Pope was, and about church attendance in France. They also asked me how the Cold War was going, who was prime minister here and there, and whether their home soccer team did well in the European championship competitions the way it did the last year they were out in the world when all their vows and white and work and joy were just wishes they had. I answered best I could.

Left to my own devices as Mila went through her evening rota of tidying up and praying before the sacrament in their chapel, I went to my room. A knock on the door heralded the little guy who brought the tea around. He didn't have any tea for me but, with all the ceremony of an emissary from the court of Cinderella's prince, he held out the shoe I'd lost the day before. It was scuffed and kind of dusty, and minus its lace, but what the hell. He offered it to me and at the same time kept a hold of it, so we had a brief tug-of-war till I fumbled coins at him. They were refused twice, and I found that very Catholic. I hastened the ritual by insisting *hard*. We both grinned at the foolishness of it as he pocketed the money and left.

My face aching from all the noises I'd had to make through dinner, I thought about the things Mila and I might say that evening. I found a vision of the hurt that lay ahead. I was trying to clear it out of my face when Mila appeared.

"So, sin," I reminded her as brightly as I could once she had sat down. "We were talking about sin."

I hinted at the story I'd evolved for myself about what had driven Milo so crazy the day after the dance. I said, "What I ask myself each time I run through this tale is, if it's the truth, what kind of person is Sister Mila Galitzka?" She said I had to judge her as I thought fair. I stared that back at her and said, "I didn't come to judge you." She reminded me that God had done that, already.

Mila said if I were a detective I'd be the nice one who offered the perp a cigarette after the bad one had finished beating up on him. With the look in my eyes and the way I wrinkled my nose and pouted, she said, I'd get the confession out of him and in the process of getting him to damn himself I'd make him feel good, at least for the moment, free of the bonds of his crime. "There's something in you," she told me. "Makes people want to tell what's in their hearts." Certain of this power in me, Mila was astounded to realize again that Milo had never told me the truth about his angel. She got a glimpse then at what kind of agony he had been living through with the secret she gave him, to have me there and yet not be able to tell.

Agony was what she had wanted for Milo though, wasn't it? The thing is, you can get yourself absolved all you like, but no priest can exorcise your memory. Mila felt those sins fall on her head again, went to the corner sink and splashed water on that face in which I'd seen them appear for a second.

After Lucy died, Mila lived under a cloud of hurt and sin. It wasn't lifting and didn't seem like it was going to. She spent most of her time in her room. I'd seen her around town. "No doubt," she said. "But doing what?" She went to the stores, walked up on the cliff, even went for a spin on her bike into the countryside, but those were things she'd always done. Everybody else her age was busy with something that would advance their lives in some way. The town was just a place full of eyes she avoided.

She helped the white sisters at their work, but she had always done that, too. The whole town thinking she was crazy hadn't been able to stop her wanting to join, and nor had her dad, once she was at the age of majority, but Milo had managed it. Every time Sister Jozefa said to her, "Are you going to join us, Mila?" she'd had to feel for the hatred she carried in her heart and see that it hadn't lifted, and say no, remain with them but not of them, like Milo and the bikers.

I said that was a difference of one little word, but it didn't matter that the sisters didn't know about the sin Mila had. *She* knew. And God knew. God knew too about the even bigger sin she would come up with a few years later. She sat in her room in her underwear and read her Bible and made teeth-marks on her knuckles. That was no way to stop that sin incubating.

"Why didn't you just go confess it?" I asked her. The answer was that she hadn't committed it yet and didn't know what shape it would take. Only God knew for sure but she didn't want to let go of it, kept it so she could unleash it on Milo someday.

"Remember I said I wanted to crawl into a corner and die?" she paraphrased, calling up those moments in that Lyceum classroom again. "Remember, that day? Well, after Lucy died, I faced every day feeling that way." I saw the face she'd kept from that time for a second, that of a lost and wretched child, saw it clearly only then.

She was in pain, she was stifled, she told me in answer to my question about what kind of person she was. She blended in with the people of Balz at last, but kept silent rather than add her voice to the hypochondriac whine of the town's jeremiad.

"I was stuck with that sin. I lived that way, in sin. I didn't even have the little joy these people here around us have. And what was Milo doing? He was getting on with his life. He came home on college vacations and was Pa's blue-eyed boy, like always, and they sat and talked about strings of numbers that didn't mean zip, spent days and nights in the yard under face masks heating up metal like medieval alchemists. Milo had taken all my joy away from me, so I had to take it back, and to do that I had to take his. I had to hurt him. No." She closed her eyes against the question I was about to ask. "There was no other way."

Later at the mission, when Sister Mila and I sang a song about soldiers lost in time

I thought Mila had hatched her plan out through those bitter years when Milo was away at college, going crazy with it as it ate her up inside. That wasn't true. It came to her like a mischievous ghost scattering dust. Once the dust settled she knew what she had to do and just went and did it.

"The masked dance was an abomination." She looked away to show me that she wasn't aiming that comment at me in particular. "It hit me that if it was the abominable that Milo wanted, then I'd give it him like he'd never had it." She didn't think of it the year before, or the year before that. She didn't know why, except that maybe she felt she wasn't up to doing anything other than keeping a lid on the wrong Milo did Lucy. She just added it to her own jeremiad, the story most of which had already been told throughout Balz with the aid of the trumpet Milo had for a mouth. "Revenge takes a *lot* of energy," she said. Even bringing the admission to words whitened her face a shade.

She thought of it a few nights before the dance. Milo passed her room, and she saw khaki, brass buttons, a cavalry stripe, saw that he was going to be a soldier. She thought of dashing sergeant Milo moving in the crowds of the dance.

"*My boy will have his big white horse*," she quoted at me, and I joined in. "*His epaulettes, his nice sharp sword, his shiny leather boots. My boy will ride off to war. Where are the boys of yesteryear?*" we sang together softly. "*All rode off to war.*"

The end of the verse brought silence. We bit our lips and came close to smiles.

Mila remembered days when she and Milo were little, sat on Glass Beach waiting for their mom or dad to finish work and bring them home, when they used to see lines of soldiers out on the flats drilling; Milo watching, mouth open. Then Milo walked out after the angel who took over the form of Sister Adelheid as it led her to her death, and at the same time invited Lucy into that fatal dance. It came to Mila then that she could bring these fundamentals of Milo's memory together and give him a jeremiad of his own. She decided to conjure up the angel he chased that day.

Her only aim was to make her angel give Milo that profane secret she had promised him on the day Lucy got buried. It was sheer improvised enthusiasm that made her present him with the moon and the stars, life and death, mind as well as body. She could see Milo falling in love and knew it would bring him down with a bump when his angel disappeared, because despite his faults he was full of love, and thought it was the one big thing we all had to have. That and a bike. He'd be in love with his angel for the rest of his life, unable to love anybody else.

The other thing that made her talk her way through what she was doing was that fear every girl goes through when about to pop her cherry, but it was Milo telling her it was his first time that clinched it for her. If she'd had any doubt about it, that blew it away and propeled her onward. She knew he wasn't just spinning a Casanova's yarn; it was Milo at his best *and* worst, free of guile.

The promise she made him from the porch on that funeral afternoon filled her ears with its somber music. The other voices she heard were those of Milo and her dad resonating through Milo's door. *Don't care who fucks me?* She evoked those words for the last time. *Hah, Milo?*

"Tell the rest," I said to her. She looked at me sharply, then away. "Tell the part you didn't tell."

"There's no more." The light from the candle on the table filled her eyes and made them liquid. "Look," she started to say, but didn't want me to look at her.

I said, "No," gently. "Tell."

"I couldn't have done it," she whispered, "if I really hadn't wanted to. And I knew." She looked frankly at me now. "It had to be good." She got up, did her statuesque part and stretched her arms and spread her shoulders and sprouted invisible wings that filled the room. My pursuing eyes drew out of her, "I had to like it."

"Had to like it," I echoed.

"And I did." She looked up, checked with God maybe, to see if it was okay to say it the way she had. "I loved it. It was..."

"It was what?"

"Oh Lord." She raised a knuckle to her mouth, turned her face away.

"One more sin," I called up to her. "Didn't make any difference, huh?"

"No. I guess not."

She was safe behind her veil and the memory of her absolution, but then I *did* want to judge her. What was more, I wanted to get up and slap her face, but I'd vowed to deny myself anger. I fought it as it rose, cautioned it that we were in a city that had enough violence of its own. What I did instead was cry, and then Mila was kneeling next to me, arms around me for a long time.

"Go on," I bade her at last, but there wasn't much more. After their performance, she watched Milo making a fool of himself with all those other women got up like angels, and knew the more ambitious reaches of her plan were working.

The other angels were a bonus, enabled her to stick around and watch in the obscurity of numbers. I told her that maybe five of the angels at the dance were my fellow-nurses at the BG. Part of my compulsion in trailing Milo after his angel was to see if it might be any of them. I saw again what I'd done that night, how I'd been prepared to help Milo go off into the dawn with his angel, even though I'd grown up with the idea of him as the only guy on the planet for me.

"That's kind of what I mean." Mila had a child's look of wonder on her face. "You're good. A good person."

"That's what good people do," I said. "Is it? And not just stupid ones?"

"No." I could see her restraining herself from waggling a finger. "*Good* people, without a single doubt. You *were* the angel – I'm telling you."

"*No.*"

"Yeah – *yes.*"

Mila had watched from a window in the Zacharov mansion, thinking Milo was about to give up and go home, to enable her to go through the final part of her plan, when she saw him run into the shape that sat on the steps of the insurance building. She could feel her sin wanting to lift but just got more and more blown out with it inside her as she fended off the grotesques who came on to her at the dance. She watched Milo and I sitting not doing anything then saw us get up and come back into the mansion's grounds. She kept track of us, and the sight of us hitting it off made her mad, made something in her sink. In the meantime, the picture of me was getting clearer. I'd been a little dark shape out on Ascension Avenue and when I came back to the mansion I was a dumb green pixie.

When Mila the angel called Milo to come down to Glass Beach, she thought I was gone and didn't see me till my head appeared next to his. That was a dangerous time; she knew I'd come with him. She cursed the idea she'd had when she saw Milo, which was that she would walk into the fog coming in over the flats with the dawn, double back and leave him wandering out there. It was the poet in her that thought of that. "I was always a lousy poet," she said. That almost drew a laugh out of me.

On Glass Beach her rhyme and meter broke up at the sight of the pixie. She'd seen her seeking out the other angels. She knew that if Milo was dumb enough to lose sight of her or was just sapped of the energy for it, the pixie wasn't. Mila had to brazen things out somehow. She got in against the cliff and put on the clothes she'd changed out of earlier. She stuffed the props behind a rock. Even caught up in the business of guiding Michael home, the thing she'd been intending to do as soon as she changed anyhow, it took all her courage to swing her way past Milo, and to raise the two violent little words that summed up their situation so aptly. It took a little bit more to avoid the curious pixie eyes that were blinking hard at her and, it occurred to her, knowing what was what. She hadn't wanted that to happen. The secret she'd wanted to give Milo had to be his alone.

From up on the cliff she looked down through a parting in the curtain of the fog and saw me and Milo loving each other. It came back to her as a shock how he'd done that to her too. What a debut for him, she thought. "Go ahead," she said to herself. "Enjoy, Milo, because after this time, every time you go through that act you're going to think of me and of the hurt you did me and the secret I gave you in return for the ones you owed me."

Next morning when she went into Milo's room, she stood over him and listened to him breathing evenly in the sleep he'd found; I'd given him that sleep. I got a flash of the deepest anger again when Mila told me how she got onto the bed, her legs either side of him, and tore him out of the last pleasurable dream he'd have for a long time. She'd gone back to the beach that morning and recovered the remnants of the angel. She dumped them onto his chest, the mask, the halo, the wings, and a square yard of angel hair freshly cut from her head, saying, "You've found your angel, Milo."

Milo looked up and remembered her in the same position the night before, listened to the voice he hadn't heard through those three years of injured silence, that had come only from his angel. "Now go tell the whole fucking town," she spelled out. It was the first time she'd seen him speechless, but she didn't wait for any words, walked out of there and left him to it. He didn't come down for lunch. Mila knew he was up in his room, crying like a child.

Her mom cross-examined her the whole morning in low tones so her dad wouldn't hear, about what she'd been doing out in the middle of the night. Mila maintained her story that she'd gone to get Michael, but her mom knew something was up.

For a start, Mila was wearing an aspirant nun's veil. When she refused to remove it, Romualda snatched it off and revealed the mess Mila had made with her clumsy, impromptu barbering. It was plain then where Mila was headed.

Mila knew her sin wouldn't be showing in her face for much longer. She replaced her veil and walked off to catch Father Vishnevski in between masses to make the confession burning a hole in her. "So tell them," she said out loud as she hurried past families in Sunday best and past the shrines that marked the way to the Holy Apostles, had Milo before her in her mind, stretched out under her. "Tell them, Milo. Go stand on the fort and shout it over the rooftops."

She heard Milo tiptoe down the stairs later and go through the hall quiet as a shadow. She went to the window and saw him wheel off down the path on his bike. Away he went, off out to chew over the last secret he'd get from his sister, knowing by then, I guess, that it was going to catch in his throat forever.

Later I made Mila's picture complete from silhouette to pixie to nurse Bronia Chambers the slant-eyed girl in blue and white who might not have been an Indian but knew how to follow a trail all the same. From Balz to the sea, from London to Paris, even to Delhi, but farther still I would go, deep into Milo Galitzki's jeremiad to reduce its pages to dust. Wise Mila Galitzka had not counted on that at all.

THIRTEEN

Now, And All The Times There Were, And All The Times That Will Be

———◇———

"The stories are behind us, Milo," I remind him sometimes, whenever I see a certain resignation in his movements, when I spot him nursing a morning headache after a glass too many of wine and not enough sleep. I tell him it's me does the nursing around here. "At least," I add, "the stories behind us are behind us." It makes him smile to hear in the north of Paris the logic that passed for optimism back in Balz.

"What stories?" he says, and I can never make out if that's supposed to be a gag or not. I laugh anyhow.

"Why, all of them," I answer. "All the stories there were."

We live in an apartment that echoes due to our lack of much furniture. I think this is to do with our having escaped from homes where we were hemmed in by useless clutter. We fill it with our impassioned talking, with friends, nurses and bike riders in mufti, with neighbors and their kids, flood it with music, step around it dancing. We empty it out when we want to and stretch out on a rug and pull muscles making love, retreat to low-lit corners, welcomed by blankets and books and thoughts. Then the stories come back. We tell only happy ones these days, rendered into French for those friends of ours.

We cross-hatch French and English to tell our stories to Anaheim, the first of the little Galitzkis. As they open boxes in her mind she didn't know she had, she grasps them and knows, for a few years at least, that the world is a spectacular place in which no bad things happen. "Whut," she says,

259

"*whut?*" when Milo looks at her a particular way. She trembles with the anxiety that kids love, guessing that he is about to sit on his haunches and tell her something that makes no sense at all if you're not a Galitzki, that she is about to laugh fit to wet herself, to fall split with giggles around the floor.

Milo knew when he'd had enough of resting. The amphetamines he'd lived on as a bike pro left his system at last, and he was able to focus once more. He became a tall figure haunting Paris quayside bookstalls, or a hunched, harassed one on rush-hour buses, arms full of books and checkered math paper. He sat in cafés, consulted his tracts on aerodynamics and design, got his pencils at his pad, sketched angles and tubes and wheels of bicycles, saddles, pedals, forks, bars. He put that aside to read his Victor Hugo, got into new worlds of nuance in those pages. He got through a lot of the writers he liked, old frowning Victor, of course, but Voltaire too, Montaigne, Montesquieu, the almost impossible Proust, Camus, Sartre, de Beauvoir and others he sometimes spied on their mumbling way to their Paris haunts and hangouts. He'd come a long way from the kid who put his hand up in class one day at the Balz Lyceum to answer some teacher's question about who wrote *The Man in the Iron Mask*, and managed, in graceless sincerity, "It was Alexander Dumbass."

In between books, he found that he was looking at his bike in its team livery, glinting in the shadows. Then it became something he rode to the store. "You're riding," I said to him, first time it happened. He scratched his head, said how it was nice out, and anyhow that I'd been using the car.

We took weekend runs together, me on the bike he built me, weighed down by its rack and basket and bell and fenders. "Race you to that tree up there, first in the row," I'd say, and if the *grimpeur, rouleur, super-domestique* Tour de France man was able to resist that, the boy in him couldn't, and he'd try to burn rubber. Sometimes he won, and sometimes, when the pins in his leg stabbed him, and if we hit a downhill and I was loaded with provisions, it was me who won those imagined sprinter's laurels. When we rode down in the valleys of France Milo only once in a while looked up at the crags that shut us in.

"Wish you were up there?" I asked him.

"Sometimes." It took him a long time to find such an inadequate word. "But you can't have it all, can you?"

He seemed happy enough with the fields rolling by, a chateau coming out of the trees, a roadside bar to stop for bread and beer and conversation. "Gal-eetz-kee," the radio-owning newspaper-reading bar owners say if they recognize him. They shake their grave, expert heads and mention legendary mountains scattered like the dead from a giants' battle around the big, beautiful country they have that only, for some of them, comes alive each July for that circus of a bike race. They punch Milo on the arm, slap him on the back and launch into men's bike-talk. Milo slips his affirmatives into the pauses and looks like that big foolish boy he used to be.

There was a job going on one of the hotshot French teams as chief mechanic. I picked up a call one day from the manager of this team, a bike legend, though if you say his name to most people they'll just go, "Huh? That's *who*?" I got over that quickly and told him Milo was out, so he grilled me to find out if it would be a good idea for him to ask Milo if he'd be up for the job, whether Milo wanted to be around bikes and riders and the kerfuffle of the teams again. I said I didn't know, and he said, "You must know. You're his wife." I couldn't dispute that, but said it still didn't make me know; he'd have to work it out with Milo.

"It'd be good to get some more money coming in," was my thought out loud, secret, as it was in English.

"He won't be an onlooker," I was assured in the lofty French style adopted usually by dandies and drinkers. I knew that and said so, and sharply, that God forbid a cut-throat business like bike racing should carry any passengers on the bent backs of the riders. "He will be a part of the machine of the race," I was ignored and told. "He will sit at the very heart of it and control its… mechanism."

"Spare me the poetry," I said. "Ask him."

Milo made a visit during which the first thing they did was challenge him to find a good reason for not taking the job. Then they slooshed wine and nibbled cheese and jabbered about materials and components and talked tactics, star riders and their legs and their magic potions and their egos. At home Milo limped up and down arguing with the walls, made Anaheim clap hands and laugh. I laughed with her, but I was sad because I knew he'd be away a lot again.

Once more, Milo built bikes and tinkered endlessly with the things, and the garage, the yard, the kitchen, sometimes, were full of bike detritus. The team liked having a bike builder around; they knew in their bones that they had some good seasons coming up, and that turned out to be true. I thought Milo found his real self again, because deep down he was still Engineer Galitzki, a designer and molder of materials, coaxing them into life with math and science, fire and metal. There lay his real talent, and there would lie his rewards, in the perennial problem of how to make the most beautiful object in the world faster than the fiercest wind. He was left to ponder another question, and that was whether, if he'd stayed in racing, he would have been the star climber the pundits saw in him or just a nearly-man, a guy who was good but not great, or even great, but not with the greatness of champions. He was happy enough to decide that impossible questions could be answered in another life.

The team would consult him about mountains, of course, but really, even I knew there wasn't much to that. That brought us back to the afternoon all those years before in the Bistra Café over Mozhay Beach when Milo fell into the trap of happenstance, and told me his climbing secrets.

"You know why Otto Dreyer got the climber's jersey that year you were sixteen?" I said. Milo said how Otto was a scarily decent rider, albeit an asshole of the first order. "Yeah, he was," I said, angry for maybe the thousandth time at myself. "But Otto knew all that stuff too." I looked up at Milo. "About how to get up mountains fastest."

Milo said, "I know *that*," and saw, I knew, Otto's ass ahead of him on the road, probably his sweetest feature.

"All that stuff you told me. How did he know?" I pressed Milo. "How did Otto get the sky in his eyes that day, Milo?"

"It doesn't matter." Maybe Milo saw me staring, sweet sixteen too, lips pursed, eyes full of inscrutable anger, white pigtails tied with red and white ribbons. He kissed my face, the one I have now with all the things it knows, and changed the subject by putting an arm around me. I knew I'd never have to mention it again.

That's what Milo does then, all the races, the one-days, the six-days, the three-week pains-in-the-ass, goes to France, Spain, Italy, Switzerland, Belgium, Holland, and the World Championships, wherever they may fall, and the Olympics, though all he sees of those places are the roads, workshops and hotel rooms. While he's doing that, I do my nursing, study for qualifications that will take me off wards and into oncology research and dull conferences. I get into a black silk dress sometimes to perform gentle pieces on my guitar at the *Academie*, and get better little by little at both, I hope.

"When are we going to see aunt Mila in India?" Anaheim asks whenever she remembers, which is often. We don't know. We remind her that visitors aren't encouraged. We tell her aunt Mila will visit us one day, if she ever gets a vacation: that if Anaheim sees a white lady come down the path in the yard one day, moving in and out of the parts of bikes, she's not to panic and go thinking of ghosts or angels. In the meantime she's to write something nice to aunt Mila to let her know we're thinking of her. "In English," I remind her.

We'll never get to Delhi, but in our long vacations we drive coast to coast over Europe, shrink it in our little car, bikes on the rack, my guitar in the back with Anaheim. We always wind up on the coast. Doesn't matter where it is, if it's somewhere grand like Istanbul or Venice, or some windswept shore of Portugal or the Baltic, we're happy long as there's some water to look at, and the noise of the waves to make known to us the wishes of the moon.

"The water heals," we tell Anaheim. She can only agree as she puts a grazed toe into it, feels the salt sting, and yelps, feels it soothe then and sighs. "And what it doesn't heal," our eyes tell each other, "it conceals." Our gorgeous laughing child will be a swimmer, we decided, even as she paddled in amniotic fluid; she will master that even before she learns to balance on a bike.

The perfect white waves inspire Milo, I know, though much of the time he keeps whatever he thinks a secret. "The darkest ever secret in the world," I tell Anaheim. She's in her time of wonder, and goes solemn and widens her eyes and makes her mouth into an o. She turns into the little sparrow that wheeled over Victor Hugo's Notre Dame church at times of great change, stupefied at seeing the whole angel legion spread its six million wings; she can say only how cool that has to be. I tell her she's right, that she is the wisest Galitzki of all, no doubt about that. We keep out of Milo's thoughts and know in the hollows of our bones that we wouldn't have things any other way. If he sometimes wakes in the night and finds himself on a rocky beach at dawn, thinking of angels, well, I do too. That is one of the dreams we share, replaced soon, happily, by others that don't belong to the black and white past at all, but stretch into the parti-colored future to wait for us there.

ACKNOWLEDGEMENTS

I couldn't have faced rewriting *The Last Thing the Angel Said*, and finessing and finishing it, without the love, support, critiques and insights of my wife Jacqueline.

I'm eternally grateful to the unswerving attention this book got all the way through its first incarnation from Hilary Hodis. Jo Armes and Jon Johnson were also there while the story was settling, and Jon showed me for the first time what it might look like as a book. Paul Lyons, my talented fellow novelist, put many things into perspective for me, as he has done for most of my books, and I can never forget the amazing support I got from another writing friend, Colin Gruzd (RIP).

I'd like to thank the small press publishers who got parts of it out there while it was still very much a work-in-progress, including Ambit's Martin Bax (RIP), Geoff Nicholson (RIP) and Kate Pemberton. Also due a mention are the editors of Breakfast All Day and Tiny Flames Press. Thank you to Krish, Auctus Publishers supremo, who agreed to bring out this very belated work, and has been a real force of encouragement.

The people of Warsaw were a major inspiration, unknowingly, unwittingly and uncaring as they passed me by during the early stages of the book – inspiring fictional characters will never be the most arresting thing that has happened to them and their city, it is safe to say, but, despite its far-flown setting, it's very much a book with the spirit of that great city at its heart.

Warsaw 1995 – Whitstable 2024